growing up gracie

maggie fechner

bonneville
springville, utah

growing up gracie

maggie fechner

bonneville
springville, utah

ISBN 13: 978-1-59955-453-2

Published by Bonneville Books, an imprint of Cedar Fort, Inc., 2373 W. 700 S., Springville, UT 84663
Distributed by Cedar Fort, Inc., www.cedarfort.com

LIBRARY OF CONGRESS CATALOGING-IN-PUBLICATION DATA

Fechner, Maggie, 1980-
  Growing up Gracie / Maggie Fechner.
    p. cm.
  Summary: As she grows up, a Mormon girl learns that lasting friendships, hidden talents, and faith in God are some of life's most precious gifts.
  ISBN 978-1-59955-453-2
  [1. Coming of age--Fiction. 2. Friendship--Fiction. 3. Mormons--Fiction. 4. Christian life--Fiction.] I. Title.

  PZ7.F2983Gr 2010
  [Fic]--dc22

                2010019848

Cover design by Danie Romrell
Cover design © 2010 by Lyle Mortimer
Edited and typeset by Heidi Doxey

Printed in the United States of America

10 9 8 7 6 5 4 3 2 1

Printed on acid-free paper

For *Gracie*, *Emmy*, *Lily*, and *Ryan*, my darlings.

And for *Dan*, my forever.

acknowledgments

I would like to thank the following people who helped make my first novel a reality: Shersta Gatica for giving *Growing Up Gracie* a chance to become a published book; Annaliese Cox for her kind pre-editing advice; Heidi Doxey for her emphasis on keeping any changes true to my original idea; the Cedar Fort design team for making my cover so much more beautiful than I imagined; and Sheralyn Pratt for putting up with numerous marketing emails from a clueless "newbie."

Thank you to Robin and Mom for reading and re-reading and always thinking I am so much more talented than I really am. Thank you to my first readers and very best girlfriends Shalie, Shauna, and Rachel, who offered encouragement and kind words throughout the entire process. Thank you to Dad and RB who love me no matter how Mormony I get.

Thank you most of all to my best friend and husband, Dan, who puts up with me spending too much time at the computer and who even read a "chick" book for me. And thank you to our wonderful children. I love you.

prologue

After the baptism was over he drove Sheila home, but I beat them there. I waited on his front porch swing, and when that truck came around the corner, I caught his eye. He smiled at me all the way up the lane. Then he jumped out of his truck and laughed as he leapt up the steps.

"Hold on," he said. Sheila stopped to hug me on her way in the house.

There was a cool breeze, but I hadn't noticed. I had my arms wrapped around my knees to keep warm.

Whatever he was doing in the house took longer than I expected. Finally he came out with a huge red and white quilt and wrapped it around my shoulders as he sat down next to me.

He stopped the swing and turned toward me.

"Gracie." He was serious.

"Yeah?" My stomach tightened. Here it was. After all this time—he was going to say he loved me too.

"What are your plans for awhile?" he asked.

"Well," I said slowly. "I'm going to keep working for the agency and living with Mom and Dad, I guess. Is that what you mean?"

"Are you going to Chicago?"

"What? How'd you know about that?"

"Your mom told me," he explained.

"I haven't decided. I'm definitely not set on going." I would stay if he wanted me to, and my eyes begged him to realize this.

"I'm leaving for awhile," he said.

"What?" I gasped.

"Kendra is home—remember, from my mission—and I'm going to meet her family and just hang out down there for awhile."

I jerked a bit, and the swing pushed back awkwardly. *Don't cry, don't cry.* I just stared.

"I didn't know you two were still close," I said flatly.

"Yeah, she's great. We always planned on doing this after our missions, so I guess now we're finally getting to."

I nodded my head.

So that was it. He'd grown into the man of my dreams, I had finally realized it, and now he just wanted to be friends.

one

Whether my first memory is an actual memory or just a moment rooted into my brain from thumbing through a stack of bent and faded Polaroids over and over again, I'm not sure. Either way, it was the summer of 1993, and I was five years old.

My best friend Liza Roberts and I were playing hide-and-go-seek on the second story of her mother's ancient farmhouse. The home had once been beautiful, I'm sure, but time had slowly taken its toll. The old kitchen was the permanent home-base for any game we played. I was barely taller than the butcher block I stood facing. It smelled of onions and pickles, and I plugged my nose as well as covered my eyes while I counted.

"Ready or not, here I come," I hollered.

The entire house was covered in its original wood plank flooring. The pieces varied in width but were identical in their foot-smoothed finish. Being sneaky in this house was nearly impossible. I attempted silence by walking on the outside edges of the stairs, clinging to the banister. *Crrreeeaaakkk.* It was no use.

At the top of the stairs I glanced right, but I knew Liza probably wouldn't have gone into her mom's sewing room. It was too messy. Instead I opened the bathroom door. I quickly slid the rosy pink shower curtain around the rod, but Liza wasn't in the claw-foot tub. To the left of the staircase were three bedrooms. My best guess was that Liza was hidden in the spare bedroom—the second door on the right. She really wasn't very original in her hiding spots, but I wanted to drag out my turn being "it," so I opened the door to Liza's mom's room. A beautiful deep green, gold, and burgundy rug covered nearly the entire floor. Her huge queen-sized bed boasted mountains of pillows in the same colors. Above the bed was the picture I loved—the photo of Liza's mom, Amy; her dad, Evan; and a baby Liza Roberts. It was taken on the front steps of this house when the house was still lovely. Both parents wore blue jeans and white shirts. A young Amy had wavy blond hair that hung to her waist. She sat on the top step with her arms wrapped around Evan, and she was positively beaming as she looked into Liza's face. Evan cradled the baby close to his chest. Evan's hair was red but handsome in a short haircut.

Amy was twenty-two in that picture. Three weeks later Evan died when his truck went off the road early one morning.

Amy's parents hadn't spoken to her since she'd joined The Church of Jesus Christ of Latter-day Saints when she was seventeen. Evan's family still kept in contact with Amy and Liza, but for the most part, the mother and daughter had been alone. Amy was the widow of a farmer, and living in the country had made her as tough as most of the seasoned men on our lane.

Staring at the picture, I backed out of the room and turned to Liza's door. It was left open. Liza's twin bed was overflowing with stuffed bears, ponies, sheep, and rabbits. The pine shelf that ran the length of the east wall hung heavy with children's books. Liza could already read.

Just as I swung open the spare bedroom door, a stifled sneeze snapped my head toward the closet, and I opened the double doors, giggling. Liza's allergies had been her nemesis on more than one occasion.

A few minutes later, Amy found us lying on the dusty floor of the spare bedroom with our feet propped up on the bed.

It was covered with an antique white beaded bedspread and matching pillows. Curtains of the same material framed the windows to either side of the bed. Amy tugged open the curtains, creating a light cloud of dust but letting in some warm sunshine. Her hair was still blond, but now it was only shoulder length. It hung in a messy ponytail. She wore Wranglers with her Justin boots and a buttoned blue western shirt.

As we watched, she walked over to the closet and slowly slid each hanger along the rod. One by one she unzipped plastic garment bags and inspected her old formal dresses. She lifted each one carefully out of its place and hugged them to her chest before laying them over a mahogany bed post. We stood up to look at them. Each gown was distinct. There was a navy blue satin dress with white glovelike sleeves. I ran my little finger over the black lace on the neck of another dress while Liza did her best to drape a sequined red one up over her neck.

Amy helped pull the elegant dresses over our cotton summer ones and stood there scrutinizing us like runway models. Before she ran for the Polaroid, she brought us high heels, costume jewelry, and a tube of lipstick—coral. I couldn't imagine a day when Amy Roberts had actually worn this stuff, but Liza and I felt like a million dollars.

⚜

It doesn't seem like I ever met Liza Roberts, just that she's always been my best friend. Back then Liza was covered with freckles. She said she didn't mind the ones on the bridge of her nose, but she could do without the ones across her shoulders and down her arms. She almost always wore her wavy light red hair down or occasionally with barrettes pinning back the sides. Unlike mine, her hair never seemed tangled. It was so soft.

Liza walked a perfect line between being strong and tender. She loved to mother—and I was usually the recipient of her care giving. I'd never heard a disapproving word spoken about

Liza Roberts. Adults were constantly commenting on how polite she was. She was the girl your parents hoped you'd be best friends with.

I was anything but strong. Dad said I was scrawny from birth. I was born with blue eyes—not the "wow" kind of blue eyes, just a pale blue. And I had long brown hair that, despite my mom's efforts, remained in a perpetually snarled state. Once Liza and I tried to match our hair colors to crayons. I longed for something exotic. I wanted burnt sienna or auburn or even ginger hair, but honestly the closest match was brown. Plain old BROWN. I wasn't exceptionally short, but I was skinny. My older brother called me Knobby Knees since before I could remember. Really, though, my most distinguishing feature was my eyebrows. It wasn't that they were extremely bushy or too thin. Rather the exceptional characteristic of my eyebrows was their shape. Both eyebrows rose to a very pointed peak directly over my pupils and then sloped back down again—I had mountain peaks for eyebrows. Mom always said I'd be famous for those brows. I would rather have had auburn hair.

Liza lived three doors down from me on Appaloosa Lane. One year my grandpa made stick horses for my sisters—there're four of them—and me. They had beautifully sewn stuffed heads (Grandma must have helped) and came complete with leather harnesses. Long polished dowels stretched from the heads to wooden wheels designed to roll behind the rider. I think Grandpa tried to match each horse to each granddaughter. Although my brown-haired, blue-eyed horse was the absolute plainest animal, I adored her. But my older sisters Hope, Danielle, and Samantha quickly grew bored with their ponies. In a week I snagged Samantha's gorgeous horse and gave it to Liza. We galloped up and down the dirt road on our "Appaloosas." It was the closest either of us ever came to owning real horses.

Dave and Julie Fremont, my parents, had both lived in Cody, Wyoming, from birth. In fact, Mom grew up in the same house I did. She still called our place the Trellais Farm even though Mom and Dad had sold off most of the farm acreage years ago.

Mom and Dad had been together since they were sixteen, only taking a break for Dad's two-year mission to Ohio. When he came home, they were married and soon moved to Laramie, Wyoming, where Dad went to college. They had two kids and a third on the way when Grandma Trellais died. Dad quit school, and they came home to take over the land.

By the time I—Gracie Ezra Fremont—was born, they were used to the whole parenting procedure. I doubt I was welcomed home with much fanfare: I was number five out of six. Besides, 1988 was a big year for Cody, Wyoming, I'd often been told. Mom and Dad brought me home from the hospital on a rainy April day, but by June the area was in a severe drought. The textbooks said the great fires of Yellowstone burned heavy through the summer and late into fall, eventually scorching three-quarters of a million acres. There were firemen camped all over town, and a steady stream of planes and helicopters. I imagine a new baby was old news when compared with the continual dusting of ash covering our little town near Yellowstone's East Gate.

Whenever she told the stories of that year, Mom would point to me and joke, "but out of the ash came a child . . ." to which she usually received an exaggerated eye roll in return. Mom and Dad were incredibly loving, hard-working, and kind parents, but they tended to be annoyingly churchy. If Dad were on his deathbed, he'd still find a way to be on time to his meetings. His completion of the regular duties of a Mormon father—family prayer, scripture study, or family home evening—often leaned toward military-ish.

My mom was sweet as pie. In fact my friends would often tease that it was virtually impossible to get Sister Fremont to yell. Still she morphed any topic she could into a gospel lesson.

Think: *not rinsing your dishes out right away is like not repenting immediately after you sin.* Mom and Dad frequently told me how special I was, but usually I felt forgotten in the Fremont family.

Hope was the oldest Fremont. She was gorgeous. She inherited Mom's board-straight black hair and olive skin. She had big green eyes. Hope was the girl every guy wanted to date and every girl wanted to be. Of course she knew this. In a small town like Cody, hers was a desirable position.

Next was my brother, Nathan. Sometimes I got so sick of how much everyone adored Nathan simply because he was the only male our parents had managed to produce out of six tries. He was a stocky, dirty-blond farm boy with big muscles and a bigger mouth.

Danielle, the second girl, was an amazing singer. She had performed in almost every concert held in our county since she was a toddler. Standing on the front of a stage, her whole body smiled. She could sing anything, but she was best at a poppy version of country music.

Samantha was timid like me, but that's where our similarities ended. In looks she was a smaller version of Hope and Mom. These two were who anyone meant when they said, "Oh boy, those Fremont girls . . ." with smirks on their faces. She wasn't as outgoing as Hope, but Samantha was gentle and sweet to everyone she met. Not a bad combination with striking beauty.

My younger sister, Alex, was only a year and a half younger than me. She kept our family young with her infectious humor. Her contribution to family time had been her own stand-up routines since she could talk. Like her name suggested, Alex had a boyish figure and was the best athlete of any of us—including my brother. It took quite a wrestling match for Mom to get Alex into her one church dress every Sunday. Any other day of the week, Alex wore sweatpants or shorts with tennis shoes.

And there was me. Gracie Fremont: the most average all-American country girl. I cried too easy, I liked books, I liked chocolate chip cookies, and I liked to ride a stick horse. And I did have those eyebrows!

two

The first time I saw Chelsea Copeland, I wanted to be her friend. Even at seven years old, I knew she was pretty. It was August, and she was sporting a deep summer's tan from playing outside. Her light brown hair had natural blonde highlights, and even in a ponytail, it hung to her waist. Chelsea had the biggest blue eyes I had ever seen. She filed into the rust-colored Primary room behind three other Copeland kids. I'd soon find out she was the youngest of seven. The youngest and the most spoiled.

Our Primary president, Sister Smeuter, lined the kids up in front of the dark wood pulpit and encouraged them to introduce themselves. Carina was almost twelve, Carter was ten, Colten was eight, and then there was Chelsea. The kids had three older brothers as well. The Copelands moved to our ward from somewhere in Utah, Sister Smeuter explained, warning us that we better all treat them like friends. There was an empty metal chair next to me, and I hoped Chelsea would take it. Instead she fluffed out her dress and carefully sat by our teacher, Sister Bowdish.

In class Chelsea interrupted Sister Bowdish's lesson on John the Baptist three times to tell everyone why she had moved, her middle name, and what her many talents were. She was quite theatrical. Whenever Chelsea turned, her long ponytail made a big swoosh around the room, and I was split between being mesmerized by the movement and afraid I was going to get whacked. Halfway through the class I realized I hadn't stopped staring at Chelsea yet. Of course, she hadn't noticed.

I inched my chair closer to Liza's as I started speculating what kind of a friend Chelsea might be. I had sat next to Liza in these small church classrooms for every Sunday as far back as I could remember. In fact, our moms often repeated the story of how our friendship began in nursery. Mom said when one of us was dropped off in the classroom, we would cry until the other one showed up.

Sister Bowdish asked Liza to show Chelsea to the restroom. Liza pushed herself off the metal chair, took Chelsea's manicured hand, and headed out the door. My feet were tapping overtime because the girls were taking way too long. My neck was starting to feel hot and red. I took a deep breath to push the tears down, but I knew the flood would open any moment. Just when I knew I couldn't hold it back any longer, the heavy wooden door opened and the girls were back. Liza sat right back where she had been. I took a loud, relaxing breath.

After class Liza grabbed my hand and pulled me over to Chelsea. Chelsea wore a perfect dress. It was white with eyelets and had little red cherries all around the edges. It hung to her knees and made her legs look the color of hot chocolate as they stretched down to her folded white socks and pretty red Mary Janes.

I stood as far behind Liza as possible to hide my tan jumper. I had never noticed how plain it was. Glancing down I saw it was no better than an oversized brown T-shirt with pockets. My hair hadn't gotten a thorough brushing before church either. Chelsea was going to think I was the homeliest girl she'd ever met.

Liza tapped Chelsea's shoulder and said, "This is my best friend, Gracie."

I craned my neck around my friend and smiled wide.

"Hi, I'm Chelsea," she said.

No kidding, I thought. *You've already told us your name how many times?*

"We're going be best friends," she added. It wasn't a question. It was a statement.

Every aspect of Chelsea Copeland's life was a statement. That would never change. She announced that she was going to be best friends with me and Liza the same way she would later announce, "James is going to be my boyfriend" or "I'm going to be Homecoming Queen." Sometimes it would make other girls hate her, but not Liza and I. She'd declared it, and so it was: the three of us were best friends.

three

"Gracie, come over right now," Liza begged in an urgent whisper over the phone.

"Are you okay?" I asked.

"Just come over, okay?"

I asked Mom's permission as I pulled on my grubby jelly shoes and grabbed the rubber band from off the mail bundle for my hair. It had been the hottest July on record in Cody in the last fourteen years, and my sweaty hair was sticking to the back of my neck.

"Be back before supper," Mom called after me as the screen door slammed. I jumped off the stairs on our wooden porch and stumbled to catch myself. Glancing around, I was pleased no one was outside to notice. As the sun hit my face, I smiled despite my clumsiness. I loved summer. I was eight this year, and it seemed my boundaries were infinite as long as I was home by supper time, which in the Fremont family had always been at six.

The pink Huffy that Samantha had just passed on to me was lying next to the mailbox, so I pulled it up by the sun-scorched handlebar streamers and slung my leg over the bar. Our houses were only three apart, but in the country that meant quite a distance. In fact, most of the lots had farm land behind their houses. Just like my parents, though, Liza's mom had sold off her acreage to neighbors. When her husband died, she tried running the land with a few hired hands, but it was too much for her. She kept the old house and divided the acreage into three parcels.

Liza wished the land was theirs again. Years before she was born, her older cousins had built a fort down on the creek about half a mile behind the house. It was at a deep spot in the water where it slowly churned around a curve. Overgrown bushes hid the spot perfectly. The boys had crafted a three-sided room from wooden pallets and then carefully laid sticks across the bottom to create a floor. They even built a crude table by lashing more sticks together. One summer Liza and I snuck down there twice, but the second time, Mr. Bowers caught us and called Liza's mom. He said to stay off his property. He was scary enough that we hadn't dared disobey.

The springtime runoff on our dirt road made bike riding miserable. Potholes the size of watermelons pocked the washboard road in both directions. For years Dad and the neighbors had been saying the county was going to pave the road, but I didn't believe a word of it. Every Saturday, Dad, in his dingy overalls, and the other neighborhood men stood out in their gardens or by the mailboxes, discussing the same topics.

Nathan got in trouble once for sauntering around the house in Dad's rainbow colored suspenders, mimicking him. He stretched both suspenders back and forth with his thumbs and in the most backwoods voice he could muster, he slurred, "Have you cleaned out ya ditches yet?" "How ya tomata's doin' this year?" And "Have ya seen how fast those darn Bronson twins drive up and down the road?"

Dad's ears turned red, and he gave Nathan a knock-it-off look, but we all noticed Mom laughing over her sink full of dishes. It was a pretty accurate imitation. Dad and the neighbors' conversations were just country talk, but as a kid, I imagined every adult's life revolved around these rural subjects.

I ditched my new-old bike while it was still rolling and ran up Liza's front steps. There was a plank missing in the second step, but it had been missing for years, and everyone who knew the Roberts remembered to avoid the hole. Liza was standing there with the door held open, pressing her finger to her lips in the "sshhhh" motion. I didn't say a word. Once inside we snuck up the stairs to her bedroom. She shut the door and let out an exasperated moan, flopping onto her bed.

"What's going on?" I asked, sliding a purple elephant out of the way to make room for myself.

"Didn't you see the truck outside?" She looked disgusted.

I hadn't noticed the two-tone brown Ford with the broken headlight, so Liza pulled me to the window and pointed to where her mom and a man were walking around near the back fence. I couldn't see his face, but his balding head looked vaguely familiar.

Liza started crying. "Jason Miza's dad is here. He loves my mom."

I immediately pressed my face back to the window as if I might catch them kissing.

"I'll bet they're going to get married. And then she'll forget all about my real dad." Liza was sobbing now. I was speechless.

"Gracie! Jason Miza is going to be my brother. I'd rather die than have him as a brother!"

I threw my bony arms around her shoulders and felt her warm tears through my pink and green striped shirt. After a few minutes, my arm started to ache from the weight of Liza's head, but I didn't let go. This was so unlike Liza. I was the one who cried. Me being the comforter was a new phase in our friendship, and I was glad to do for her what she had done for me so many times. She lifted her head, revealing swollen red eyes. It was the first time I noticed her freckles were fading. In fact I only counted five across her nose. I considered telling her this, but then she gasped.

"Oh no," she looked mortified. "Will they change my name to Liza Miza?"

The possibility of a new rhyming name instigated a deafening wail. Fortunately Mr. Bower's combine buzzing through the field muted Liza's death cry enough to keep her mom from hearing it outside.

It turned out Bruce Miza was only talking to Amy about remodeling their basement. He was a general contractor in town whose wife had died of breast cancer a few years back. It was true, Bruce could use some motherly help with his son, Jason, but he never caught Amy's eye. Still, she didn't refuse the friendly discount when he crafted a huge food storage room in her basement.

It would be years before Amy was ready to marry again. She would one day; I think Liza always knew that. But Liza wasn't herself again until Bruce Miza loaded his table saw and leftover plywood into the back of his Ford and didn't come back.

four

Chelsea showed up at school wearing makeup on the first day of fourth grade. She didn't actually leave her house with it on; instead, she slumped low on the green leather bus seat and pulled out a tiny fuchsia-rimmed hand mirror to make herself over. When the bright yellow doors opened, she emerged from the bus a new woman with plum eye shadow and a puckered smile of ruby lipstick. Her cheeks were too tan to show the blush, but that lipstick was flaming.

Of course Chelsea's parents didn't allow her to wear makeup yet, but her older sister Carina could. After Carina descended the stairs for breakfast, Chelsea had snuck into the bathroom and loaded up her backpack with supplies from Carina's tackle-box-style makeup holder.

"What is on your face?" Liza asked first. We were slowly making our way from the bus lines toward the soccer fields.

"Cover Girl, of course," Chelsea said, as if she had been wearing makeup every day for her entire life.

"You're going to get in trouble," Liza said. "The teacher will call your mom."

Chelsea didn't seem worried, and she didn't offer any more explanation for her makeover, so Liza dropped it. As we neared the blacktop four-square court, Jessica Rouster, Mary and

Holly Mending, and Savannah Ritchey were clustered together in conversation. They shut up quickly.

"Hi," Jessica said to none of us in particular. "Did you have a good summer?"

She never looked our way and obviously wasn't interested in our responses. Jessica was the leader of this foursome—the most popular girls in our grade.

Holly, one of the Mending twins, was really the only pleasant one of the bunch. The rest of them spent any spare moment teasing and making fun of other girls. Last year two of them had been sent home for sticking gum in Roberta Wild's hair. Of course, Chelsea never realized these girls didn't adore her because she just assumed everyone did.

"My summer was fantastic," she answered enthusiastically. "I went to Disneyland for vacation, and we got to go to the beach in California, and also my dad bought a boat this summer, so I spent most of the time out on the lake."

Liza and I feigned interest, but we'd already heard the details of Chelsea's summer a hundred times. We were only jealous. The rest of the girls didn't seem to care either. Chelsea didn't notice. Instead she just smiled. "Well, see you around." Chelsea led Liza and me over to inspect the new playground equipment. As we walked away, I heard the girls snickering about Chelsea's makeup.

"I'll race you to the fence," I screeched in a too-loud voice to cover up the girls' comments. It worked; Chelsea didn't hear a word.

When the bell rang, we raced toward the peach metal double doors with the rest of the Sunset Elementary student body. Our school had a policy we all hated—class rosters weren't announced until the first day of school.

So far, Liza and I had been lucky. Since morning kindergarten, we'd been assigned the same classroom every year. Trying to follow the no-running rule, Liza, Chelsea, and I speed-walked down the brightly decorated hallway to the class list that was posted on the first door. The three boys standing in front of us were slow as molasses. I started tapping my feet and wringing my hands. The purple door was Mrs. Stellar's door. She was by far the favorite fourth grade teacher. Every kid wanted to be on that list. If Liza—the tallest of us three—stood on tip toes, she could see over their heads.

"Yes! I'm in her class," she yelped.

I jammed my head between two boys' backpacks and searched frantically. *F, F, F. Let's see . . . Lucy Folder, Rachel Frampton, Michael Harris. Oh no, there has to be one missing. Gracie Fremont. It should be there.*

It has to be there.

I scanned the entire list, starting from the top. *Maybe they just got my name out of alphabetical order,* I ventured. I went down the list again.

It was hopeless. Gracie Fremont was not on that list. But right there in the C's was Chelsea Copeland. My two best friends looped their arms around each other and danced a circle in the hallway. They were positively giddy to be in the same class with the best teacher. In fact, Chelsea wouldn't shut up about how this was going to be the best year ever. But Liza knew I was hurting. She walked with me down the hall to find my own class. I just stared at the green and white flecked linoleum floor, embarrassed, as tears streamed down onto my new pink-striped overalls.

My name didn't show up until the third blue door, which was Mr. Nibard's class. No one wanted Mr. Nibard. The sixty-something, gray-haired teacher was one of the oldest in the school. He wore thick glasses and polyester pants that were habitually too short. My sister Samantha had him a few years before, but even worse—my mom had Mr. Nibard too! I remember Sam coming home to complain that her class had studied maps every day of the fourth grade. Where Mrs. Stellar's room was decorated with a rain forest theme, Mr. Nibard's walls were covered with every type of map I could imagine. I wondered if the décor had been the same when Mom was here.

To make matters worse, it looked like Mr. Nibard had the

smallest class. Out of seventeen kids, it only took a second for me to count that there were only six girls. Dejected, I stood there in front of the blue door, shaking my head. I put my purple new-old backpack—another hand-me-down—in the locker and found the desk with "Gracie" taped to it. I sat down, folded my arms on top of my desk, and put my face down. There was still ten minutes until the bell.

"Come on, Gracie," I heard Chelsea say. "Come with me." She gently grabbed my arm and pulled me up out of my seat. I moped behind her as we made our way past the classrooms and around the corner to the door marked GIRLS. "It will make you feel better."

I knew what she had planned, and I knew I wouldn't stop her. She leaned her backpack against the green tile wall and began pulling out cosmetics. My eyes grew wider as she kept unpacking, but the eight-foot window-sill offered adequate counter space for her products.

"Don't worry," she said. "We'll wash it off before we go home."

I took a deep breath and closed my eyes as Chelsea got to work. My head jerked back in surprise when she first tapped it with the powder puff.

"Sorry," she said.

Next she carefully colored my eyes with emerald green eye shadow on the tips of my lids to the crease, and then a lighter green shade nearly to my unusually arched brows. She chose a rose blush for my cheeks but then wiped it off with rough toilet paper. Instead she went with Summer's Kiss. When I opened my eyes, she was smiling. Chelsea thumbed through the lipsticks to find the matching shade and then instructed me to pucker up. Apparently my lips were a bit flimsy because this process took several tries and more toilet paper.

Chelsea put her hands on my shoulders and spun me toward the huge mirror, and I felt beautiful. She sprayed too many squirts of Vanilla Romance on my neck, and I stepped out of the bathroom a bit more ready to face my challenge.

I guess our teachers were too busy with the first day of school to notice our flashy faces. No one said a word. That was the last time my face saw color until I turned sixteen, but I can't even count the number of times Chelsea was sent to the bathroom to scrub her face that year.

⟡

The silver lining in the gray cloud called Mr. Nibard's class turned out to be Cade Rawlings. I had known Cade forever. Our mothers were best friends.

Cade had more friends than me—by a landslide. He wasn't shy. He was cute, though, and most girls thought so. Just like all the Rawlings, he had the lightest blond hair and fair skin. He was tall and skinny, even for a fourth grader. But Cade's most unusual quality was that he was friends with all the kids at school—not just the cool ones.

I never had a crush on Cade like most of the fourth grade girls, including Chelsea. I had known him too long, and he was almost like a brother to me—except of course, better, because he didn't tease me mercilessly like my own brother.

Around the beginning of October, Mr. Nibard announced we could move our desks into groups of four with our friends. The kids cheered, but I was mortified. Almost imperceptibly, I slunk lower and lower in my green plastic chair until the crown of my head barely peeked over the desk. I didn't have a single friend in this class—let alone four! Of the other five girls in the class, none had ever even talked to me.

Cade and his two best friends pulled their desks together. I knew Josh from church, but I'd never talked to him. And the other boy, Riley, was new to Sunset this year.

I didn't get up from my desk. I just sat there in the back row of what were no longer rows. My face was burning, so I stared down at my frozen limbs. When I glanced up, Cade was standing there.

"Come sit with us," he said.

I had to boost myself up in my seat to even get a good look at him. I lowered my eyebrows questioningly. I wanted to be sure he wasn't joking. Cade nodded, and I slowly swung my left leg and then my right out from under the desk and stood. I folded my arms across my chest as Cade lugged my desk over to his waiting group. Still unsure, I stood almost paralyzed in the same spot. Josh and Riley waved me over, so finally I dragged my chair slowly behind me to the group and shuffled into my seat.

There was one extra kid in the class, so Mr. Nibard let the other five girls make one "pod." They were overjoyed to be a female-only group. I didn't feel left out, though; rather, I hoped they all noticed Cade, the coolest kid in the class, had picked me to sit with him. The bell rang for morning recess, and I was the first kid out the door. I left my new jacket on the hook in the locker.

"You're so lucky," Chelsea said. "Cade is so cute."

"No, he's not," I countered, disagreeing out of principle and not honesty. "But you should have seen the other girls watching me. Cade and his friends were so nice."

There was no denying I would have exchanged a pretty hefty birthright for a chance to join Liza and Chelsea in Mrs. Stellar's room, but I decided this was the next best thing.

I think Chelsea was the only kid in our grade with more siblings than I had. I thought six was plenty, so when Mom and Dad told us we were having another one, they were met with little enthusiasm on my part.

It seemed whenever the subject of siblings came up at school, kids would make comments like, "Why do Mormons have so many kids?" or "Whoa, that's crazy!" I never knew how to respond. Usually, Chelsea responded for both of us with a "shut up" or "none of your business."

My sister Hope was now sixteen. Nathan was fifteen. Danielle was twelve. Samantha, eleven. I was nine. And Alex was seven. I never even considered the idea that Mom might have more babies. Alex was just the baby, and we all knew it.

The announcement came during family home evening just before Thanksgiving vacation. We were talking about eternal families, and Dad had just finished reading the Proclamation on the Family. Nathan had a red beanie on to hide his headphones and Hope was painting her toenails. I was reading my favorite book, *Where the Red Fern Grows*, under the table, trying not to get caught. It was my third time through it, and I was just about to the part where Rubin Pritchard falls on the axe, trying to break up the dog fight. Whatever Dad had to say couldn't be as exciting as this, I'd figured.

"Well, we were going to wait until Grandma's and Grandpa's house for Thanksgiving, but now seems like a better time to tell you guys," Mom said. I was speed reading to get to the climax of the scene before someone stopped me.

"We have an announcement," she said.

That snapped everyone to attention—including me—but still, I held my pointer finger in the binding of the book to mark my spot. Mom and Dad were met with puzzled looks all around the table. She turned toward Dad, and he smiled.

"We're going to have a little Fremont baby in June," she blurted out.

The six of us looked around at each other to make sure we'd heard right.

"Well, what do you think?" Dad asked after the long pause.

Still no one answered.

"Mom and I are very excited. It was a surprise, but we're still excited. And we know you'll all be excited too when we meet this new baby," he said.

"Hey, Dad, can you say excited one more time?" Hope asked sarcastically.

Mom jumped up and nearly ran to get the lemon bars from the kitchen. I stared at her stomach. Nope, there was no sign of life in there yet. No bump. Maybe she was wrong. The silence was filled with our chewing, and then Nathan grabbed Yahtzee from the closet. He passed out score cards and pencils quickly and shook the dice in the red plastic cup. The noise seemed much louder than usual. No one said anything about the baby news for a week.

The next Sunday we were eating dinner when Hope dropped her fork obnoxiously onto her plate. She looked up at Mom. "You know I won't have much time for babysitting with yearbook and cheerleading practice, right?"

Mom nodded. "Of course, honey."

A huge grin spread across Dad's face, and he started his

infectious barrel laughter that got us all going. Soon we were all asking questions. Nathan: Do you think it will be another girl? Danielle: Can I pick the name? And Alex: How long until she can play basketball with me?

※～❦❧◈❧❦～※

Mom and Dad picked out Joseph's name as soon as the ultrasound determined he was a boy. It wasn't until spring break that they knew Joseph wasn't okay.

Bewitched reruns blared from our TV set and captivated the whole Fremont clan. I was sprawled across the family room's brown carpet in a pair of black shorts and an oversized teal T-shirt. Hope, Danielle, and Samantha were all crammed on the fifteen-year-old beige suede couch while Nathan and Alex shared the thread-barren recliner. I heard the garage door rattle open and shut but didn't look up when Mom and Dad walked in. They had been at another one of the "tests" they were always whispering about.

I heard sniffling, and I barely caught a glimpse of Mom's bloodshot eyes as she scurried through the house and straight up to her bedroom without even saying hello. Dad slowly walked in front of us and turned off the TV. At bedtime or homework time, this action would have been met with serious protests, but I think we all sensed something serious was going on.

"The baby is sick," he announced. "We don't know if he'll live through the delivery." I had never seen Dad cry—not even when he was bearing his testimony in church, which I was thankful for. Dave Fremont was the portrait of strength in my mind. But now I could see tears coming to the corners of his eyes. It had been a long time since I'd really looked at my dad's eyes. They were so blue, I decided. Almost like I imagined an Alaskan glacier would look. When the tears peeked over his lids and dripped down his reddened cheeks, my tears came too. I pulled the pillow from behind my head and held it over my mouth to suppress the sobs.

Alex sprang from the recliner and ran to Dad. She threw her arms around his waist. He pulled her up in a hug and let out a little moan. Legs dangling, my little sister buried her face in Dad's whiskered neck, crying right along with him.

"Momma is real sad right now, guys, so we all need to do our best to help her," he choked out.

After Dad sat down for a few minutes, he told us about how the baby's heart was weak and how this was a common problem in older mothers. He used some long words to describe the disease, but I had already blocked out his voice. Every time he started to talk about Joseph again, his tears would resurface. I didn't want to hear any more of it. I wanted the baby and my mom to be fine. But mostly I wanted my dad to stop crying.

I ran out the front door and toward Liza's house, but I stopped in the middle of the road. Her house was where I'd always gone in times like these, but this was different for some reason. I stood there, staring at my right foot planted deeply in a mud puddle. No, I couldn't go to Liza with this. I guess because of her dad, she didn't seem like the right person to talk to about death.

Instead I crawled through the barbed wire and ran as fast as I could through a field of tall weeds. I came to another fence and went through that one too, but this one caught on the back of my shirt and ripped a small hole in the shoulder. I stopped to inspect the damage until the weeds began to itch my legs. Then I started running again. I ran and ran and ran.

The tears were streaming hard, and I could barely see where I was going. I knew I was getting close to the Rawlings old cabin, though. When I came over the hill, I saw it down by the tiny blue pond. The log and mortar cabin had been built long before any of our farms. In fact, my dad always called it the homesteader cabin. Inside it was one room with a wood floor that was added sometime after the original owners left. There was a small loft to the west side where four mattresses were laid out under the low eaves. The main room had a large

26

stone fireplace with a smoke-blackened bar, meant to hold a pot or tea kettle. There were two couches, a queen-sized iron bed, and a huge picnic table.

I stumbled down the hill and out onto the aging dock where I stood, trying to catch my breath. My tears and breath were so loud that I didn't even hear him behind me. But when I felt a hand on my shoulder, I screamed and jumped forward, nearly falling into the weedy water.

"Gracie, it's me. It's Cade," he yelped out.

I glanced back but then quickly turned back around. I didn't want anyone to see what I must have looked like.

"I'm sorry," I sniffled. "I didn't think anyone would be here."

"You remember," he said. "Mom and Dad always make us come out here for spring break. You know, to clean the place up for summer."

I didn't remember, but I nodded anyway.

"What's wrong, Gracie?" he asked. I shook my head. "Come on, tell me. I won't tell anyone."

I hesitated for a moment. "Not even your mom?" I asked.

"I promise."

I sat down on the dock and pulled my bony legs up to my chest. It felt good to rest my feet. Cade unhurriedly squatted down next to me. I still avoided his eyes, but I'm sure he knew I'd been crying. I figured I could limit my explanation with a simple, "Mom's baby is going to die." But soon I was staring into Cade's gentle face, and he was so easy to talk to. I told him about the baby, but I also told him how I wasn't even sure I had wanted a new brother in the first place. And how I couldn't stand the brother I did have. And how I didn't really belong in the Fremont family anyway.

"But now I feel awful," I cried. "I wish I could just die instead of Joseph. No one would even notice."

Cade stretched his arm around my shoulder and said quietly, "I would."

We dangled our feet into the pond and sat with our tennis

shoes soaking for the longest time. I talked until I couldn't talk anymore, but he seemed to understand even what I couldn't say.

For the next few years on Joseph's birthday, which was also his death day, I would run to the pond. It was June 16—Father's Day that first year. I sprinted toward the cabin almost as wildly as I had the first time. But when I got there, I felt much more at peace. I rolled my jeans up and threw my sandals onto the grass before I walked out on the dock. I wondered aloud what Joseph was doing in heaven. Sometimes I wondered why Heavenly Father let a little boy die. And I worried about how Mom must feel.

When Joseph would have turned two, the Rawlings were at the cabin, but I went down to the dock anyway. Cade came down with two 7-Ups, and we sipped soda for awhile. Then he left me alone, so I could talk to Joseph. I told my baby brother about the lives of each of his siblings on Earth, and I told him I loved him. I promised Joseph that one day I'd see him again.

As far as I know, Mom and Dad never tried for any more children. Actually it was a huge relief to all of us. Losing one sibling—even though we each had only held him once—had shaken the Fremont kids. Besides, I don't think Mom and Dad knew how fast their first grandchild was on his way.

six

"My fingers are going numb here, Hope," Danielle said. "You better appreciate this."

My older sister had enlisted Mom, Danielle, Sam, and I into folding invitations: 50 graduation and 250 wedding.

Spring of 1998 was a busy time for Hope. She turned eighteen on May 19, she graduated from high school on May 26, and she married Anthony Sterling on May 31. They had been dating since she turned sixteen, and despite their parents' protests, they had quickly decided to date only each other.

Anthony was a Cody High School star basketball player, who graduated one year before Hope. Hope and Anthony had remained temple worthy throughout their two years of dating, but Anthony opted against a mission. No one was pleased with his decision. No one but Hope, that is.

Even as a little girl, all Hope ever talked about was being a wife. When the rest of us wanted to play school, hospital, or office, Hope would only play house, and of course she had to be the mother. Mom and Dad spent many late nights begging her to send Anthony out into the mission field.

The weekend after their sealing in the Idaho Falls Temple, they had a big reception at Anthony's parents' place. The Sterlings lived in a large brick house in town with a swimming pool. They couldn't have asked for better weather—84 degrees and not a cloud in the sky. The DJ played an upbeat mix of pop and country. The deck railings were embellished with white bows that mimicked those on Hope's train. She looked radiant. It seemed like the sun just refused to go down that night. In fact, Mom and Dad had to drag us kids out of the pool at 11 PM.

After watching Hope and Anthony that first year, I wasn't sure I ever wanted to get married. I remembered their dating days when Anthony would come to our door and Hope couldn't wipe the smile off her face if she tried. Anthony would undoubtedly be carrying a bundle of roses or tulips or even lilies. Late at night after Mom and Dad would go to bed, I'd see Hope sneak down to the kitchen to call Anthony. They couldn't get enough of each other.

But shortly after saying "I do," or whatever it was they said in the temple, Hope and Anthony weren't much fun anymore. Anthony started school at the community college in the fall with aspirations of becoming a financial advisor like his dad. But after Christmas break, he didn't go back. Hope explained there were too many bills with a baby coming. He'd just have to go to school later. Anthony started roofing for Peters Brothers. He worked long hours—sometimes sixteen in one day—and Hope was bored at home alone. It seemed she was at our house every day when I came home from school. When I saw her maroon Civic in the driveway, I was tempted to turn around. Mom and Hope talked about pregnancy all the time. I'd gone from being clueless about pregnancy to being an expert on the ailments of the first, second, and third trimesters. Every conversation revolved around swollen feet or back pain or eating pickles. It was so annoying! Soon though, Michael arrived, and from then on, I loved to see my sister and her little one.

Hope and Anthony's son, Michael Anthony Sterling, was born February 28—raising more than a few eyebrows. Some family friends were entertaining the idea of a pre-marriage "mess up" in the Fremont/Sterling case. But there wasn't. The butterball was just born three weeks early. He had red hair and huge cheeks. Even three weeks early, he weighed nine pounds. After a thirty-hour delivery, Hope swore she'd never have another baby.

I was in the sixth grade, and I adored my chubby-faced nephew. I could spend hours studying him. But even though I was old enough to babysit him, Hope usually selected Danielle or Samantha because they were older.

I'd tickle his little feet and blow on his tummy. Liza loved him too. We took turns feeding him bottles, burping him, and rocking him in Mom's wooden glider. Liza treated Michael like the brother she'd never had.

One day that summer, Dad came in from watering the lawn, and Hope was crying at the kitchen table. She sat across from Mom and sobbed.

"There are just so many bills with a baby, Mom!" she wailed. "How are we supposed to pay for all this? I wish Anthony had just kept going to college."

I saw Dad shaking his head out of the corner of my eye.

"Now we're going to be poor and live in that tiny apartment for the rest of our lives," Hope whined.

Dad strolled over to the table and pressed both hands down on it. Mom and Hope looked up at him, and he took a loud breath.

"Honey, we love you, but you and Anthony chose this life when you got married and pregnant at eighteen. Your path might have been easier if you had gone to school and if Anthony had served his mission. The Lord blesses us for our willingness to obey His commandments."

Hope looked shocked and started crying even harder. Mom put her arm around Hope's shoulder, but she nodded her head in agreement with Dad.

"Now, you and Anthony are good people, and you'll make it through this tough time. But right now you need to be with him," Dad said. "You need to talk with *him* about what's going on in your marriage, not your mother. You two will make it, but you can't run away to your family every time it gets tough."

Hope wiped her eyes on the back of her hand and stood up from the table. She walked to where I held Michael on the couch and grabbed him from me. He didn't wake while she buckled him in his car seat and reached her arm through the handle. She walked out the door without saying a word.

No one heard from Hope for two weeks. It drove Mom crazy, but Dad kept telling her not to call.

One afternoon, the phone was ringing as we walked in the door from church. Alex ditched her scripture bag on the couch and leapt in front of Nathan for the receiver. It was Anthony. He said they hoped they could come over for dinner, and Dad said of course they could.

Mom made our favorite family dinner—chicken broccoli crepes—and Danielle, Samantha, Alex, and I made a double batch of chocolate chip cookies. Anthony, Hope, and Michael came with pictures of the baby. I couldn't believe how much he'd changed in just two weeks. Anthony did most of the talking for the Sterlings throughout dinner. But afterward we played charades, and Hope couldn't help but break into a smile at Dad's impression of Snoop Doggy Dogg. The funny part wasn't him trying to be a rapper—it was that he'd never heard of Snoop and so was instead trying to imitate Snoopy. He pretended to climb on top of a dog house and pull out a typewriter. Needless to say, the boy's team lost.

seven

GRACIE EZRA FRAM. I practiced writing it over and over in my journal. *MRS. JUSTIN FRAM.*

My brother, Nathan, graduated that spring, but I didn't care as much about him graduating as I did about Justin Fram. Justin had been Nathan's best friend for the past few years, and he lived about two miles down the road from us. He picked Nathan up for seminary, and I'd actually get up at 5:45 AM just so I could catch a glimpse of him.

He was gorgeous. Justin's dad was a real farmer so Justin worked outside all summer long. This meant he was tan, muscular, blond, and the object of my twelve-year-old dreams. His dad paid him well, so at sixteen he bought a black Ford pickup truck. I pictured myself sitting next to him in that truck, driving down the old highway that was so bumpy it made me laugh.

After graduation Nathan worked with Justin on their farm for the summer. The effects of the work were the same on my brother's body, and there were a few young women who quickly grew interested in him. But he was either too self-absorbed or too embarrassed to acknowledge them because Nathan never went on a date before he left for his mission that January.

Justin was young for their class, though, and wouldn't turn nineteen until the next summer, so he moved to Rexburg for a year of school. I remember his last Sunday at church in August. He was just three rows ahead of us. It was fast and testimony meeting, and his mom had been nudging him for the past thirty minutes. He kept giving her the knock-it-off look, but she wasn't relenting. He finally stood up and made his way to the pulpit. His church shirt looked so tight against those biceps.

It was the first time I had ever seen him bear his testimony, and it was the first time I cried in sacrament meeting. It wasn't that I felt the Spirit; I just didn't want Justin to leave. All he said was something like, "It's been great. Thanks. I'll miss you all." But, nonetheless, my trademark hot tears streaked from my eyes.

I was so embarrassed I got up and stared at the orange carpet as I rushed toward the bathroom. Liza saw me go, so she slipped out the back of the chapel and followed me.

"Are you okay?" she asked.

"No! I love Justin Fram! And now he's leaving, and I'll never see him again."

Liza stifled her laughter and hugged me. "He'll be back, Gracie. Hey, don't forget he'll have to give a farewell for his mission here next summer."

She did have a point.

"And maybe when he gets back, you two will get married," she said seriously.

"How old will we be then?" I asked.

"Let's see, we'll have to be at least about sixteen by then," she said.

I started to bawl again. "That's not old enough to get married. I don't want to be like Hope!"

"Well, maybe after high school you can go to BYU, and he'll be there, and you can marry him after a few years."

"Okay, yeah, maybe I can."

She wiped my tears on the sleeve of her denim dress, and I looked in the mirror. I always looked awful after crying. My blue eyes would turn turquoise with all the redness—it was so obvious. Liza wandered the halls with me until she swore my eyes were all clear. Then we silently went back in.

If Justin Fram can just wait for me at BYU. . . . Yeah, that's what we would do. He would go on a mission and then to college for a few years, and I would marry him after that. Yes, this could work! There was only a miniscule flaw in my plan—Justin Fram didn't even remember my name.

As soon as we got home from church, I snuck into Mom's sewing closet. I found two colors of embroidery thread that she hadn't opened yet: a periwinkle blue and a yellow. I grabbed the first needle I found and went upstairs. I kicked off my black church shoes with the little white bows and wiggled my toes. *Those are starting to get tight,* I thought. I quietly shut the door and got comfortable on the bed. I separated the blue string into three strands and threaded the needle. I jumped down again and found a pencil on the desk. This would surely look better if I took my time. I grabbed my white lace pillow that had been a Christmas present last year and pulled it onto my lap. Carefully I etched "The Frams" across the front. *This will be a fantastic decoration for our first home,* I thought as I pushed the needle up through the pencil line.

I sat on the front porch in my pajamas at 5:00 AM the next morning because I knew he'd be leaving. I snuggled the pillow close, pleased at how it'd turned out. I softly ran my fingers over the periwinkle "The" and the egg-yolk-colored "Frams." Finally I saw the headlights turn from their driveway onto Appaloosa. I quickly flipped off the flashlight, so I wouldn't be seen. Tears dripped onto the pillow as he made his way past me.

In his absence, my crush grew exponentially until October, when I heard Mom and Dad downstairs in the kitchen.

"Fram sold his farm," Dad said.

"What?" Mom asked. "I didn't know it was for sale."

"I guess it wasn't, but some Californian came and dropped a load of cash on his table, and he took it." I could just imagine Dad shaking his head. If there was one thing the men of Appaloosa Lane hated more than potholes it was Californians moving in.

"They're moving down to Boise right away," Dad said.

"Well that's too bad," Mom said. "Gracie will be crushed."

I dove onto my bed and buried my face in our family pillow. *Am I that transparent?*

eight

When I heard I could take wood shop as a class during my first year of junior high, I was thrilled. My Grandpa Fremont had been boosting me onto his work bench in his dusty shop since I was five years old. I sipped pop while I watched him craft cabinets and cribbage boards and a rocking cradle that was meant to be used by all the great-grandchildren. I always wanted to learn how.

Wood-working came naturally for me. Our first project was a pencil holder, and I finished it in two class periods. Next we completed a peg game, a child's stool, and a planter box. The picture frame was a bit more interesting, since I was able to use a router, but still I whizzed through it.

My marble maze was the best in the class. And when Mr. Andrews called me to the front of class with my cutting board, I wished I could slide under the door and away from the attention.

"That turned out really cool," a boy I didn't even know said. "How did you get the curves around the edges so even, though?"

I smiled and began speaking in a language I'd never even known I possessed.

"I made a template out of the radius of a quarter-inch

masonite and copied it onto the four corners. Then I cut it out with the band saw. I sanded them even with the spindle sander and rounded over the corners with a half-inch bit on the router."

The girl closest to the front sat slack-jawed, staring at me. I smiled and took my seat.

Since Dad had only one boy, my newfound talent was like a loaded gold mine to him. Each Saturday he'd wake me with one instruction: get dressed and come out to the garage. We started easy, with instructions on how to correctly read a tape measure—I promised him I already knew. And then he had shown me his trick for ensuring a straight cut when hand sawing. I told Dad there were power tools for this, but he'd insisted I master the basics first. We'd practiced staining, sanding, and restaining projects, and finally we'd moved onto the good stuff. He'd mark two-by-fours with a flat carpenter's pencil at two-foot intervals and then teach me how to make clean cuts on the miter saw. We practiced straight cuts and ones on the forty-five. Dad drew circles on sheets of plywood and made me change the bits in his cordless drill to make the holes. He'd bring in rough two-by-sixes for me to polish. I liked the lighter disk sander, but Dad urged me to learn belt sanding. He also wanted me to master the Sawzall, but my skinny arms would shake so bad I had no control with the thing.

"Maybe next year," he said, smiling and unplugging the cord.

On the Tuesday before Thanksgiving, Nathan's mission call came in the mail. Mom, Dad, Danielle, Sam, Alex, and I huddled around, waiting for him to open it, but he surprised us when he held the envelope high over his head and said, "No, let's wait until Thanksgiving Dinner."

"What?" Dad asked. "This is the kid who's peeked at his Christmas presents for the past nineteen years! You really want to wait?"

Alex was leaping futilely in the air, swinging for the envelope, but Nate tossed it back and forth between his hands.

"Yep, I really want to wait." Nathan grinned, animated by the response he was getting.

"No!" I shouted. Alex stopped jumping, and everyone looked at me, confused. I stammered, "I just . . . I just want him to open it now."

Nathan shook his head.

"This is ridiculous," I said, stomping up the stairs. My family just stared after me. I slammed the door, and a framed 8x10 photo of Liza and I fell from the wall. I was fuming.

It wasn't that I was dying to know where Nathan was going. He could go to Timbuktu for all I cared. But I did not want my brother to save his news for Thanksgiving Day! I had my own plan for Thanksgiving Day, and it would be just like a Fremont sibling to ruin my arrangement with his own show.

I looked down at my hands and saw they were trembling. The skin on my right thumb, pointer, and middle fingers was red and sore. I'd been slaving over a cornucopia in wood shop for weeks, and I was hoping to unveil it at Thanksgiving.

This was my masterpiece. After the first few months of class, I'd grown bored with novice projects. I finished everything so much quicker than the other students and just ended up sitting around in the shop. I was thumbing through an old text book when I saw the cornucopia. I knew immediately it was much more advanced than the rest of the class assignments, but I'd also known I could do it.

Mr. Andrews agreed to help me with it after school as long as I kept up with the class work. That was no problem, I assured him. Mr. Andrews had used his own lathe to roughly shape the fruits, vegetables, and horn. Then I refined the shapes at school with a jigsaw. I sanded and textured them carefully with tiny Dremel tools. When I brought them home, I used my mom's old acrylic paints in my room at night to make them look realistic. After several coats on each piece, I was certain it looked fantastic. The cornucopia was hiding behind the broken down Corolla in the garage.

I'd finally found a hobby I was really good at. This was my

something that set me apart in this family. Now my surprise would mean zilch compared with Nathan's news.

Still, every few hours I went out to the garage to check on my creation. Running my hand over the dimpled leaves of the peaches and pears made me smile. The golden shade of yellow I'd used on the corn was so realistic. The plump tomato looked almost good enough to eat. It was so beautiful.

Whenever I walked out of the garage and into the house, my smile quickly disappeared. I drug my feet slowly through the house, answering questions with one word. I stared lifelessly at the TV football games, even though I didn't know a thing about either team. I was moping with all the power I had. But in all the excitement and anticipation, no one even noticed my mood.

Grandma and Grandpa Fremont came down from Casper on Wednesday night. That dumb white envelope was the object of every conversation. Everyone guessed where Nathan might be sent and what language he would be called to learn. Grandpa got the great idea of making a big list of everyone's predictions and awarding the winner a twenty-five dollar gift certificate to Pizza Hut. I just smirked when they asked for my guess. Honestly, I wished he'd already left.

Undeterred, Grandpa had Mom round him up a huge poster board and black Sharpie.

"Italy," Hope guessed.

"Ireland," Samantha followed.

"Chicago!" Alex screamed. "Then you can meet Michael Jordan! I heard he has a huge 23 on the gate at his house. You have to take a picture of that for me, Nate."

I slid into my moccasin slippers and snuck out the sliding glass door. The wind swirled around me, and I pulled the hood of my sweatshirt tightly around my face. I stood still for a second at the bottom of the steps and looked up into the dark night. There was no moon, but the stars were innumerable. For a moment I remembered Dad sitting with me on his lap on nights like this and pointing up to the stars. He had showed me

40

Orion and Taurus, Andromeda and Pisces. He taught us how to always find the North Star, but tonight all I could find was the Milky Way. It streamed across the sky in a huge arc, and I traced it backward until I nearly tipped over. I went back inside and went to bed without saying good night to anyone.

The next morning Hope, Anthony, and Michael showed up. I lay around watching TV while the house filled with noise, laughter, and the aromas of Thanksgiving dinner. Eventually I slipped back outside. I walked around to the side door of the garage and reached up high to unlatch it. I wondered for the first time why there was a lock on the outside. I sat down Indian-style behind that old car, and the tears started falling as I stared down at my cornucopia. I loved it, but nobody else cared.

I fingered a crack in the concrete and watched the digital clock up on Dad's work bench tick past 1:00 PM—dinnertime. Did they even notice I was gone? At 1:15 I heard Samantha yelling out the back door, "Gracie, Gracie, come on its dinner-time." At 1:20, from under the car, I saw Dad's sturdy legs as he opened the garage door and looked in the minivan. A few minutes later, I heard Mom walking around the driveway with the cordless phone in her hand. "Amy, have you seen Gracie? She's not here, and we're about to have dinner and open Nathan's mission call." A pause. "No, we haven't opened it yet." Pause. "Yes, we are so excited." Pause. "Oh well, I'm guessing Spanish or Portuguese. What do you think?"

Oh give me a break! Even when they were trying to find me they couldn't focus on me.

"Well, I'm sure she just went out to play or something and lost track of time. No, we're not worried. I guess we'll just go ahead without her." Pause. "Well, if you hear from her give us a call. Okay, thanks. Bye."

She went back in the house, and the tears streamed. I sat still and I cried.

By 3:00 PM my behind hurt so bad from the cold, hard concrete that I got up on my feet and crouched. I'd been looking down at the cornucopia so frequently that my neck was getting stiff. I looked up to the rafters and rolled my head from shoulder to shoulder a few times. I wasn't crying anymore—that was a step—but I still couldn't believe they had gone ahead with Thanksgiving dinner without me.

I blew out a heavy breath and watched the white puff of air fan out in front of my mouth. I licked my lips and wrapped my arms around myself. I should have brought a blanket. I was ready to go inside—not to face everyone, but at least to warm up—but I didn't know how to get out of this situation now. If I just walked in the house, I knew I'd face huge trouble. I could just imagine Dad: "You're too old for this charade!" But I didn't know how much longer I could stay out here. It was getting really cold. Inside my slippers, my toes felt numb. I pulled them off one at a time and rubbed my toes hard with my red fingers.

It was too late to give up now. I was in too deep.

At 3:29 I heard the slider glide along the tracks. I didn't know who came out, but I could tell whoever it was, was in the backyard looking around. When I saw the clean white Nikes at the end of the garage, I knew it was Nathan. He too opened the minivan door and looked in. He looked in the Corolla and when he didn't see me, he started heading to the front of the car. I held my breath. Nathan, more than anyone, was going to hate me for this.

"Hey there, Gracie. Whatcha doing?" he asked coolly, as he stepped around the car, facing me head on.

"Nothing," I whispered. I started shivering, from cold or nerves, I wasn't sure which.

"Wow, what's this? Did you find this back here?" he asked picking up my wooden ear of corn. "This is really cool."

"I made it."

"What?" He opened his eyes wide and stared at me.

"You made this? Oh my gosh." He put down the corn and picked up each piece, inspecting it with scrutiny. The apple. The potato. The carrots.

"This is awesome, Grace. It looks like it came from a store. You should show everyone."

I shook my head. "I'm so sorry, Nathan. I wanted to show everyone but I knew no one would care once they heard about your mission." The tears were pouring now. "That's why I didn't want you to wait until today for it."

Nathan carefully placed the pear back in its box and lifted me up in a huge bear hug. My feet must have been a foot off the ground, but he held me like that a long time. My eyes shed a few tears, but just a few. Mostly I was in awe. This was the first time I ever remembered Nathan hugging me, and especially when he should have been so mad! He finally lowered me back to my spot and gathered each piece of my cornucopia. I watched in wonder as he gently laid the cornucopia on the white tissue paper and arranged each piece neatly inside it.

"So where are you going?" I finally asked as we walked out the garage door.

"Hold on," he said, holding his hand out to stop me. "Even as cool as your wood thing is, there is no way you could trump this . . . Ogden."

"As in Ogden, Utah?" I asked.

He almost choked because he started laughing so hard.

I took a deep breath before I slid the door open. When I did, the smell of pumpkin pie almost bowled me over. For the slightest moment, I forgot the trouble I was in and heard my stomach growl at full volume. I had almost missed everything! But just as quickly, every eye turned to us, and my hunger ebbed.

Dad set down his fork mid-bite, and his beautiful blue eyes seemed to cloud over. I knew I was grounded. Before anyone could say a word though, Nathan practically jumped in front of me.

"I found her. She was so busy making us this great gift that she didn't even know she missed the feast."

I smiled pleadingly. Dad picked up his fork and chewed while he considered Nathan's words. The whole room seemed to be waiting for his judgment. Even Grandpa seemed to plead with Dad on my behalf.

"Well, you'd better get some pie, missy," he finally said.

Mom squeezed out from the mass of bodies around the table and hugged me tight. "Don't ever do that again," she whispered in her sternest voice, which wasn't stern at all.

Dad polished off his piece of pie and held his hands out for my box. He shuffled a space between the pecan, apple, and what had been pumpkin pies. First he pulled out the cornucopia and turned it over and over in his hands. He nodded approvingly as he felt the smoothness of the wood. Then he set it down softly in the center of the table. I tried not to smile but couldn't help it. By the time the last fruit—the peach—was settled into the horn, I was beaming. Grandpa and Dad were thrilled, but even more surprising, my sisters were impressed too.

"Isn't she amazing?" Dad asked his own parents.

I turned to the counter to grab a pie plate from Mom's stack of china, and I noticed Nathan for the first time since we came in. He was leaning back against the kitchen sink, watching his family from across the room. He was completely content to let me have my moment, and in it I realized Nathan was ready. He would make a great missionary—even if it was in Ogden, Utah.

nine

Chelsea had been sneaking makeup to school and hiking her miniskirts up after she left the house for years, but it wasn't until the summer of 2001, just before eighth grade, that she got in real trouble. Liza and I didn't hang out with Chelsea much that summer. She was permanently attached to her cell phone—the first one of the three of us to get one—and neither Liza nor I had much control over our families' home phones.

Getting a ride to town was like pulling teeth, it seemed. I swear Mom was on a driving strike. I begged and begged, but unless it was a multi-tasking trip to benefit all the kids, she wasn't up to it. Amy would have taken us to town whenever we asked, but Liza was starting to figure out her mom didn't have much money. She said she felt bad asking for rides all the time when gas cost so much.

So our average summer day was spent being lazy at each other's houses. Neither of our homes had air conditioning, so we were usually forced outside. We sunbathed on our porches or on blankets spread out in the grass. When it finally cooled off in the evenings, we'd move to our bedrooms, turn on our radios, and listen to "Love and Desperation," the local country music request show. We memorized songs and flipped through countless *Seventeen* magazines—tearing out and completing any quizzes we could get our hands on: "What kind of friend are you?" or "Would you make good girlfriend material?" We munched popcorn while watching movies and summer TV reruns. But our biggest accomplishment that summer was planning a road trip using Liza's uncle's atlas.

Liza and I made a pact that when we turned sixteen we'd take this trip. We intended to drive all the way from Southern California to Seattle along the coast. We planned to camp on the beach and meet cute guys. We used a pink highlighter to trace the highway from our house across the country and back.

We were content without too much activity, but there was no way Chelsea was going to sit around the house all summer. Without Liza and me, Chelsea started hanging out with Jessica Rouster and Savannah Ritchey. These girls had traded in their Target fashions of elementary school for more expensive and exclusive name brands. Instead of cheap makeup, they now took trips to the mall in Billings to buy Clinique. But besides these changes, they were the same as they had been in fourth grade. They were pretty. They were popular. And they were mean.

That Sunday Liza rode to church with us because her mom had the flu. As we walked into sacrament meeting, Chelsea shot us a look I could read like a billboard. It could only mean one thing—we need to talk! Throughout the meeting Liza and I whispered about what could be going on.

"Do you think she's moving?" I asked.

"Or maybe her parents are getting divorced," Liza ventured.

I don't think the "amen" was completed before Liza and I shot out of our seats and speed-walked to the hallway. We waited for Chelsea and set off for the stage. We had shared so many secrets behind the heavy red curtains, and we knew we'd be safe there. We got settled in on the floor, and Liza and I stared expectantly at Chelsea.

"I'm grounded for the rest of the summer," she announced.

"What?" I asked in disbelief. None of us had ever actually been grounded.

"I've been hanging out with Jessica—"

"Rouster?" Liza gasped.

"Yes, Rouster. And we snuck out on Friday. We drove around with Scott—you know her boyfriend—and his friend Mike. And finally I ended up walking home at two in the morning."

"Chelsea, what were you thinking?" I asked without a hint of empathy.

"Here, read this," she said, handing me her journal. I hadn't noticed she was carrying the thin black notebook. "This is what I was thinking, I guess. I wrote it all down."

I gave her a questioning look. "You want me to read your diary?"

"Yeah, both of you. It's easier than telling the whole story again," she said.

Liza and I flipped over to our stomachs with our legs out behind us and opened the book. Chelsea turned it to the right page, and Liza read it aloud.

Oh man have I done it this time!! I am so dead. Dad said he'd talk to me about all this tomorrow, but I know they're going to ground me for life and probably take away my phone and my clothes and everything else in this world. Well, anyway, here's the story.

Jessica lives a block away from us, and I stayed the night at her house for the first time last night. Well, I was supposed to stay the night, that is. We were watching MTV in Jessica's room at about 11 when her parents walked by the door to say good night. As soon as Jessica heard her parents' bedroom door click shut, she turned to me.

"We're going to sneak out," she whispered.

Jessica tip-toed across her carpet and softly shut the door. She slid the huge mirrored closet door open and began thumbing through her choices. She held a purple V-neck shirt to her chest and asked me, "How about this one?"

"Not your color." I mean, I had to be honest!

So she chose a banana yellow halter top and a really tight pair of dark denim jeans.

"What are you wearing?" she asked me.

"You're serious about this?" I said.

"Yeah. Come on, I do it all the time, and they've never caught me yet," she smiled.

I went to Jessica's closet and found a knee-length brown corduroy skirt and a white button-up shirt that had puffy capped sleeves.

Jessica locked her door and led me into the adjoining bathroom. We left the TV on for noise. We put on fresh coats of mascara and lipstick and then she stood on the toilet and opened the small window above it. My heart was racing as I followed Jessica out the window and onto a lawn chair she must have set up earlier. Once we were outside the back gate, Jessica started laughing.

"See? Easy, huh?" she said.

We ran down the alley to where Scott was waiting in his Mustang. He's sixteen. My legs were shaking when I climbed into the back seat, but there was no way I was going to tell them no! It was still warm outside, but not warm enough to make me sweat as much as I was. I wished I had put on another coat of deodorant. Scott squealed the tires, and I spun around to look out the back window, but Jessica didn't seem worried at all.

I knew right then I should have just went home, but I didn't want them to think I was chicken or something. And I knew Jessica would hate me if I left her.

Anyway, we picked up another older guy, Mike, who I guess likes me. Jessica hadn't told me about this part of the plan. My legs stuck to the sticky leather seats as I tried to make room for Mike. He flashed me a smile and then asked Scott for a dip. I was so disgusted to see him pull out his lower lip and fill it with the stinky black tobacco. Scott and Mike were both spitting in Mountain Dew bottles, and the minty smell *made me want to puke. The chewing must not have bothered Jessica though because at almost every stop sign, she leaned over to kiss Scott. I stared out the side window, but I could tell Mike was slowly inching closer and closer to me. The band screaming from the back speakers was giving me a nasty headache.*

Scott made his way to Main Street, which was mostly empty by then and cruised down the road. We went around the corner at Webster's Chevrolet to make the loop on one end of town and then did the same thing around the city park across from the high school on the west side. Only two of the lights on the street were still flashing red, yellow, and green, the rest of them were doing that yellow flashing thing they switch to late at night.

At first it had sounded fun to be out so late and with older guys. But at 1:00 AM when we had been "cruising main" for two and a half hours, I'd had enough. I was super bored and seriously so mad I had risked getting in trouble for this!

"Take me home," I said. It was the first thing I'd said all night.

"What?" shot Jessica. "You'll get caught."

"I don't care. This is stupid, and I'm tired."

"You're just scared," Jessica said, and the boys started laughing.

"I'm not scared. I just said this is stupid, and I want to go home," I had to scream it over the music.

Scott said to Jessica, "Didn't you say this girl is Mormon? What made you think she'd do anything fun in the first place?"

Now, that really made me mad!

Liza put the book down and looked up at Chelsea. "Chels, I'm sorry they were such jerks to you!"

I rolled my eyes. This was all a bit too dramatic for me. I could tell Chelsea was reading my mind.

"Just keep reading," she sneered.

I swear Jessica looked completely evil.

"I thought she was a cool Mormon," she said, glaring at me over her shoulder. "But I guess she's lame like the rest of them."

"I'm getting out," I said. "Stop the car!"

Scott pulled into the Chamber of Commerce parking lot and skidded to a stop. I practically flew out of the car.

Jessica screamed out the window, "If your parents tell my dad, I'll kill you. You won't have a single friend next year, you loser!"

Scott peeled out, shooting gravel against my shins. My face was burning, and right there, I started bawling.

I walked to the street and headed up the hill toward my house. I knew I was at least two miles from home, but I didn't care. I would have gotten out of that car in the middle of the desert if I had to.

I looked up to the old clock near the roof of the tan brick court house when I heard the first "bong." It struck twice—2:00 AM. I fished through my purse for my phone and opened it, but the dang battery was dead. I could have found an old pay phone, but even if I did, I was way too scared to call my parents in the middle of the night. What was I going to say when I got home? How would I even get in the door? I was going to be in so much trouble!

The roads were mostly deserted, but pretty soon I heard a car start to slow behind me. Oh no, I thought, Scott and Jessica are back. I started walking faster. When the car didn't pass me, I started running and crying. But then it pulled up beside me.

"Chelsea, is that you?" a man's voice said.

"Who is that?" I was out of breath. I tried looking in the window, but it was too dark.

"It's Brother Staten. Are you okay?"

Brother Staten is in the bishopric of our ward. He's a doctor in the emergency room and has late shifts. He pulled his black Suburban over in front of me and got out of the car.

"What's going on?" he asked.

I have never been so embarrassed in my life! "Can you just take me home?" I asked.

"Of course. Get in."

I was silent on the way home. I'm sure Brother Staten was freaking out, wondering what the heck a thirteen-year-old girl was doing out alone at two in the morning, but he didn't ask me any questions. When he pulled up to our house, he asked if he should wait. I said no and just thanked him for the ride.

I walked up to the red double doors and took a deep breath before I rang the bell.

Nothing.

The church floor was getting uncomfortable so I rolled over onto my back. I was hoping Chelsea's story was about to get to the point.

I squeezed my hands together and tapped my foot frantically. My heart was racing. I rang the bell again and again. Finally the orangey front light turned on, making me squint. I was praying Mom would come to the door, but instead Dad swung it open and stared in disbelief.

He pulled me in the house and sat me down in the living room. He took a deep breath and looked me over.

"Are you all right?"

I just nodded.

"Then I want you to go upstairs and go to bed, young lady. I am very upset, but we will figure this whole thing out in the morning."

I walked upstairs and here I am, counting sheep and bawling an hour later. I cannot fall asleep! Oh my gosh, I can't imagine what tomorrow will bring!

Liza closed the book and handed it back to Chelsea. We both just stared at her.

"Well, who am I supposed to hang out with? You guys never come to town anymore, and there are no other girls our age from church," she said.

"Well, that doesn't mean you had to sneak out."

Chelsea smiled for a second and said, "I thought it might be cool. I mean look how popular she is."

I shook my head in repulsion.

"But . . . But then I realized it was stupid and that it was wrong. I chose to go home, Gracie, so lay off."

"So what happened in the morning?" Liza asked.

Chelsea's parents had almost lost it, she explained. None of the older kids in her family had ever rebelled, or at least they had never gotten caught if they did. Her dad had even called the bishop to set up an appointment for his daughter. Chelsea apologized, and they settled on a month of grounding. When they threatened to call Jessica's parents, Chelsea begged them to extend her grounding until school started instead. Eventually, they agreed.

"Guys, I think Jessica is still going to tell everyone, though," she said. "Don't you dare leave me alone next year."

ten

By the time eighth grade started, the sneaking out fiasco had been forgotten, and Jessica's clan was back to ignoring us. I preferred it that way.

I spent most of the year doing two things: writing Nathan letters and building things in wood shop. This year there were only three girls in my class. I didn't mind, though; in fact, I liked it better. Cade was in the class, so I had someone to talk to while I worked. We started with basic projects to refresh our memories, but I got bored, so I moved quickly through the peg board and piggy bank. Soon Mr. Andrews had me helping other kids run the jigsaw and setting their pieces with wood glue and clamps.

During the final semester, I made a bird house covered in tiny cedar shakes and painted blue and white. I gave it to Mom for Mother's Day. Dad hung it in the maple next to the fading deck in the backyard. We planted that tree when Joseph died, so it was a special place for me.

That Thanksgiving Day with the cornucopia had turned my jerky big brother into one of my closest friends. I wrote him almost every Sunday after church for two years. On the few times I did miss, I wrote him an extra long letter the next week. I was amazed that he always responded.

He also wrote to Mom and Dad all the time, but not to the other kids.

Nathan wrote about the families he was teaching and about his companions. He said when they were bored, they would try to think of weird concoctions to make for a new breakfast or lunch. Nathan was surprised there were many people in Utah who didn't know very much at all about the Church. He said some people who had grown up there still thought we encouraged polygamy. I laughed at that.

But then a few weeks later he was transferred to a rural area, and he actually ran into a polygamous family. They invited him and his companion in and said they were members of the Church. As more and more children and more and more women joined the conversation, Nathan got more and more confused. Finally, his greeny companion asked, "Now, how are you all related?"

Nathan's jaw hit the floor when the oldest woman began introducing her cousins and sisters as "Mother Sarah," "Mother Janie," "Mother Elsa," and "Mother Margie."

"We are Samuel's wives. I am the first wife," she said before listing her sixteen children.

The missionaries kept their cool, but when they began going over the Official Declaration in the Doctrine and Covenants forbidding plural marriage, the father, Samuel, came home. Needless to say, Nathan and his companion were kicked out and not invited back.

Still, Nathan was in that neighborhood for several more months, and Mother Elsa watched for him to pass the house. She'd come outside with hot bread, cookies, or cinnamon rolls. "Don't worry about me," Nate wrote. "My Momma #2 is keeping me well fed."

I told Nathan anything I could think of in my letters. I wrote when Chelsea snuck out, and his return letter was one of a worried, protective older brother. He warned me to stop hanging out with her if she kept it up.

"It's easy to follow when your friends start going down the

wrong path, sis. Even for a lumberjack woodsman like you! If you want to serve a mission someday—and even if you don't—keep yourself in line!"

I giggled at the idea of me serving a mission. But as far as standards went, I knew Nathan was barking up the wrong tree. As much as I loved the attention from him, he didn't need to worry about me doing what was right. For the most part I always had. There would be Chelsea out dangling on the edge, but then I had Liza, who was firmly planted on the safe side of the rod. I knew if I ever had to choose one friend, I'd walk with Liza. I loved Chelsea, but that was just the way it was.

I laughed as I walked by the kitchen table that fall and saw my wooden cornucopia set up so obviously. Not that it wasn't good. It was still a great piece, and I was still proud of it. But I laughed at the memory of that day two years ago when the pieces of wood meant more to me than my brother's mission call. It seemed so childish now, but if it hadn't happened that way, Nathan and I might not have gotten so close. He teased me about that darn decoration any chance he got. With Thanksgiving being right around the corner, I was sure his next letter would be full of the joking.

Sure enough, a week and a half later, I got a letter. Mom had left it on my dresser, and I saw it as soon as I came in the room. I kicked off my shoes and grabbed a pillow to prop under my chin as I plopped down on the bed.

Hey Gracie,

Sorry I'm late, but I hope all is well with you and everyone else. I sincerely hope I didn't miss any Thanksgiving time fiascos this year. I trust that you ate dinner with the family at the table this time and didn't brown-bag it in the garage.

Just kidding, sis.

His ward had messed up and scheduled them for two dinners on Thanksgiving Day, he wrote. Nathan and his companion didn't mention the mix up and hit two feasts. The first was at noon and the second at three.

"I swear I could have just ditched my bike and rolled down the road that night," he wrote.

Because I was cracking up, his next paragraph caught me off guard:

So since it is the day of giving thanks, I wanted to tell you what I am thankful for: I am thankful for Heavenly Father. I am thankful to know that He loves me. I am thankful to know that He cares about every tiny detail of my life.

I am thankful for the Book of Mormon. I am amazed at how a book written so long ago can be applied to our situations today.

I am thankful for the gospel. To know that what we've been doing all these years is worthwhile. I am thankful that I can have an opportunity to be tested and that if I pass this test I can live with Heavenly Father and Christ.

I am thankful for Jesus Christ. I can't bear to think of the pain I personally caused Him as He hung on the cross. I know it happened. I know it happened for me.

I stopped reading. Hold up, was my brother turning Mom-and-Dad-churchy? I started over and read it slower this time. Then I continued.

Gracie, do you know this is true? I mean, do you, personally, know?

I know we've known it and been taught it all our lives, but at one point, you have to know for yourself. For me, when this happened, it made life worth living.

Sorry if this was too preachy for you, Grace, but I felt like I should write it.

I love you. Write back. Nate

My older brother, who before two years ago didn't even know I existed, was opening his heart to me. It felt like the testimony he shared was heartfelt and wasn't easily formed into words. It was beautiful.

On the other hand, why was Nathan questioning my own beliefs? Of course I knew for myself. I had known it since I was a Sunbeam. *Now that he's a missionary, it doesn't mean he needs to preach to the choir. Right? I mean Mom and Dad always say—*

Mom and Dad?

"Wow, what if he is right?" I said out loud to myself. Had I ever really asked for myself? Right then, I folded the letter and sat up. I shut the door and put the toe of a tennis shoe under it to serve as a makeshift lock. Then I knelt down next to my bed and folded my arms.

"Heavenly Father, I think I know the gospel is true. I've always lived it, and I've never really questioned it. But now, Nathan says I need to find out for myself. Please help me to know if the gospel is true. I say these things in the name of Jesus Christ, amen."

Okay, that should do it, I thought. I sat up on the bed and looked out the window. I could see Alex helping Dad rake the leaves underneath Joseph's maple. I glanced at the digital alarm clock—4:12. I watched dad and Alex some more—4:17. And then I got up and took the shoe out from under the door.

So when exactly was the answer supposed to come, I wondered? I took a stack of my friends' pictures out of my backpack and replaced last years' photos around my mirror. 4:23.

"Gracie, come snap these beans," Mom yelled up the stairs.

I guess today isn't my day. I flipped off my light and bounded down the stairs.

⋆⊶✦⊷⋆

"Heavenly Father, I've been praying about this for a whole week now, and I haven't felt much. I honestly feel the gospel is true, but please give me a confirmation. In the name of Jesus Christ, amen."

Again nothing came. I found myself in the same place I'd

been almost every night this week—sitting on my bed with tears streaming down my cheeks.

Maybe the gospel wasn't true. Maybe I'd just been spoon-fed it all since birth and robotically believed what I heard. I almost wished Nathan had never brought this up.

It was getting late, but I called Liza anyway.

"Hey, sorry to call so late, but I need to talk. Can I come over?" I asked.

"Sure, just don't knock, Mom's already in bed. Or I guess I'll just wait on the porch. Wear your coat. It's freezing outside."

I hung up the phone, went back upstairs, and grabbed my tennis shoes and a Cody High School sweatshirt I had inherited from Hope or Danielle, I wasn't sure. Everyone was watching TV in the living room, so I just whispered to Mom that I was leaving.

Liza waited on her porch, wrapped in a navy blue sleeping bag. She had one out for me too.

"Nice hat," I teased her about her hunter's orange wool stocking cap.

I unzipped the top of my bag and snuggled down into the cozy flannel interior.

"Is everything all right?" she asked.

"Yeah, I just . . . I don't know. I need to ask you a question."

"Okay."

"I know we've always had the Church in our lives, but do you think you personally know it's true, or is it just what you've been taught."

"A little of both, I guess," she said. "I mean if I hadn't have grown up with it, I probably wouldn't have known it was true, but I've also received my own testimony."

"How?"

"How what?" she asked.

"How did you receive your own testimony?"

"Well, when I conscientiously make a choice to follow the

gospel in some way—like pay tithing or pray sincerely—I feel good about it. And you know that one scripture says that if something brings you peace and happiness then it's a good seed. That's how I get my testimony," Liza said.

"I never really thought about it until Nathan wrote me this letter about knowing for myself. So I've been praying about it all week and I haven't gotten any kind of an answer . . . I don't know."

She shuffled in her sleeping bag so she could lean back against the house.

"Gracie, it's different for everyone. I get the confirmation that something is true when I feel happy after doing what I'm supposed to. Some people know after they talk about things with the missionaries." She looked at me kindly. "Maybe for you it's going to take more work than just praying."

"What do you mean 'more work'?" I asked.

"Well, maybe if you do some work on your end to find out if the gospel is true, Heavenly Father will do some work on His end and let you know."

I looked up at the stars and pointed out the Little Dipper to Liza. Finally, I climbed out of the sleeping bag, stood up, and gave her a hug. The night air nipped at my face.

"Thanks for being here for me. I hope we never live more than three houses away from each other."

"Me too," she said as I side-stepped to avoid the stair with the broken plank.

When I got home that night, I said good night to the family and went upstairs for a particularly lengthy prayer. I poured my heart out to Heavenly Father, telling Him I wanted to know with all my heart if the gospel was true. I was willing to "work" for it, like Liza said, but I needed His help to know what I should do. I went to bed feeling not much better than I had all week.

At 5:30 the next morning, Danielle pounded on my door.

"Gracie, we have to leave in fifteen minutes. Are you even awake yet?"

"I am now," I shouted back. I must have forgotten to set my alarm.

I pulled my hair into a ponytail and grabbed my favorite jeans and a white sweater. I'd have to forgo the shower this morning. I slid the books off my desk and into my backpack, brushed my teeth, and grabbed a bagel out of the fridge on my way to the car.

"Why can't we live in a town with release-time seminary?" I groaned.

"Quit whining," Danielle shot back. "This is my third year of it!"

We were studying the Book of Mormon this year, and Brother Batterly read a quote from President Benson that caught my attention, "There is a power in the book that will begin to flow into your lives the moment you begin a serious study. . . ."

I felt a pang of guilt. My family had probably read the Book of Mormon four or five times, but I hadn't ever really studied it. On the contrary, I was usually daydreaming until Alex nudged me to read my verses. I was contemplating the "seriousness" of my studying when Liza tapped me from behind.

"Listen, maybe this is for you."

I turned forward and looked at Brother Batterly, who was staring at me and clearing his throat.

"Like I said, Gracie, I'm issuing a challenge for every student over christmas break. I would like you to read the Book of Mormon in one week."

Yeah right—that's like 1,000 pages a day, isn't it?

"If you will pray that Heavenly Father will help you get through it, I am confident you will gain a greater knowledge of the gospel and have your testimony strengthened."

It sounded like this could be what I needed, but did I really want to go through the hassle? I mean one week was almost half of the vacation, and I would be reading night and day.

"Remember, Gracie, maybe you need to work for it," Liza whispered from behind. Sometimes that girl could read my mind. I just nodded my head.

"Beep, beep, beep."

It was the first day of my Christmas vacation, and I woke up to the alarm.

"Oh, give me a break," I mumbled and pushed the snooze button to get at least nine more minutes of rest. I rolled back over and when I opened my eyes to look at the clock I saw my Book of Mormon sitting there. Oh yeah. I didn't want to do this, but I did want an answer to my prayers.

As I pulled on my slippers, I noticed a hole wearing in the right toe. *It's about time for some new ones*, I thought. I quietly went downstairs. Everyone was still sleeping, so I nabbed a Pop Tart and warmed up a mug of water for hot chocolate. I trudged back upstairs, propped a bunch of pillows against my headboard, and snuggled back into bed. 1 Nephi, chapter 1. *Okay, I can do this.*

I'd figured out the night before that I would need to read around eighty pages a day. I didn't think that was too bad. I knew it wouldn't be the same as reading *The Great Gatsby* in a few sittings, but I could handle this.

At 7:00 I looked up and noticed my hot chocolate had gone cold and I'd only eaten half the Pop Tart. I was making progress, though. At noon Samantha peeked her head in to ask if I wanted to go sledding with some kids from the ward. I said no but realized I needed to get in the shower. I was to 1 Nephi chapter 20, though, so I decided to finish that book before quitting.

I went downstairs, still in my pajamas, and grabbed two triangle grilled cheese sandwiches off a blue glass plate on the counter.

"You sure slept in today, huh?" Mom laughed.

"No. I woke up at six," I said.

"What? Then where have you been?"

"Just reading."

"Really, what are you reading?"

"Scriptures." I was going to make her beg for any information here.

I wolfed down the sandwiches before walking up the stairs and starting the shower.

I had read 1 Nephi many times, but I was surprised at how much I was enjoying it. This was the first time I'd read it like a story instead of just a chapter at a time.

In the shower I imagined Lehi's family as the Fremonts and tried to decide who would play what part. We didn't really have a Laman and Lemuel, I knew, but still, it was fun to imagine me and my sisters drawing straws over who would contend with Laban. Of course it would be Alex who chopped off his head. I was far from Nephi material. But once it was time to build the boat, I would definitely be the most qualified. I could just imagine using Nathan as my slave laborer. He would love that!

I shut off the water, tugged on sweatpants and a long sleeve shirt, and laid back down. I wasn't even dreading my task, I was actually excited. I dove into 2 Nephi. But my excitement hit a wall an hour and a half later at chapter 7. How could I forget the Isaiah chapters? This was surely going to take longer than a week. I slowed my pace a bit since these chapters took more focus. Besides, I was on page 69 already, and it was only 2:30.

There were major chunks I was unsure of, but I think I was getting the general drift of Isaiah when Mom yelled up that I had a phone call.

"Hey Gracie, how's reading going?" Liza asked.

"Pretty good, I guess. I'm already on chapter 7 in 2 Nephi. What about you?"

"Wow, you're fast. I just finished 1 Nephi. Hey, I was

wondering if you wanted to come over tonight and we could read together."

I hesitated for a moment, not wanting to hurt her feelings, but I knew she would understand.

"That would be much more fun, I'm sure, but I think I really need to do this on my own. You know?"

"Okay. You're probably right. Hey, don't forget to pray too."

We said good-bye, and I was up the stairs in three leaps.

"What are you up to, Gracie?" Mom yelled after me. I pretended I didn't hear her and shut my door.

Isaiah had slowed me down a lot, so I got to chapter 11 at five that night. That was eighty pages. I'd gotten through the first day. I knelt to say my prayers.

"Dear Heavenly Father, I'm trying my best to find my own testimony. I really am working at it. I've been reading the Book of Mormon all day and I feel great about doing it. Just help me know if it's true. I truly want to know for myself. In the name of Jesus Christ, amen."

❦

At the end of day two I was at Alma chapter 13 and I offered the same prayer I'd been praying each day. Was gaining a testimony really supposed to be this hard? That afternoon I was so tired I felt like I had to hold my eyelids open to keep going and twice I had fallen asleep mid-chapter.

The hardest day was Sunday, though, because we had church at eleven and I accidentally slept in until ten. I didn't even get started reading until that afternoon when we got home. The wars and battles of the Nephites and Lamanites seemed never-ending. But when I finally finished Alma, I got a second wind and flew through Helaman to chapter 14.

I only had two days left. Was Heavenly Father going to come through on His end of this deal?

At 10:30 PM when I closed my book, I went out on the back porch. It was freezing, and I could see my breath, but the fresh air felt good. I prayed for the second time that night, and when I again felt nothing, I grew frustrated. I clenched my teeth and balled my fists up. Wasn't I doing my best? Was it too much to ask for a simple answer? Maybe it was all just lies. Why else wouldn't I be feeling the Spirit when I was working so hard for it? Why was I wasting my time this way if there was nothing behind the words on the pages?

I jumped when I heard Sadie, our black lab, scratch at the slider. She wanted to come outside with me, and it looked like she had something. I let her out and snagged the soggy paper from her mouth. It was wet and crumpled, but before I unfolded it, I knew what it was. Nathan's letter. That was weird. Sadie must have picked it up off my floor, but I was sure I'd put that letter away in my desk. I read my brother's words about me "knowing for myself" again. Dejected, I went back inside, tossed the letter in the trash, and collapsed onto my bed.

The next morning I woke rejuvenated. It was my last day of reading, and I decided to fast. If the answer didn't come, I didn't want it to be because I didn't try. My family was having dinner when I reached Moroni Chapter 10. I read verses 4–5 over and over. ". . . and if ye shall ask with a sincere heart, with real intent, having faith in Christ . . . ." But I had done all that, hadn't I? And I still didn't know the truth. "He will manifest the truth of it unto you, by the power of the Holy Ghost."

I knelt down and began to weep.

"Heavenly Father," I choked out between sobs. "I have the strongest desire to know if the gospel is true. I have read the Book of Mormon. I have lived the gospel standards. I have never questioned the reality of Christ and that He died for my sins. Please, please help me to know."

I continued to pray and beg Heavenly Father for almost forty minutes. When I tried to stand, my knees almost gave out, they were aching so badly. I just crumpled onto my bed and hugged my knees up close. It had been the longest, most heartfelt prayer I'd ever said, and I knew it was my last hope. If I didn't receive an answer after this, then the gospel wasn't true. With all of my heart I hoped it was.

I was physically and mentally exhausted. I dozed off as I lay there, staring at the stitches on my antique pink and white quilt. It was 10:30 PM when I woke up to Mom pulling my covers out from beneath me and tucking them in around me.

"Good night," she said. "I love you."

I watched her as she walked out of my room, her head hanging down. Through the hallway light, I could see her pause, shake her head, and turn back to me.

"Gracie, read 2 Nephi 22:2," she said. Then she shut the door.

I rolled off the bed, flipped on my desk light, and looked in the mirror. I looked awful. My hair was piled up on top of my head like a nest with a ponytail buried somewhere in the mess. A crusty white drool line ran from the corner of my mouth toward my chin. My eyes looked bloodshot. I pulled the chair out from the desk and turned it backward. I straddled it, leaned my chin on the wooden back, and stared at my tattered scriptures. I honestly didn't know if I could read another verse. Nothing had worked so far.

I slowly opened the leather binding anyway and thumbed my way to page ninety-three. I read it quickly and then reread it, concentrating on every word.

"Behold, God is my salvation; I will trust and not be afraid; for the Lord Jehovah is my strength and my song; he also has become my salvation."

My eyes were wet, and a warm glowing feeling began radiating out from my chest. My hands were even a bit tingly. I pushed my scriptures back on the desk when a tear fell to the page. The tears slowly trickled down my cheeks and dropped on the desk. I grabbed a tissue from the drawer.

This feeling reminded me of two years ago in the garage

when Nathan hugged me close in my time of need, but now it was much stronger. It felt like someone had just placed a warm heavy blanket around my shoulders. The whole room seemed lighter, and I felt free of the stress and worry I'd harbored over the past two weeks. Sitting in my room alone, I felt so loved I was almost confused. Was this the Spirit?

I read it again.

The Lord is my strength and my song and my salvation. I knew that was true. I knew it. I felt it. And I knew that the Holy Ghost wouldn't comfort me like this if I wasn't on the right path. I didn't need to be afraid because I had the Lord's gospel in my life. This was His church and He was pleased that I was trying my best to know that.

He was answering my prayer. Finally. I knew He was answering my prayer. Suddenly, almost instantly, all the pain was gone. The gospel was true!

I jumped out of my chair and ran for the door, but I stopped short.

I rushed back, knelt down, and thanked Heavenly Father for helping me know the gospel was true. I felt that same, warm-blanket-love feeling I had just received.

I had to catch Mom before she went to bed.

She was in her bathroom, and I knocked softly.

"Yes?"

"Can you come downstairs for a minute before you go to bed?" I asked.

"Sure. I'll be right down."

I waited for her on a kitchen stool. I knew I had the biggest smile on my face when she stopped halfway down the stairs and looked at me strangely.

"What's going on?"

"Mom, why did you tell me to read that scripture?" I asked.

She paused like she was trying to figure it out herself.

"Well, I'm not sure. I mean I had to go look up that scripture after I told you that just to remember what it said. I was leaving your room, and the Spirit whispered to me to tell you that. When I was a teenager that scripture used to be a favorite of mine, but I must admit I haven't really read it in years," she said. "Did you read it?"

"Yes!" I jumped off the stool and gave her a hug. "Thank you so much. I did read it, and it changed everything."

"Gracie Fremont, you've been a little sneaky this week, and I've noticed you've been reading an awful lot." She smiled. "It's time to tell your mom what's going on."

I was hoping she'd ask. I recounted the whole story from Nathan's letter to Brother Batterly's challenge. When I got to tonight, she had tears running down her face.

"Mom, don't cry" I said, embarrassed. "I'm *happy* now. I'm *so* happy now, in fact."

"I just wish you would have told me while you were having such a hard time finding your answer," she said.

"I couldn't, though," I answered. "Then I wouldn't have found out for myself. You know?"

I hugged her again.

"I love you so much, honey. I'm so proud of you. Hey, we better go to bed—it's almost midnight."

I nodded my head and followed her upstairs. She kissed me good night and went into her room. I lay in bed with my eyes wide open, smiling until my face hurt. Twenty minutes later, Mom opened the door a tiny bit, "Are you still awake?"

"Yeah, you too?"

"Do you want to do something?" she asked, surprising me. Mom had never been much of a night owl.

"Like what?"

"Just come on."

We went downstairs, and she found two huge Hershey's bars at the back of the freezer. We went into the den, and I got comfy on the floor. She pulled down every photo album on the shelf. She laid them out in front of us and dusted off the light blue one—it was mine. I'd looked at it hundreds of times, but never with just Mom and me. She told me stories to go along with each photo that I'd never heard before. She pointed out how my eyebrows were peaked, even as an infant. We lounged on huge pillows on the floor until four in the morning.

The next day—Christmas Eve—we picked up my brother Nathan from the airport. His two years were up.

eleven

James Fromberg was probably the best-looking guy in our class. He was six feet tall and had movie-star eyes and a strong, square jaw. His rigorous weight-lifting schedule had earned him chiseled abs—a feature he loved to flaunt. I swear his T-shirt was permanently removed from May until September.

Even as a sophomore, James was the star wide-receiver at Cody High School. Over the past few years, he'd worked his way right through the list of popular girls to date. Jessica Rouster and her gang had all made the list, along with the elite of the senior, junior, and freshman classes.

"Fremont" and "Fromberg" were close enough that James's locker was always close to mine, so I was frequently an unwilling witness to James's daily dose of fondling with his current lady. Even though I could admit James was cute, my admiration stopped there. I'd had biology, algebra, and eighth-grade English with him, and he seemed about as deep as a cookie sheet. Sometimes I wondered how he'd actually passed those classes.

Chelsea had a different perspective. Since sixth grade she'd been telling us, "James will be my boyfriend." Liza and I would just nod our heads, knowing that if Chelsea proclaimed it with such vitality, she could probably make it happen. We never discussed it, but I think we both hoped he wouldn't go for her.

Chelsea would turn sixteen in October—the first of us three—so by Labor Day weekend, she was concocting a plan to get James to ask her out.

Just as she had been at six, Chelsea was still beautiful. Between junior high and high school she had become an all-the-way blonde, swapping in her natural highlights for the bottled version. She also bought colored contacts to make her already green eyes pop even more. Chelsea was the only one of us who had tried sports, and it turned out she was a natural at tennis. Her already Californian tan was bordering on Hawaiian now.

Chelsea was definitely on James's level, but we didn't hang out with his crowd. Instead, she was the girl everyone knew was beautiful but who no one quite connected with. No one but us, that is. She was lost in her own world and had a confidence unlike any other teenage girl I knew.

This was the first Labor Day I ever remembered being warm in Cody, and we were taking full advantage of it. The three of us were sunbathing on oversized towels on the gravelly beach of the Buffalo Bill Reservoir. Brown, dry, deserted hills surrounded us, but the clear sky was brilliant. It stretched out forever. I could see Chelsea's dad jetting around in his sparkling red and black Mastercraft not too far from shore; her brother Colton trailed behind on a wakeboard.

"Okay, girls, we have less than one month until I turn sixteen. What are your ideas?" Chelsea asked. She had one hand in a bag of potato chips and another on a can of soda.

"Hmmm," Liza said, propping herself up on her elbows. "Maybe you could help him in geometry. You said you have that class together right?"

"Hmmm," I mimicked. "Maybe you could go out with a Mormon who isn't a jerk." I rolled my eyes and flipped over onto my stomach. I could feel the fronts of my thighs beginning to burn.

"Oh, come on, Gracie, he's not a jerk. Just because someone is popular doesn't mean he's a jerk. Besides, what Mormon would you suggest I date?" She laughed. "Like there's anyone in our ward!"

Instantly I pictured three guys from our ward that I wouldn't mind going out with, but I knew they wouldn't be up to par for Chelsea. The only one I knew she'd agree to dating was Cade Rawlings. And even though Cade had only been a friend to me, I didn't want to share him. He was the only cool thing I had over Chelsea and Liza.

"Nope, James is the one, Gracie. James is the one."

<hr/>

A few weeks later, James invited Chelsea to go out on her birthday, and we didn't talk about anything else for the next week. Her over-the-top excitement was so annoying. She spent every pass time speculating on what he would wear, what he would say, what he would do. At first I tried to hold it back, but as the day grew nearer, I couldn't hide my aggravation. As Chelsea forged through the hall toward the gym, I walked behind her, rolling my eyes and whispering under my breath. Liza snagged me by the sleeve and whispered in my ear.

"Seriously, I know he's not a great guy, but let her be happy, okay?" she said. "It's her first date." I decided to drop it.

After school Chelsea's mom picked us up in their Four-Runner, and we drove to their huge house on the golf course. Walking up the brick walkway, I couldn't help but compare our houses. In a word, the Copeland house was fancy. The arched entryway must have been sixteen feet high. Inside the heavy double doors was a marble foyer leading to a wide oak staircase. Professional portraits of the kids lined the walls, and beautiful pictures of the Savior were everywhere.

We shared in their family birthday dinner of prime rib and mashed potatoes, and then it was upstairs for Primpfest 2000. Liza and I were given strict instructions to pick out a cute outfit while Chelsea showered. We easily selected a blue and white sweater with a pair of jeans and tan sandals. Our choice was immediately tossed aside, though, because Chelsea deemed it "way too ordinary." Instead Chelsea began her own arduous task of picking clothes that ended after a half hour and twenty or more changes. Liza and I worked like servants, rehanging the tops and refolding the jeans.

Chelsea finally decided on a baby pink top with darker pink lace around the bottom and a little black skirt. When she walked downstairs, though, her dad demanded she put on a skirt that was knee-length or longer. Chelsea pouted but eventually complied. She chose a calf-length flared denim skirt. Next, it was onto the makeup and hair, all of which required six hands to master. At length Chelsea's desired look—drop-dead-gorgeous—was achieved, and the three of us sat on the stiff floral couch in the family's living room.

I hoped Amy wouldn't pick us up until after James came for Chelsea, but she showed up first. Liza hugged Chelsea and wished her good luck, and I squeezed her hand as we walked out to Liza's mom's car.

"Keep your cell close," I whispered. "We're calling at 10:30 for the details."

⁑⁂⁑

Back at Liza's house, the two of us were bored out of our minds. We watched *Grease* and recited most the movie from memory and then went out to the porch. We had nothing to talk about except for Chelsea and what she was probably doing.

"Who do you want to go on your first date with when you turn sixteen?" Liza asked me. My birthday wasn't until April, and I hadn't even considered my options yet.

"I don't know," I said. "I can't exactly imagine a ton of offers on the table."

"What are you talking about?" Liza humored me. "You're going to have to fight them off."

Later that night we snuck the cordless phone up to Liza's room. She covered the speaker holes while she dialed the number. After four rings, she hung up.

"What in the world? She's not home yet," Liza said. "She better not be in trouble."

A few minutes later we tried again, and this time Chelsea answered. She was almost euphoric. Liza held the phone out so we both could hear.

"He's gorgeous, don't you think, guys? Oh my goodness, I swear, he is the hottest guy I've ever seen," she swooned. "So do you want to know all about it?"

"Of course!" Liza prodded.

"Well, his truck is so nice, first of all. But, anyway, okay, he paid for the movie and we went to see *Into the Fast Lane*," she paused. "Don't worry, Liza, it's PG-13."

Liza laughed.

"Before the movie started, he asked me if I wanted popcorn, but I was too nervous to eat, so I just drank a pop. I swear, I don't have a clue what the movie was about because I was just watching him out of the corner of my eye the whole time! In the middle of the movie, he put the arm rest up and sort of slid over closer to me."

"Oh, wait, here comes Dad." There was a long pause while Chelsea held her breath.

"Okay, never mind, I'm good. So anyway, after the movie we got ice cream. He told me about his truck and football and that sort of stuff. He said maybe he'd come watch one of my tennis matches sometime. I sort of hope he doesn't, though, because I'd be so nervous, I'm sure I'd play awful."

Liza interrupted, "So you like him, it sounds like?"

"Are you kidding? It was amazing. He was so nice, Gracie, not what you thought at all." I didn't answer.

"I better go," she said. "I hear my dad out there again."

"Happy birthday," we both said in unison.

"Thanks, guys. Oh yeah, James said he would call me tomorrow. I'll let you know! Bye."

We hung up and giggled at Chelsea's enthusiasm. Still, I hoped it was just a fleeting crush.

⁕—◦⊱◦⊰◦—⁕

After two weeks, I was so sick of the name James Fromberg, I could've screamed. They had gone on two more dates, and Chelsea talked about him constantly. The Copelands were starting to raise their eyebrows.

"'We don't want you to get serious with one boy when you're sixteen,'" Chelsea said, mimicking her mom. "I mean, they're being ridiculous!"

"Hey, maybe they're right," Liza said.

"Why? James has high standards," she said. "Anyway, it's not like we're going to get married. I wish they would just lay off." Her face begged our concurrence, but she could tell she wasn't winning us over.

"If it starts to get serious, I'll tell him I can't date him anymore, but for now I'm just having fun. I mean, I waited until I was sixteen, for goodness sake," she said.

The day after Halloween, which she spent with James instead of Liza and me, Chelsea described their first kiss.

"We sat under the stars on the tailgate of his truck, and it was so quiet," she said. "The wind was blowing a little, so I'll bet my hair looked all flowy like in the movies. We were talking about his Dad, who he totally hates, and then mid-sentence he just turns to me and stares at me. I started to say something, but he just put his finger to my lips to stop me. He leaned toward me, and I closed my eyes, and then he kissed me. It was more romantic than anything I ever could have dreamed up."

Gag me. This was about enough for me. Liza and I looked at each other, and Chelsea sensed our concern.

"Oh, come on," Chelsea said. "It's just a kiss. My goodness, lighten up."

In two days "just a kiss" became a hallway make-out session.

And from three lockers down, I witnessed Chelsea becoming the next Jessica Rouster on James's list. Watching their groping—out of the corner of my eye, of course—didn't seem a bit romantic to me.

By mid-November Chelsea and James were inseparable. She'd rarely make plans with Liza and me anymore, or when she did, James dropped her off and picked her up a few hours later. Honestly, I didn't blame Chelsea for not wanting to hang out with us anymore because when she did, Liza morphed into Mrs. Mom. No matter what angle Liza tried though, Chelsea had only one answer: "It's not serious. We're just dating!"

Being on James's wrist had elevated Chelsea's status in school dramatically. She got invites from girls we had never hung out with before. She attempted diplomacy at first, making sure we were allotted just as much time as her new friends, but by Christmas break, Liza and I barely saw her any more. She'd call one of us every now and then with an I've-been-so-busy excuse, but we didn't make her explain.

Liza turned sixteen in November and went out with a guy from the ward. She wasn't interested in him, and I think she only said yes out of pity. It hadn't held the same excitement as Chelsea's dating life. Liza didn't plan or primp, and we didn't stay up late that night talking about her miniature golf outing.

I hated to admit it, but without Chelsea, it was turning into a boring winter and spring. I stayed busy with a curio cabinet I was building in wood shop, and Liza took a job as a busser at a restaurant. We went to movies or school games on the weekends, but when Young Women's activities became the highlight of my week, I knew something was missing.

In February Chelsea stopped showing up to Mutual. One night she called Liza and said she was too sick to come. That night we went to a college volleyball game and saw her driving by in James's truck. I never mentioned that we'd seen her, and I'm sure Liza didn't either.

A few days later at school, their make-out session was maddening. Seriously, couldn't Chelsea at least come up for air? I took a breath as I grabbed my gym bag, shut my locker a little too loud, and had to face them to walk by. James's hand must have been glued to her back pocket. Of course she didn't notice me as I passed, but I couldn't stand it any more. Just a foot from their meshed faces, I stopped and stared.

Finally, she turned toward me and giggled.

"Yeah?"

I didn't know what to say. I just glared.

"What in the world was that for, Gracie?" Chelsea asked.

"I just think it's gross the way you two grope in the hallway. That's all."

"Give me a break. Get off your high horse and live a little."

I spun on my heels and headed toward the nearest bathroom. I knew the tears were coming.

⋆⟶⟤⟣⟥⟵⋆

From then on, Liza talked to Chelsea on the phone, but I left her alone. As far as I was concerned, she had become one of the mean popular girls I didn't like. She laughed when the jocks tripped kids and she made fun of less-attractive girls right along with her new friends. When I saw her wearing trendy strapless tops and super short skirts, I could only imagine the fighting going on at the Copeland home.

The worst part was on Mondays when I had to listen to Chelsea, James, and the rest of their clique talk about the parties over the weekend and what they couldn't remember from being too drunk.

I wanted to punch Chelsea, but at the same time, I ached for her. She had been sucked in, and I didn't know if she'd ever come back.

A few days before my birthday, I stood at my locker, searching for my history notebook. I could've sworn I just had it. From behind me, I could hear James and a few other guys talking at his locker.

"Yeah, she's hot, huh?" James said. "I don't know though, man."

"What? What?" The guys lingered on his words.

"I mean she won't put out. I've spent the better part of sophomore year working on her, and it's hardly paid off. I don't know how long I can stick with this."

The guys laughed. "Fromberg can't get none," one of them screeched.

I felt sick. Chelsea's "romantic" boyfriend, who she thought was so sweet, was considering breaking up with her for having a shred of morals? I waited until they walked away and almost ran to Chelsea's locker. She stood with her shoulders back, applying a coat of lipstick in her mirror.

"Chelsea, I know you hate me, but I need to talk to you."

"I don't hate you. I just think you're a little too strict, you know?" she said, her eyes never leaving the mirror. "What do you have to talk about?"

"Well, um, I just heard James talking to his friends, and he said if you don't put out soon he's going to dump you," I told her honestly.

Chelsea twisted the top back on her lipstick and set it down on a miniature shelf she had stuck up in her locker. She shifted her weight back and forth between her legs without saying anything. Then tears welled up in her eyes.

"That is such a low blow, Gracie," she said. "I can't believe you would lie like that just to break us up! Seriously. What's wrong with you?"

"I'm not lying. It's what he said."

"James loves me, so leave me alone."

Chelsea shoved by me and ran down the hall.

It was less than two weeks later when I heard James talking to those same friends.

"Fromberg ain't gettin' any," the same obnoxious kid leered.

"Shut up, Smith. I don't know. Something's changed with her . . . It's like Chelsea all of the sudden ain't so prude anymore."

The guys shouted, slapped shoulders, and gave high-fives all around.

What? No.

"Yep, she's definitely different." He smiled.

My warning to her had totally backfired. Instead of getting her away from him, it drove her right into his arms. Chelsea knew I was telling the truth, but she cared more about losing James than anything else.

If Chelsea didn't hate me before, she did now. Every time we passed in the hall, she either ignored me or looked at me like I was something stuck to her shoe. When I was around, she'd talk extra loud about staying out late with James or what she'd been drinking last weekend. Her new friends were in on it too, and mean girls love having someone to hate.

My sixteenth birthday had come and gone without event. Lucky me, my birthday fell on a Monday, so Mom and Dad planned a big embarrassing family home evening about chastity. First they showed us this white rose and how beautiful it was. Then they passed it around for everyone to touch the petals. They showed it again and how it wasn't beautiful and pure anymore. Dad explained the analogy to being morally clean and then gave me a new white rose. The whole scheme was mortifying.

There was no first date to primp for, no party, no driver's test. Instead, Liza and I went to *Two Strangers*, a boring and predictable love story.

Before I went to bed that night, Mom and Dad came in my room to give me my present. I tore open the paper—Mom's signature brown grocery bag decorated in marker—half hoping for a cell phone, but knowing better. Instead, I found a 25-piece Dremel Kit. It was fantastic. I couldn't wait to get out in the shop with it.

Before Mom left she said I was allowed to wear makeup now if I wanted. But all I added to my morning routine of deodorant, lotion, and chapstick was a bit of mascara.

By the time school was out, I still hadn't been asked on a first date. At least Liza hadn't gone on any more either. Chelsea was riding high though—she was at the top of every guy's list now. Too bad her heart belonged to James.

twelve

"Slow down, Grace," Nathan yelled. "You're going to hit the canal."

I pulled on the brake lever way too fast and flew over the handlebars of the four-wheeler. I landed on my back in a heap of weeds and dust about five feet from my machine and only a few feet from the water. It hurt, but not so bad that I couldn't laugh. Nate jumped off his four-wheeler and ran to me.

"Are you okay?"

I couldn't answer him, I was laughing so hard.

"I guess so," he said.

I stood up and brushed the dirt from my rear and legs while Nathan wiped off my back.

"Sorry," I said. "I had no idea we were getting so close to the canal."

Nathan just laughed. "No big deal. Just be careful, I doubt your paycheck would cover the cost of a sunken four-wheeler."

The first break in my year of boredom was when Nathan and Danielle came home from school in May. Danielle and I had never been close, but over the past four years, Nate had become my closest friend next to Liza. He got me a job working with him for Gregory Farms that summer. It was the

80

hardest work I'd ever done, but I loved it. My arms earned muscle for the first time in my life, and I was so tan I could have given even Chelsea a run for her money. Mostly, though, I loved being with Nathan.

Mr. Gregory had us doing odd jobs—feeding chickens, mucking stalls, and fixing fences. But mostly we were in charge of setting irrigation ditches, which gave us plenty of unsupervised time to play on four-wheelers. The 500-acre farm was predominately flat, but we had found one steep, sandy hill to race up and down. There was always something to talk about with Nathan. For some reason he was especially interested in keeping up with the Chelsea/James gossip.

⊶⊰⊱⊷

At the Fourth of July parade, Nathan, Liza, and I climbed up the town's eagle statue at the west end of Main Street to get a good view. Nathan had tried to get me to climb it when we were younger, but I had never been strong enough until now. We watched with a bird's eye view as the rest of our family meandered through the crowd toward us. I held up my hand to shield the sun and saw Mom talking to Sister Copeland in front of the Irma Hotel. Sitting there on the curb was Chelsea and her dad. "Look," I pointed out to Liza, "no James in sight."

Throughout the parade I kept one eye on Chelsea, half waiting for James to come whisk her away. The high school band marched by, playing an especially noisy rendition of "Louie, Louie." Liza pointed out a few friends, and we waved, unseen. I turned to see if Chelsea was watching, but instead she had her head down on her folded arms. She was shaking. It looked like she was crying. A few seconds later she got up and ran inside the restaurant behind them.

Liza had watched the scene unfold too and said we should go check on Chelsea.

"I don't know," I said. "She hates me, Liza."

"Fine. Well, I'm going," she said, scrambling down the rocks.

My flip-flops slapped the sidewalk as we ran toward the restaurant. Liza shouted something over her shoulder to me, but I couldn't hear over the wailing fire engine sirens. We were getting close when the parade ended and suddenly we were encased in the thick crowd. Everyone but us seemed to be moving west. We pushed through the crowd, but by the time we got there, Chelsea and her parents were gone.

The next day was Sunday, and it was the first time I'd seen Chelsea at church for most of the summer. The Copelands were there early and so was Liza, so she got the gossip first.

I caught up with them after sacrament meeting. When I saw Chelsea's swollen eyes, my heart dropped. Whatever she was going through was much worse than my damaged pride. Still, I didn't know what to say. She read my mind.

"Gracie, please let's not be in a fight right now. I've got too many other things to deal with. Just be my friend, okay?" she asked.

"I'm so sorry," I said and hugged her tight. Chelsea shook in my arms, and I knew she was trying to keep her sobs silent. The three of us walked quickly to the stage and found a dark corner behind the curtain.

"I knew you were right, but I didn't care," she sobbed. "I know you guys think I'm stupid, but I love him!"

Chelsea rehearsed the whole story to us, and it had played out just as I'd imagined it would but hoped it wouldn't. Chelsea didn't want to lose James, so she did what she knew would keep him around. And it did. For awhile, but eventually a new girl came along, and James was through with Chelsea. I nodded my head, and tears slid down my cheeks. We hugged for a long time.

By the time school started, our friendship seemed back to normal. Chelsea was struggling through her repentance process and was getting back to our confident, fun-loving Chels. She made Liza and me two promises: she would never date another nonmember, and she would never give up our friendship again.

One Saturday a few weeks before school, Liza borrowed her mom's Jeep Cherokee, and we drove to Billings for school shopping. The blue sky seemed to stretch forever, and we cranked the radio up loud. There was no AC, so we rolled our windows down, even though we were going sixty-five on the highway. The car filled with whipping hair and singing—or rather screaming—girls.

We hit the mall early, and I was finished in about an hour. I bought three new pairs of jeans and several short-sleeve shirts. I found two sweaters I loved and a new pair of brown leather shoes with straps and pink stitching. Liza completed her shopping shortly after I did, but Chelsea was another story. She combed through the racks of Abercrombie and Buckle and then spent hours in Vanity and Maurices. After she accrued twenty bags and more than six hundred dollars on her dad's credit card, she was ready to hit Old Navy. Liza and I insisted we eat first, so we pulled into Applebee's and were seated immediately at a tall table with three stools.

We each ordered a strawberry lemonade, mozzarella sticks, and a blondie—our favorite dessert.

"Okay guys, so I've been thinking," Chelsea said.

"Uh-oh," Liza laughed.

"So I know I was a jerk to everyone last year."

"We're definitely not going to argue with that," I said.

"Listen, listen. So I know I was mean and everything, but I want to make up for it this year."

"What exactly do you have in mind?" Liza asked.

Chelsea lifted her green corduroy purse off her lap and set it on the table. She pulled out a folded pink sheet of paper.

"I made this huge list of everyone I want to apologize to,"

she said, unfolding the paper. "And that's not all. I want to make tons of new friends too."

"Oh, great, here comes Mrs. Popular again," I said.

"No, no, not that. I want to make friends with new people. Different ones that we've never been friends with before."

Liza looked at me, suspicious.

"Let's just try it, guys," Chelsea said. "Maybe it'll be fun."

Just then the waiter brought the cheese sticks, and Chelsea snagged her camera from her purse.

"Could you take a picture of us?"

We leaned into each other and smiled at the waiter, who happened to be cute.

"Say 'cheese.'"

After Old Navy, we stopped by a sports outlet for Chelsea to pick up a couple of new tennis skirts and then we got back on the highway. We were all worn out, so the two-hour ride home was much less exciting than the one that morning. However, we did stop once when I spotted a cow with the biggest udder I'd ever seen. We took a picture of the poor thing, whose swollen udder almost dragged on the ground. Oh, the fun to be had in Wyoming. We pulled into Chelsea's driveway just before 10:00 PM. It took all three of us to unload her new school clothes.

"Talk to you tomorrow," I said, turning back toward the Jeep.

"Hey, I was serious about my plan," Chelsea said. "You watch. I'm going to be nicer than you two! Hey, by senior year, I'll probably be homecoming queen."

I thought Chelsea was joking, but I glanced back over my shoulder and saw that starry look in her eyes. I knew Chelsea was making another proclamation, one she entirely expected to unfold. Yep, Chelsea was back.

thirteen

"Have you guys ever been in the Ag Shop?" Chelsea asked. "It's really, um, interesting."

Liza and I looked at each other and laughed.

We sat in a back booth at Burger King, munching on Whopper Juniors and fries. Chelsea wadded up her paper wrapper and walked to the nearby garbage. On her way back to our table, she pulled a pink paper from her pocket.

"My list of sorry's is finally done," she said.

In ticking off her list, Chelsea had already made friends with nearly every clique in school. The amazing part was, she wasn't being fake. She was taking a genuine interest in new people, and I have to admit, our lackluster social calendar was getting a whole new spice. Liza and I caught her bug, and it seemed we had a year's goal of becoming friends with as many new people as possible. We watched a garage band practice; we went to swim meets; we helped the student council make posters for lockers.

I mostly focused on the guys in wood shop. These weren't the jocks of the school, but most of them had a lot more character—and a few were really talented too.

Quentin Libbert was one of them. He was almost painfully shy. It was obvious from his clothes that he didn't have a lot of money, and his bright red hair had earned him a slew of nicknames. He wore wire-framed glasses that were a bit too big by today's standards, and they only magnified the oodles of freckles he had sprayed across his cheeks. He was taller than me and thin too. I'd worked near him for most of last year, but we'd never talked.

"Hi," I said.

Nothing.

"Hi," again.

"Oh." He looked up confused. "Were you talking to me?"

"Yeah."

"Oh, hi, then, I guess."

I waited for more, but that was it. He turned back to his graph paper and ruler and continued drawing a set of plans. That was our first conversation.

Every day started like this, but one day I finally broke through. I was routering the edges of the top piece of a night stand I'd been building. When I looked up, I saw him watching me.

"You're pretty good at this stuff for a girl," he said.

"For a girl?" I raised my arched eyebrows. "Or for anyone?"

"Yeah, I guess," he said. "How'd you learn woodworking?"

"When I was little, my grandpa let me watch him in his shop. I thought it looked kind of fun."

"Does he live here?" Quentin asked.

"No, he lives in Casper, but when we were little, my sisters and brother and I would stay with my grandparents in the summertime."

"Sisters and brothers, huh? How many of them do you got?"

I smiled. Was Quentin actually conversing with me?

"Just one brother but four sisters."

Even with a guy as quiet as Quentin, a family of six kids usually got the talk flowing. Soon we were gabbing about my siblings and our "farm," and whether we had three sets of bunk beds.

"That must be kinda fun," he said as he turned back to his work. "We just got me and my mom."

❧⁓✦⊙✦⁓❧

I brushed my hand across the smooth finish of the walnut bowl I'd been turning on the lathe. The sides were still too thick, so I grabbed a U-shaped bowl gouge and started again. After a few minutes, I heard the bell, so I switched off the lathe, unclamped my bowl, and took off my safety glasses. I hung my apron on the hook and grabbed the broom to clean up my sawdust. Just then Quentin tapped my shoulder and caught me off guard.

"Gracie, why do you talk to me? You know I don't have any friends, right?"

"Um, yes you do," I said. "I'm your friend."

When he blushed, the redness of his cheeks almost completely hid his freckles.

"I don't know what anyone else thinks. But I think you're a really interesting guy. And besides, I believe we're all God's children, so you're not too different from the rest of us. You know?"

He just nodded his head and waved as he left the shop.

Two days later I was almost ready to wax my bowl. I softly rubbed any remaining sawdust off with a cotton rag. Quentin was leafing through magazine plans for bookshelves. He looked up and said, "What do you mean we're all God's children?"

"Well, exactly that. God created every person. He created you, and so He knows all about you."

"How do you know that?" Quentin asked.

I put down my rag; I knew this conversation might take awhile. But then I changed my mind.

"I'll tell you what. Every Monday my family gets together

and talks about stuff like this and then we do something fun. Do you want to come tonight?"

This must have been the first social invite Quentin ever had in his life because he looked dumbfounded.

"Um, well . . ." he stammered.

"It's not that weird, Quentin," I laughed. "I invite. You say 'yes.'"

"Okay, yes."

He tore out a corner of the magazine, and I jotted down directions. I told him to be there at six. Quentin helped me with the wax, and the bowl turned out beautiful. It was the one skill I'd admit he was better at than me. I wanted to take it home right away, but I didn't want to risk smudging it, so I carefully set the bowl on a high rack to dry.

❦

"Mom?" I yelled as I walked in the door. I tossed my backpack in the front closet. I needed to make this sound as nonchalant as possible or I knew they'd get the wrong idea. Mom stepped out from the kitchen wearing yellow rubber gloves.

"Hi, honey," she said. "The sink is stopped up again."

"Um, I invited someone over for FHE tonight. Is that all right?"

"Of course. Do I know her?" Mom asked.

"Oh, actually, it's a *he*. And no you don't know him," I said, grabbing an apple from the basket on the table. "His name is Quentin."

"Aaahh." Mom smiled. "Who exactly is this 'Quentin,' Gracie?"

"Oh please. Trust me, Mom," I grimaced. "He's not that kind of friend."

I ran upstairs and changed my sweater for a T-shirt. I kicked my shoes into my closet. Mom's comment got me wondering if Quentin was getting the wrong idea about our friendship.

To make sure he didn't, I quickly dialed Liza and told her she had to come over that night too. Alex and I were the only ones left at home now, but Hope was bringing her family over that night as well.

I tried to do some homework, but for some reason I couldn't concentrate. The more I thought about it, the more I imagined my family ruining a good missionary opportunity. I called Dad at work and told him to tailor his lesson a bit.

At 6:05 we were all ready in the living room, and I glanced out the picture window. Splashing through the mud on our road came the loudest, biggest, rustiest pickup truck I'd ever seen. Quentin's 1970-something Ford had huge tires and a lift. The body though, was in the mid-stages of repair. Besides the forest green passenger-side door, the rest of the truck was a chipped orangey-red color.

"Is that him?" Hope laughed as I nodded.

Quentin came in, and I introduced him to everyone. The house wasn't hot at all, but he was sweating. He looked so nervous I could've sworn he was about to pass out.

"Could we have the activity first tonight and then the lesson?" I suggested. Maybe that wouldn't be so intimidating.

"Sure," Dad said.

It was Alex's turn for the activity, and she pulled out the same game she had chosen every time for the past three years: Pig Mania. In Pig Mania you roll two rubber pigs that serve as dice. The way the pigs land determines how many points you rack up. In normal circumstances, the Fremonts get carried away with the pigs, but thankfully everyone kept their cool. Quentin still hadn't said much, but by the end of the game he had stopped sweating and his shoulders had dropped a bit. Mom brought out caramel corn and milk, and Dad started the lesson.

Dad spoke about Heavenly Father and how much He loves us. That was it—and I was so glad. Quentin sat on the front of his bench with his elbows on his knees and his chin in his hands. He leaned forward, almost eerily focused on every word.

In fact, I wondered if he'd ever heard much about God before. At the end of the lesson, Dad asked if anyone had any questions. Quentin didn't ask any, but I think he took the comment as a clue that it was time to go.

He swung his heavy boots over the bench, stood up, and said "Thanks for having me over. It was nice to meet you all."

I walked him out.

"You're so lucky to have a family like this," Quentin said.

"And you've only met half of them." I laughed.

Our *family table has seen its day*, I decided. It was huge—four feet wide and eight feet long—and was built by Dad in a picnic-table style. The wooden benches were each close to 150 pounds. Everyone who came to our house commented on that table. And it was beautiful, I had to admit. But looking close, its wear was obvious. Dad used pine, even though it wasn't a hard wood, because Mom loved light wood. Consequently the table was covered in pock marks and divots. There were fork and spoon marks from impatient toddlers, remnants of math equations from years of homework pressing through the paper, and the prints of shoe toes kicked into the legs. I would love to take this out to the shop and sand it down, refinish it, for Mom. But then again, the marks also told the stories of all of us Fremonts growing up, and I wasn't sure she'd want those removed.

I glanced across the table and could hardly believe it was only a month ago that Quentin walked into our house sweating bullets. He seemed right at home.

"Yahtzee!" he yelled. "You know, you guys aren't very good at this game."

Every Monday night, Quentin was acting more and more like part of the family. He joined in asking questions and making comments, and he always ate a healthy portion of Mom's treats or my chocolate chip cookies.

Between cutting, turning, and sanding, we'd talk about the gospel at wood shop. I was amazed at how much I was enjoying our friendship. Before the "Chelsea Friendship Challenge" as Liza and I called it, I probably never would've talked to this kid. But now I was finding out he was a really great guy—and even more, he was interested in the gospel!

One day at the end of class he asked me if I wanted to go "mudding" with him. I was hesitant, wondering if he considered it a date. I think he read my mind because he said, "It's not that weird, Gracie. I invite. You say 'yes.'"

I started laughing. "Sure, I guess. But what's mudding?"

"And you call yourself a country girl," he teased.

The next day after school I walked around to the parking lot behind the gym. Quentin's truck was impossible to miss. I stood outside it, waiting for him, and caught some interesting looks. When Jessica Rouster and her clan drove by in a white convertible with the top down, she pointed at me and laughed. I smiled widely and waved over-enthusiastically.

Just then Quentin came running toward the truck.

"Hey," he called. "I'm glad you didn't chicken out."

He crawled in the driver's side and leaned over to unlock my door. I was glad he hadn't opened it outside, date-style. I pulled open the creaky door, grabbed onto the gray rubbery handle, and hoisted myself into Quentin's big rusty truck. He was embarrassed when the engine roared to life and his stereo was blaring. He quickly turned it down.

"Sorry," he said. "What kind of music do you like?"

"Chris LeDoux is just fine with me," I said, laughing.

He gave me a surprised look when I started singing along to "Cadillac Ranch."

"So maybe you are a country girl after all."

Quentin made his way down Beck Avenue and then turned right up the Greybull Hill. He drove out to a place he called Diamond Flats and told me to buckle my seat belt. There was a road, that much I could see, but anything else on this prairie was entirely hidden by sagebrush. Growing up in the great state of Wyoming, one gets used to sagebrush, but this was different. I'd never seen a field of the silvery-gray bush blooming like this. The bushes were huge, probably close to six feet tall, and were covered with yellow flowers. It had rained the night before, so I rolled down my window to smell the sage. The aroma filled the truck in an instant.

Quentin stepped on the gas, and in no time we were flying down an old road with deep, muddy ruts. I flinched when mud splattered on my cheek. We both laughed, and I hurried to roll up my window. In a matter of seconds the windshield was covered in mud. He switched on the wipers, which only smeared the mess even more. Quentin grabbed a bottle of water, unscrewed the lid, and leaned out his window to douse the windshield. With the windshield only a bit better, he took off again. We went airborne over a hole, and I screamed when I bounced a few inches off the seat with a thud.

"Guess your belt's not tight enough there," he laughed. I used both hands to cinch it down.

We wound our way around the narrow road, and I wondered if it really led anywhere. It didn't matter. I was having a blast. A few minutes later, we went around the bottom of a hill, and I noticed the sagebrush was gone. Instead this was an open prairie, decorated only by variations of brown sand, dirt, mud, and clay. Suddenly Quentin flew off the road to the right and raced out into the prairie. There were no tracks where we were going, but he acted like he'd been here before. He turned one more time, and I found us face-to-face with the base of a nearly vertical hill. He didn't even pause. The truck hurled toward the hill. About fifteen feet up, the truck slowed dramatically. Quentin was downshifting and staring ahead as we began the upward crawl. I knew at any moment we were going to go rolling end over end backward. But Quentin was unfazed. Finally, we inched our way over the peak, and he slowed to a stop. I gulped a huge breath and stared at him.

For a moment I imagined what we must look like from a side view: an old multi-colored truck, high-centered on a tiny pinnacle. Ahead I saw the dented hood and in front of that was only blue sky.

"We're going down that." Quentin grinned, nodding his head forward.

"Oh my gosh, no." I must have looked horrified. "Are you serious?"

"I've done it a thousand times," he said, attempting reassurance.

"We can't," I said. "We'll die."

"Gracie, look behind you." I didn't want to but I slowly turned my head. It was the same story behind us. Nothing but sky.

"It's just as steep either way. It's up to you—backward or forward?"

Now I was the one sweating. It was a terrifying yet exhilarating panic. I trusted him, but still I closed my eyes.

"Let's go." My voice was barely audible.

Quentin yelped out a little "Yee haw!" and tipped the nose of his machine down what he called Deathtrap Dropoff.

"Open your eyes," he yelled.

I did and braced my feet hard against the floorboard. It felt like a mixture of roller coaster and what I imagined sky diving to be. Either way, the only thing that kept me from being sprawled out across the dashboard of that truck was my seat belt. I didn't quit screaming until I felt the pickup return to horizontal. At the bottom of the hill, he threw the truck in neutral and shut off the engine. We burst into laughter.

"Don't ever do that to me again!" I screamed.

"Oh, come on. You loved it."

"Yeah, I did," I agreed. When we finally caught our breath, Quentin handed me what was left of the water bottle, and I chugged it. Then I looked over at him. "Along with Liza, you're probably my best friend, Quentin," I said. "You're amazing and don't let anyone tell you otherwise."

Quentin smiled, turned the truck back on, jammed into second gear, and we took off again.

❦

For the Fremont's next family home evening we would be hosting special guests, I told Quentin. He guessed right—the missionaries.

He shook the elders' hands confidently and followed their discussions with rapt attention. They invited him to church, and he agreed immediately. I was amazed when the Young Men of our ward accepted him right away. Whatever Quentin's status had been at school, it was all forgotten. He was one of the guys. I thanked Cade profusely because he seemed to initiate the camaraderie.

❦

I'd predicted Quentin would say yes, but I was still so nervous! Dad told me the missionaries had reached the point where they invite the investigator to be baptized, and it would probably happen tonight. I was sure Quentin didn't know it was coming.

We were having them all over for dinner, and I helped Mom make the French bread pizzas. She pulled a bag of green beans from the freezer and dropped them into a small pot of boiling water. When the timer on the oven beeped, I jumped.

"What's with you tonight?" Mom asked.

I finished grating the cheese and wiped my hands on a towel.

"I don't know. I'm just worried I guess," I said. "What if he doesn't want to be baptized? What if he gets mad at me?"

"Gracie, Quentin thinks you're the best. You're offering to give him something that makes you happy. How could he possibly be upset with that?"

An hour later we sat around the table, blessed the food, and dished up. It was one of my favorite meals, but I couldn't eat much. Quentin gave me a questioning look when he saw the uneaten food on my plate. He knew I loved pizza.

We moved to the family room and got right into the lesson. I nearly choked when Elder Baum asked me to bear my testimony.

"Thanks for the warning, Elder," I said sarcastically. I couldn't take my eyes off the carpet, but I bore a simple testimony. I could hardly breathe waiting for what came next.

"Quentin, Elder Jessen and I know that what we've taught you is true. The Fremonts know the gospel is true too, and they live it. That's why you've felt the Spirit here in their home," Elder Baum said. "Quentin, are you ready to be baptized?"

Quentin flew off the couch and grabbed Elder Baum in a bear hug. Mom and Dad started laughing. A huge grin spread across my face, and I felt tears at the corner of my eyes.

"I was starting to wonder what a guy had to do to get that invite around here," Quentin joked. "You could have asked me two months ago. Of course I'm ready to be baptized."

***

Dad baptized Quentin on February 17, 2005. The Spirit in the room was almost overwhelming. I couldn't imagine how he must feel to be so clean and new. Even stoic Dad shed a few tears in the baptismal font.

It was the first time I met Quentin's mom, Sheila. I was dishing up brownies and pouring punch when she walked up to me and took both my hands in hers.

"I just want you to know when Quentin started talking about the Mormon Church, I was really worried. But then he told me about you. His eyes lit up when he talked about what a special person you are and how your family really loves each other."

I could feel my eyes stinging. Hers were tearing up too.

"Do you know Quentin has never talked about someone being nice to him? Never. He's never had a friend in school. I just want you to know that I love what you have done for him. I love you."

We hugged, and I felt like I'd known Sheila for a long, long time.

After everyone said good-bye, Quentin and I took a drive. We didn't go down the hill again; somehow, it seemed irreverent right after his baptism. Instead, we drove out to the McCullough Peaks, a barren set of peaks in the badlands south of Powell. We were looking for the band of wild horses that lived there, but after an hour of bouncing through the four-wheeling trails not finding anything, we parked out on a bluff for a long time. We could see the lights from Cody, Greybull, and Powell, but even better were the millions of stars. For the first time in awhile we didn't talk much. Instead I felt a silent understanding of love. This kind of love ran deeper than friendship, yet it wasn't the kind that meant couple-dom either. It was a love that felt to me like eternal gratitude.

fifteen

"Seriously, Grace, you better take a few weeks off," Nathan teased. "You're starting to look like a body builder."

I dug my shovel into the dirt and leaned it against the wall of the horse stall. I held both arms up, flexing.

"I'll quit as soon as I can beat you at arm wrestling," I said.

It was the summer before my senior year, and Nathan and I were working at Gregorys' again. This year Danielle was working with us too, saving money to leave on a mission in the fall. The house had livened up this summer with my siblings back home.

The time I wasn't working I spent with Quentin, tirelessly searching for new "mudding" country. We spent hours trolling down the dusty back roads of Park County. Quentin knew me better than anyone. He'd finish my sentences, and I'd pretend I was his fortune teller, forecasting where he'd be in five or twenty-five years. I could be so real with Quentin. I was still just average Gracie Fremont, but that was enough for him.

The day before Joseph's would-be birthday, Quentin and I sat on the grass outside the Dairy Queen eating Blizzards. The front tables and benches were occupied by the kind of tourists Cody teenagers love to make fun of. A family of four licked double cones at a table near us. The fifty-something father wore khaki shorts, a Hawaiian print shirt, and a cowboy hat he probably bought at Walmart just for this trip into cowboy country. The mother wore monstrous jean shorts that were hiked up just below her chest and hung past her knees. Her purple CODY shirt was tucked in. Even worse was the humongous fanny pack she wore around her ultra-high waist. Quentin nudged my shoulder and looked at me confused.

"Even someone as nice as you couldn't help making a comment about that fanny pack," Quentin whispered. "That is so 1990!"

I shrugged my shoulders and giggled. "I know. It is pretty bad, but I'm just not myself today. Sorry."

"What's up?" he asked. "You've been awfully quiet."

"I've just got Joseph on my mind," I said.

"Joseph . . . Smith?" Quentin asked.

"No. No. No," I laughed. "Joseph, my baby brother who died."

Quentin's forehead creased, and he looked lost. Had I really never told him? I set my strawberry cheesecake ice cream concoction down in the grass. It was melting faster than I could finish it. I filled Quentin in on how Mom and Dad lost their newborn a few years back and how every year I remembered him on the anniversary of it.

"Tomorrow is the day?" he asked. "Are you sure?"

"Of course I'm sure," I said, annoyed. "How could I get the day mixed up?"

"No, I didn't mean that. It's just—"

"What, Quentin?"

He shook his head back and forth before answering. "It's so weird."

"What?" Now I was getting frustrated.

"You know how I told you my dad died three years ago?"

I knew where he was going with this. "No way," I said.

"Yep. Tomorrow's the day."

With all that we'd been through and all that we'd shared,

we'd never talked about his dad before. Quentin told me about witnessing his dad die over the course of a year: first at home and eventually at Deaconess Medical Center in Billings. Alan Libbert had smoked for twenty years and died of lung cancer. Quentin bottled up his pain, he said, to try to make it easier on his mom. Sheila had nearly lost it when Alan was diagnosed. She was even committed for a mental health watch for a week. Thankfully, Alan was still fully functioning at the time and was able to take care of her and his son. By the time Alan passed away, Sheila had come to terms with her own grief.

Quentin stood up, tossed both our cups in the trash and sat back down.

"Gracie, I do something on June 16 each year to remember my dad," he said.

"What's that?" I asked.

"Well, I know it's corny. Don't tell anyone, okay?"

"Okay."

"I . . . I write him a letter and send it into the sky in a balloon. Mom and I did it at his funeral."

For some reason the image of this brought tears to my eyes. "That's not corny at all. Do you think I could do that too?"

"I was going to ask you," he said, standing up.

The next morning we stuck notes inside our balloons—mine baby blue and Quentin's white—and let go of them from the fifty-yard-line of the high school football field. I had to shield the sun with my hand, but I watched our balloons until I couldn't see them any more. We spent the rest of the day reading books on a blanket underneath Joseph's maple.

***

Before school started, Quentin and I agreed to go to our senior dances together—as friends, of course, since neither of us had ever been to a high school dance.

Homecoming was just a week away, so Chelsea, Liza, and

I met at my house. Mom brought out the sewing machine and made us matching cavewoman costumes for theme day. Liza and I stretched out on the couch with a bag of pretzels between us, and Chelsea sprawled out on a body pillow on the floor. We were watching *Oprah*; it was her special "Favorite Things" episode when she gives away tons of prizes. When a commercial came on, Chelsea rolled onto her elbows to face us.

"The vote is in just two days," she smiled.

"What vote would you be referring to, Miss Chelsea?" Liza teased.

Chelsea tossed a pillow at Liza's head. "I wonder what the crown looks like."

Liza and I rolled our eyes at each other.

On Wednesday afternoon, after the senior class finished skits, the nominees for Homecoming King and Queen were revealed.

"Jessica Rouster and James Fromberg; Savannah Ritchey and Cade Rawlings; Mandy Miller and Donovan Snyder; and Chelsea Copeland and Michael Heatherly." Liza and I screamed so loud, Chelsea may have been embarrassed for the first time in her life.

On Saturday night, the three of us had a triple date to the dance. I wore a burgundy, floor-length formal with a high waist and flowing skirt. It had thick straps that wrapped around my neck, so Mom had fashioned tiny cap sleeves and a more modest back for it. Hope came over to help me get ready, carrying a suitcase of beauty products inside like a woman on a mission. She curled my straight brown hair into ringlets and did a fantastic job on my makeup—making me look stunning, yet not overly made up.

Liza was getting ready at home so Amy could share in the moment, but Chelsea arrived early to finish primping at my house. Quentin showed up in his Wranglers and got ready at the house too because he was borrowing Nathan's black tux. After he finished changing, he sat in the family room, watching TV with Alex and Mom and Dad while we finished up. When we sashayed down the stairs and then twirled for effect, Quentin stood up. I stopped mid-twirl. Quentin looked the best I'd ever seen him.

"Geez, Quentin, you clean up pretty nice," I said.

But Liza stole the show when she walked in our front door wearing Amy's red sequined formal we'd tried on as little girls.

"You all look beautiful," Quentin said. I knew the comment rolled right off Chelsea's shoulders. She'd heard that her whole life. But I allowed myself to fully embrace and relish it. I didn't remember ever being called beautiful before. Liza and Chelsea's dates showed up, and the six of us squeezed in the Copeland's Four-Runner.

At the dance we shed our jackets in the makeshift cloak room and headed through the glass double doors. The gym looked fantastic. The theme was "A Night in the Stars," and it was nearly black inside. The community college had loaned the school their planetarium equipment, so constellations danced across the entire ceiling. Gobs of tulle hung down the walls and outlined the faux sky. Tiny white lights, more tulle, and white lilies lined the tables around the edges of the dance floor. The scene was almost serene, but the music was loud and exploding with energy. Garth Brooks's "Ain't Goin' Down (Til The Sun Comes Up)," blared from the speakers. I only had half a moment to inspect the room before Quentin grabbed my hand and pulled me onto the dance floor. *I hope he knows what he's doing*, I thought. In a few seconds he had my arms twisted up in a pretzel that I prayed he knew how to get out of. He did. He swung me around the floor like a rag doll, spinning me behind his back and cradling me in dips. He somehow formed a window with our arms and peered through it at me while walking me in a circle.

No way. I was stunned. *Quentin Libbert knows how to dance?* He was amazing at the jitterbug and great at the two-step too. I didn't know the steps, but it didn't matter. He was so good, he even made me look good. When a pop or hip-hop song came on, Quentin politely bowed himself out, and I danced with Chelsea and Liza. But as soon as the country songs returned, he grabbed me. About an hour into the dance, I was beginning to pick up the steps. I ran out to the cloak room to ditch my shoes and then came back in for another round. He snatched me by the hand and we picked right back up where we left off. Suddenly I felt my feet leave the floor and go wheeling through the air. I wasn't ready, but Quentin flipped me before I could protest. I stopped screaming when he righted me again. I was sure my face was as red as his hair, but he just grinned from ear to ear.

I stepped back to catch my breath and noticed for the first time that our classmates had formed a huge circle around us and were clapping to the beat. *Thank goodness it's dark,* I thought. I couldn't even begin to imagine the shade of crimson I'd turned.

"Come on, come on," they yelled.

Nervously I glanced at Quentin's face. He was beaming. He held out his hands, and in no time we were swinging again.

I ducked out of the circle after the next song and went outside for some fresh air. I was having the time of my life, but I was completely sweaty. I knew my ringlets were wilting. I silently decided to wear my hair up for prom. Liza joined me with two bottles of water, and I downed mine in two swigs.

When I came back in, Quentin found me and brought me back onto the floor. "Wonderful Tonight" by Eric Clapton was playing. Finally we could slow down. I closed my eyes and leaned my head on Quentin's shoulder. I felt myself slipping into the moment. For the first time, I felt a spark for Quentin that meant more than friendship. At the end of the song, he held me longer than necessary. He looked into my eyes, and for a moment I thought he might kiss me.

I wanted him to.

But I didn't want him to.

I wanted the moment to end, but I wanted it to last forever.

I shook my head and took a step back. Then I felt an arm on my shoulder.

"Gracie, come help me get ready. They're about to name the royalty." It was Chelsea.

I breathed in and silently thanked Chelsea. What did I want here? He was the greatest guy I'd ever met, but he was Quentin!

"I'll be back in a bit," I said as Chelsea dragged me to the bathroom.

We fluffed her hair and reapplied our lipstick. She was recoating her mascara when she looked at me in the mirror.

"What's going on with you and Quentin?" So I wasn't the only one noticing that spark.

"What do you mean?" I asked. "You know he's just a good friend."

"Uh-huh." She said sarcastically. "He doesn't look like just a friend out there."

I rolled my eyes and changed the subject to a topic I knew would distract Chelsea.

"So are you going to get that crown or what?" I asked. "It would make a nice decoration for our dorm room next year."

"Well then, I guess I'd better, right?" She smiled at herself, and we walked out the door.

Liza and I found some chairs so we could sit down with our dates while we waited for the royalty to be ushered in. I hoped Quentin would let me act like that last moment had never happened, and he did. In fact, he didn't say a word.

I glanced at Liza and saw she looked just as disgusted as I did when James Fromberg was announced as homecoming king.

"And the Cody High School homecoming queen is Chelsea Copeland."

sixteen

Chelsea wanted to decorate our college apartment with pink polka dots. She'd been petitioning for this since we were fourteen. Liza and I wanted a color scheme that was a bit less "Barbie," but we both knew that when it came down to it, we had little persuasion over Chelsea.

The three of us had dreamed of sharing an apartment at college forever. We'd planned out the theme parties we'd host and the treats we'd bake late at night. We'd even compiled a list of must-have movies for our college collection.

But by the beginning of senior year, we knew we wouldn't be going together.

Liza had straight A's. In fact, she was one of the seven class valedictorians in our year. While I was busy in wood shop every semester, Liza had been taking advanced placement courses in English and math. We all knew she would be going to BYU even before she applied.

Chelsea's plans were still gray. She had decent grades, though, and with her family's money I knew she could go pretty much wherever she wanted.

I didn't know what I was going to do either. I couldn't get into BYU with my average grades and particularly my below-average ACT scores. I was certain of one thing, though—I didn't want to work at Gregory's for the rest of my life, especially if Nathan wouldn't be there with me.

✲⁓✦◯✦⁓✲

Over Christmas vacation Mom brought home applications to the community college, University of Wyoming, and BYU-Idaho. I wasn't thrilled about any of the choices, but to please her, I did the paperwork. I was excited to spend some time with my family over the holiday, though.

Hope's fourth baby—another boy—was born two days before Christmas, so we had Michael, Mattox, and Miles as house guests. Matthew was the newest Sterling in the line-up. Alex told Hope over and over that names beginning with the same letter were so out of style, but Hope didn't care.

We spent most of the holiday afternoon talking to Danielle on the phone. She was serving in Tegucigalpa, Honduras, so the letter exchange had been frustrating at best. It was a relief to use modern communication for a change. In contrast from Nathan's phone calls, Danielle just seemed really homesick. She had a stomach flu for the first month and a half of her mission and was just getting into the teaching part. She said her Spanish was horrible. The only positive thing Danielle had to say was that her president had picked her to sing in the next zone conference.

Mom was so excited for the holiday that she decorated three Christmas trees and wove evergreen boughs throughout the banister. The house smelled fantastic. Dad did the usual outdoor display of the old large bulbs around the eaves, front door, and windows. The house was bustling with Hope's kids, but the Fremonts were paying much more attention to two special guests. Both Nathan and Samantha had brought home "friends" for the holiday.

Samantha's boyfriend, Damon, was no surprise. She was beautiful—he was gorgeous. He was a football player at the University of Utah where she was going to school. Alex was

106

Damon's hugest fan because of his vast sports knowledge. I couldn't imagine anyone but Alex being able to really talk to this guy, but Samantha seemed like she was in love.

They only stayed the first week, and then they were going to visit his family in North Dakota. After they left, Dad let us all in on the secret: Damon had asked Dad's permission to propose.

"Yes," Alex yelped. *Well, at least they'll have cute kids*, I thought.

When Mom informed me Nathan was bringing home a girl, I was so disappointed. The friendship we'd cultivated would be gone now; I knew it. Nate was in Colorado beginning pharmacy school when he met Sarah. They'd been dating since the fall. Sarah didn't have much chance to impress me—I decided to dislike her before she even walked in the door.

Sarah was pretty but simple. Not much unlike me. She grew up on a farm and knew plenty about animals. She loved hiking and had taken Nathan all over the trails of Colorado. She was usually quiet but witty when she did speak up. As hard as I tried, I couldn't find a single trait not to like about her.

I knew I'd be disgusted if they were hanging all over each other. Instead their affection seemed mature and loving. She helped me fold laundry, and she helped Mom with the dishes after every meal. She looked through scrapbooks with me, and we talked like old friends. Frustratingly, Sarah felt like she was another Fremont already.

On the morning they planned to leave, I pulled Nathan out back. The steps were covered with ice, so we stood. It was cold, but the fresh air felt great after being in the house with more than ten people for the weekend.

"So, umm, when're you going to do it?" I asked.

"Do what?" he responded coolly.

"You know what. When are you going to ask her?"

"Whoa. I'm not that far yet." He looked surprised.

"You're not?" I was amazed. "But you brought her here for Christmas, and she's perfect, isn't she?"

"She is great, but I'm not sure about marriage yet."

"Really? You know you're almost twenty-five. You don't want to be a 'menace to society,' do you?" I asked.

"Don't pull that one out on me." Nathan laughed.

"Promise you won't tell anyone?" he asked.

"Sure."

"Sarah's been married before."

I was floored. Maybe this girl wasn't so great after all. "What?"

"Yeah, it was hard for me to take too," he said. "Most of it wasn't her fault. She was married to this jerk who threw her around and treated her awful. It only lasted six months."

"Wow," I said. "Can she still be married in the temple again?"

"Yeah. That one was annulled. But I don't know. It still feels weird to me. You know? I mean I never imagined I'd marry someone who'd already been married. I'm not sure what to do."

"Are you going to tell Mom and Dad?" I asked.

"They know."

"What did they say?" I asked.

"Just to follow my heart and pray about it."

"That's a lot of help." I laughed as I hugged him. "Well, I'll be praying for you too, but, Nate, if you want my opinion—marry her."

seventeen

Samantha looked absolutely stunning in her beaded white gown. Her long hair was pulled back and hung in a beautiful fishtail braid. Even though it was crowded, the house looked fantastic, decorated in white with deep red roses for her reception.

The bridesmaids' dresses weren't my personal favorite, however. Hope, Alex, and I wore floor-length red gowns Samantha's new mother-in-law had made. This deep red was nice for flowers and streamers, but on a body it resembled a trauma victim. Plus, she had made mine too big in the chest area—where I was never terribly blessed. Thankfully, Liza had tailored it for me the night before.

Damon was starting to grow on me, and the fact that he looked like a model in his white tux didn't hurt his case either. *So maybe he isn't the smartest fellow on the block,* I reasoned. *He did serve a mission, and he did take my sister to the temple to be sealed.* As we stood in the torturous receiving line, I heard my bride sister answer the same questions over and over.

"We met at a singles' dance."

"We both have two years left of school."

"Yes, it is too bad Danielle couldn't be here."

And Damon: "It looks like P.R. I'm going to try to work for an NFL team or something."

In my little-girl wedding dreams, I had always hoped for an outdoor summer reception with a big dance. But if Samantha attempted that right now, there would be seventy-five guests up to their knees in snow and mud. For February, though, this was a pretty nice party, I had to admit.

After the receiving line broke up, I found my brother and tore him away from Sarah. We sat on the top stair in the hallway, out of sight of the party.

"So when are you going to have a shindig like this of your own?" I ribbed.

"I don't know, sister," he said. "Not for awhile, it doesn't look like."

"Why?" I was surprised.

"I don't know, Gracie. It's hard, you know? You dream your whole life of what your bride will be like, and then sometimes life doesn't work out that way."

I laughed. "You mean little boys dream about flowers and cakes and decorations too?"

"No. Not about that stuff. Just, you know, about your wife."

I gave him an I'm-not-getting-you look.

"You know. That she's a virgin too, like me." It looked painful for him to say.

"Oh, I see," I said.

We sat there in silence for a few minutes.

"Nate, can't you get past that? It's not like she was just out being a wild child. She was married for heaven's sake," I said.

"There's more I didn't tell you Gracie," he said. "She has a daughter."

"Oh." Now his hesitation made a little more sense. "Didn't you say she was only married six months?"

"Yeah. But she had just gotten pregnant when she left him. Her daughter is two now. She is so cute too. The dad isn't involved with her at all. She stayed with Sarah's parents both times we've come up here," he went on. "I mean, you should see this girl. She's just a tiny pixy, but she's so smart. She knows her whole alphabet, and she's just two years old. She even says prayers already."

I fiddled with a piece of carpet that was starting to come loose on the stair.

"Nate, if you love her, all of this shouldn't really matter," I said.

"I know. I know. It's just not as easy for me. I mean, I love her. I really do. But it's just so different than I planned. You know? It's just something I have to work out in my mind. That's all."

"Well, you work it out. I want cake," I said as I started down the stairs. Nathan stayed there, staring at the floor.

A couple stairs from the bottom, I looked up, "What's her name?"

"Emmylee." He smiled.

The rest of the night, I wasn't very talkative. I didn't mingle with the guests. Instead I watched my brother and Sarah. To me, she seemed perfect. Knowing she was a mom didn't change a thing for me. In fact, I was more impressed. She still seemed young, fun, and spunky. At the same time, though, I watched her with Hope's boys and realized she was a natural.

It was less than a month later when Nathan called home. I got on the phone and waited for the news. He hem-hawed around and finally I couldn't stand it.

"So, are you getting married?" I asked.

"Oh, I don't know about that yet," he said. "But I do have a question for you."

"Yeah?"

"What's your graduation date?"

"June 4, I think. Why?" I asked.

"Well, Sarah and I were wondering if you could come to Colorado for a weekend at the end of June."

That sounded fun. "Sure, why?"

"Well, because we're going to need a babysitter for Emmylee while we take our honeymoon."

"I knew it!" I screamed. Mom and Dad started giggling.

He must have already told them. "So you finally came to your senses, huh?"

"Yeah, I guess so. With the help of a pesky little sister and the Holy Ghost, that is."

I agreed to babysit and gave the phone back to Mom. I kept nudging her to hurry up though. I had to call Liza and Quentin with the news.

eighteen

I pulled a pen from my drawer and folded a flowered sheet of paper in half.

Dear Chels,

This isn't a good-bye letter or anything, since neither of us are really sure what we're doing. But instead it's more of a thank-you. You have made my last year of high school the best! Thanks so much for getting Liza and I out of our comfort zones. You made me realize how much better life is when I stop worrying about what people think and start worrying about living. I'm going to miss the three of us so much, but I know you'll have a blast in California. Just remember we love you and that Heavenly Father loves you too!

Love,

Grace

I stuck the note in the envelope and tucked it into the tissue paper in a purple flowered gift bag. Inside was a framed 5x7 of the three of us standing under the "Welcome to Wyoming" sign on the Belfry Highway.

Chelsea was awaiting her acceptance letters to two expensive schools in California. I couldn't count the number of times she'd tried to talk me into going with her. There was no way my family could afford it, even if I wanted to go. But somehow the idea of all those people packed into tiny spaces seemed ridiculous to me. The Fremonts had been to Disneyland once, but that was as much of the Golden State as I could handle.

In April, Liza found out she was accepted to BYU. It was no surprise, really, but we still celebrated with huge ice cream sundaes at Scoops, our favorite dessert restaurant. Amy came with us. She tried to hide her emotion, but we could all tell the idea of her daughter leaving was really hurting her.

I had shared my whole life with these two girls, but still, it was Quentin who I found myself opening up to the most. I could be so honest with him—and he adored me no matter what I said. Our friendship was everything to me.

Toward the end of our senior year, Quentin started talking about a mission. I hadn't brought it up, because truthfully I didn't think he'd be going. It wasn't that he didn't have the testimony—there was no question about that. It was just that he was so new to the gospel, and I knew the money would be an issue too.

Quentin never even considered these obstacles. He turned nineteen in July, but he was planning to work at the lumber yard for the whole summer to save money. He hoped to leave in October.

On May 1, I got an acceptance letter from BYU-I. Mom and Dad hoped their excitement would transfer to me, but it didn't. A few weeks later I knew I could go to UW too. Thinking or talking about college and life without Liza, Chelsea, and Quentin just depressed me, so I avoided it at all costs.

A week before school got out, Mom brought some college paperwork up to my bedroom and sat down on the bed. I was kneeling over some newspapers hand-sanding a jewelry box I had been working on.

"Honey, I think we need to be figuring out what you want to do about college," she said apprehensively. I was so sick of this conversation I wanted to scream.

"Why?" I asked. "There's still time."

"I know that, but the quicker we accept one of these schools, the more scholarships you'll be able to apply for."

"I don't know, Mom, okay?" I said.

"Well, you know Dad and I think Ricks would be great. But wherever you want to go is fine as long as we can afford it."

"I'll think about it," I said, encouraging her to leave. "And, Mom, it hasn't been Ricks for a long time, remember?"

I put down my work and slid into a pair of flip-flops. I hadn't ridden a bike in ages, but when I walked out the front door and saw Alex's lying there, I picked it up. This mountain bike, a blue Mountain Trek, had been Nathan's, Danielle's, Samantha's, mine, and now Alex's. The once shiny paint was completely worn off across the handle bars, and severely chipped down the bar. I wondered how many times my dad had been coerced into resetting the chain on that thing or how many spring afternoons he had spent pumping the tires. I gripped the black handles, started running up the dirt road, and hopped on like I hadn't done since I was a kid. I hoped Liza was home.

"What's wrong, Gracie?" she asked. I guess I didn't look too great.

"Life. I mean, why do you always just know what to do and I never know what to do?" I asked. "Your life just falls into place the way it should."

"What are you talking about?" She sounded offended.

"I don't know. I just don't know what to do about school. My mom wants me to decide, and I don't really even care about it. I just want to stay here and have life stay the way it's always been."

"First of all, my life doesn't just fall into place," she said. "Do you have any idea what this is doing to Mom? She thinks she's going to die with me leaving here. And second of all, it's just as hard for me to make decisions as you."

It was a tone I had rarely heard Liza use.

"I'm sorry, I didn't mean that," I said. "I just don't know what to do."

Her voice softened. "You *do* know what to do. Pray."

"I know," I said. "I have been, but nothing is coming to me."

"Well, maybe the traditional path isn't right for you. Maybe you shouldn't go to school," she said.

"Wouldn't people think I was lazy, though?" I asked.

"Who cares?" she said. "It's not their life, is it?"

"I just don't want to think about it anymore. Can we look at your scrapbooks?"

Liza laughed. "How many times have you asked me that over the past ten years?"

She opened her closet and dragged out the books that catalogued our childhoods. We flipped through the pages until after 10:00 PM when I made my way home. I prayed hard and slept little that night, and by the morning I knew what I would do.

Mom and Dad sat completely still when I announced, "I'm not going to college for awhile. I'm going to work here instead."

Dad said, "Gracie, what if you don't get married? You'll need an education to make money."

"Dad, this has nothing to do with getting married. I'm not planning on doing that for a long time either. I just don't want to go to college right now." I almost yelled it.

"You still have a little while to think about it, honey," Mom pleaded.

"Can you two leave me alone? I prayed about this okay? I have been praying for months. This is my answer." I ran out the front door with a piece of peanut butter toast.

I rehearsed my apology the whole day, but when I walked in the front door that afternoon, it was Mom who initiated it. I hadn't even dropped my bag before she hugged me with tears in her eyes.

"I'm sorry. You're right. This is your decision, and if you prayed about it, then it's right for you. We're sorry."

I hugged her back and said I was sorry too. I hoped I was making the right choice because my pride wouldn't let me back down now.

⊱•⊰❖⊱•⊰

The "Pomp and Circumstance" of my graduation was nearly drowned out by Nathan and Sarah's upcoming "Wedding March." And I was fine with that. With both events so close together, most of my siblings couldn't travel home. That Saturday morning, I totally slept in and didn't even get a shower before Mom was shouting that it was time to go. I kneeled between Mom and Dad and used the mini-van's rearview mirror to apply a splash of mascara and lipstick. Then I crawled to the back seat and pulled my cap and gown from its plastic wrapper and slipped it over my shorts and T-shirt.

"Aahh," my mom gasped. "Gracie Ezra Fremont. You mean to tell me you haven't even ironed your gown?"

"Um, nope," I said.

I looked down at the grid of perfect squares pressed into my gown and laughed.

"Oh, I'm a failure," Mom sighed. "I'm so sorry, honey. I've been so busy with all this wedding business I didn't even think about your outfit. Not to mention your invitations were sent out later than anyone else's."

Dad grinned at me in the mirror but put his hand on Mom's thigh.

"Seriously, Mom," I said. "Don't even worry about it. Obviously, I'm not too concerned." I swept my hair into a high ponytail and slid back into the car seat.

The graduation speaker—some governor or senator or something—was extremely uninteresting. I spent most of his speech scanning the bleachers for any familiar faces. Liza's two-minute speech brought tears to my eyes, though, and tossing my cap in the air was magical. The Cody High School Class of

2006 meandered out the doors, together for the last time, to the sound of Alice Cooper's "School's Out."

I vowed to get out of the crowd as quickly as possible, but still, I didn't completely dodge the questions about my future.

Adults and students I'd barely ever talked to seemed suddenly absorbed in what I had planned for next year. My "work" plans hadn't materialized into anything concrete yet, so these superficial discussions of the transformation from high schooler to adult left me speechless.

⁂

Nathan called to say congrats but couldn't drive home. He and Sarah were busy planning their trip to Salt Lake where they were being sealed. I loved my brother, but riding in a minivan all the way to Utah when I couldn't even go inside the temple seemed pointless to me. I had no choice, though, because my flight to Denver left from Salt Lake City.

The idea of being so far from home and in charge of myself and Emmylee had my stomach in a knot. I had met Sarah's daughter a few weekends ago when Nathan and Sarah came home to introduce her to everyone. Nathan was right—she was adorable. Emmylee was so petite and had the sweetest little voice. Her thin hair was nearly white and the underneath layers were totally curly, but the top ones straight. This left Sarah dumbfounded when it came to styling Emmylee's hair. Usually the two-year-old's head looked like it had just been through a windstorm, but she totally pulled it off. In addition to being cute, she was the most polite kid I'd ever met.

Mom, Dad, Alex, and I hesitantly walked up the path toward Sarah's parents' house outside of Orem. They'd invited us to stay with them. The empty, weeded lot to the side of the house held close to twenty cars, parked every which way.

"I guess we aren't the only ones staying here," Dad ventured.

The tan farmhouse with a wraparound porch looked like it would fit in perfectly on our road back home. Dad rang the bell, and when the door swung open, the hullabaloo going on inside almost knocked me over. Emmylee burst through the masses and greeted me first, though, with a huge hug. I picked her up. Mrs. Shetfield stepped out next and softly closed the door behind her.

"I know its crazy in there, but it's just family, so don't be shy," she said. "You're family too now, so come on in."

Emmylee tugged at my hand. "You going to come home to Cowowado with me Aunt Gwacie?" she asked.

"Yep, and we're going to have so much fun," I said.

"Yeah!" she shrieked.

That night the masses of Shetfields and Fremonts descended on the Shetfields' backyard for a huge spaghetti dinner. There were three long church tables covered in butcher paper and gigantic bowls of spaghetti, sauce, and salad. Each table held four baskets full of French bread too. After everything was cleaned up, we made our way back inside to get some rest. Anyone unmarried or under twenty-five was relegated to the basement floor. Emmylee laid her Jasmine and Aladdin sleeping bag out between me and Alex and fell asleep after four run-throughs of "I Was a Child of Got." I'm pretty sure she meant "I Am a Child of God."

The cowbell that was used as a wakeup call the next morning seemed to come too soon. But to get that many bodies through the shower-and-shave routine, we had to rise at dawn. I was about eighth in line and finished my ice-cold cleansing in record time. I slipped on my dress and decided to loosely braid my hair. It was the quickest hairdo I could think of. Sarah's six sisters were running around like mad hens, and I didn't want to cross their path.

"Where's the hair spray?"

"Who took my earrings?"

"When am I going to be the bride?"

It was almost nauseating. I had been ready for over an hour

119

and sat on a folding chair in the front room, watching the chaos. I made a mental note to reassure Nathan he had definitely picked the right Shetfield girl.

Dad sat next to me, flipping through a coffee-table book of temples with Alex. Then Mom walked in the front door, followed by a spiffed up version of Nathan, and you would have thought a bomb was detonating.

"Oh my gosh, get out of here!" shouted Shauna, the oldest sister.

"Yeah," chirped Stacy. "You can't see her yet!"

"Sorry. Sorry." He laughed. "You can't blame a guy for trying, right?"

The girls shooed him out the front door, and I followed. He looked great, and I told him as much. We sat on the front steps of the house.

"So, are you nervous?" I asked.

"Are you kidding? I'm shaking," he replied. "But it's the kind of nervous where I'm so happy I just want to get the show on the road."

"So, no hesitation anymore?" I asked seriously.

"No. Sarah is the most amazing woman and what happened in the past is in the past. I'm just looking toward the future."

I hugged Nathan. "I knew you'd come to your senses. Besides who could resist a little girl like Emmylee, *Dad*."

"Hey now, don't start in with that 'Dad' stuff yet. I'm still a young bachelor for at least two more hours," he said, pulling up his sleeve to check his watch.

Mom, Dad, and Alex came out the door and told us it was time to go. We all loaded up and headed toward the temple where we would meet Samantha and Damon and Hope's family. With all of those sons and Emmylee to keep us distracted at the temple, Alex and I were going to have our hands full.

The more "grown-up" folks of our party quietly filed into the temple while Alex and I took the boys and Emmylee out to the reflection pool. Of course the boys couldn't resist splashing each other, but Emmylee just delicately touched the water with her pointer finger.

"Can you believe all of those boys are your new cousins?" I asked.

She stuck out her tongue in a "yuck" gesture, and we both started giggling.

The reception was beautiful. Sarah's huge family was starting to feel like an extension of our own. It was a hot evening, and the Shetfield's backyard was the perfect setting. There wasn't much in the way of decoration, but it felt homey and comfortable. When Nathan and Sarah danced their first dance, I felt tears splashing down my cheeks. She was definitely right for him—it was obvious.

The newlyweds spent that night in a fancy Salt Lake hotel and the next morning the four of us flew to their apartment in Colorado. If it wasn't for Emmylee, I would have felt terribly intrusive, but she clung to me like I'd been her aunt forever.

Nate and Sarah stayed at the house one night to prep me on Emmylee's routine. Then they left for their weekend cruise to Mexico.

nineteen

Emmylee and I spent Saturday morning in our jammies in front of the TV. I spread out a not-too-new-looking Winnie the Pooh blanket and set out two bowls of Cocoa Pebbles. I hadn't had that cereal in such a long time. Sarah had strict rules on which cartoons were appropriate—mainly *Dora the Explorer*, and *Blues Clues*. I knew lounging around eating sugar all day wasn't exactly part of her normal routine, but I didn't think the newlyweds would mind.

Around noon I changed Emmylee's nightgown for a red gingham dress with cherry buttons on the shoulders. It was so much fun dressing a little girl. She pulled out her sparkly red shoes—think Dorothy—and her outfit was complete. I was much less concerned about my own look. After all, I figured, I was in a place where no one but a two-year-old knew me.

We left the complex and walked three blocks north and one east to a park I'd spotted when we came from the airport. I held Emmylee on my lap on a swing and gave her instructions not to wiggle. I started out gently pumping my legs, not wanting to scare her. But she screamed "higher, higher."

Long after I did, Emmylee grew bored with the swing, and I dragged my feet through the bark to slow us down. As I lifted her off my lap and set her down, Emmylee pointed to a red sports car with white racing stripes.

"Vroom, vroom," she said.

I laughed but kept my eye on the car. I knew I had seen that same car driving slowly by on our way to the park. I watched it as it turned down the second side of the park. I twisted all the way around in the swing to track it, but it went down a side street and out of my view.

Emmylee begged me to "airplane" her on my legs over and over again. Then she lay down beside me in the grass and we watched the clouds peacefully rolling by. By the time she finished her peanut butter and jelly sandwich, Emmylee was starting to rub her eyes. I completed a quick rub down with the baby wipes, packed the lunches, and started for home. On schedule or not, this girl needed a nap.

About a block from the park, I saw the red car leisurely drive down a cross street in front of us. I was getting nervous. I lifted Emmylee to my hip and picked up the pace. Even as light as she was, it didn't take long for me to realize the whole mom thing required muscle. When we were almost home, I reasoned with myself that I was just being paranoid. The driver was probably looking for an address. Emmylee had fallen asleep on my shoulder, so I unlocked the door quietly and laid her in her toddler bed. I poured a cup of water and flipped open one of Sarah's parenting magazines.

Later that night, after I put Emmylee to bed, I looked out the window and saw it. The red car was parked across the street from the apartment. Just then I heard a heavy knock at the door and I froze. He knocked again. I wasn't sure if I should answer it or call the police. I crept to the door and peeked through the peek hole against my better judgment. I couldn't see much because the man had turned, like he was checking something over his shoulder. I backed away and stood quiet.

"Sarah," he yelled in the door. "Sarah. Come out here."

The TV was turned up pretty loud—he knew the house wasn't empty.

"Sarah," he yelled louder.

I didn't want Emmylee to wake up to this, and if I didn't tell this oaf that Sarah wasn't home, I didn't know what he might do.

I took a deep breath and prayed my voice wouldn't crack.

"She's not here. I'm just the house sitter," I yelled through the door.

"Where is she?" he screamed.

"I don't know. She just hired me to watch her house," I lied.

"You're lying. I saw you with Emmylee."

Oh no. Could this creep be Emmylee's dad? But Nathan said he hadn't seen her since she was born. *Maybe I could trick him*, I thought.

He pounded both fists on the door.

"Let me in. She's my daughter," he shouted. I stood immobile with tears falling down my cheeks.

He pounded again, and it felt like the whole apartment was shaking. I heard Emmylee coughing in her room.

"Sarah took Emmylee with her. The girl you saw me with is my own daughter," I choked out.

"You're lying. Let me in." The door thudded even harder, and I knew he was kicking it. The man cursed and then said, "I know she got married. Tell me where she went!"

By now my tears were streaming down. He was so big. I knew he could somehow get through this door. I ran to the kitchen and grabbed the phone. I dialed 911 and spoke as quietly as I could.

"There's a man trying to break into my apartment. Please hurry." As the woman on the line gave me some instructions, I snuck back to the front door. Through the peek hole, I could see the man was over near the sidewalk, picking something up from the ground. I gave the dispatcher Sarah and Nathan's address and kept my eye on Sarah's ex-husband.

The woman told me to stay on the phone, but I dropped it when a rock shot through the living room window. It shattered, and I heard Emmylee scream.

I raced to her room and slammed the door. I yanked her from her bed and shoved it and the dresser against the door. My adrenaline was pumping so fast that the tears were gone. Emmylee was crying hysterically for her Mom, and I could hear the guy outside climbing through the glass.

"It's going to be okay, honey," I said. "The police are coming to get him."

I held her tight, but she couldn't calm down.

"Can you get in the closet for me and hide?"

She nodded her head and curled into a tiny ball on the floor of her closet. I quietly shut the door behind her and braced myself against the dresser.

"Please hurry, please hurry, please hurry," I realized I was whispering it out loud.

Thump. It shuddered through my whole body. *Thump.* He was pounding on the door. *Thump.* I felt the dresser shift.

"Heavenly Father, please help us. Please help us," I cried.

Thump. All I could do now was pray. Emmylee's cries were almost blistering to my ears. I waited for the next bash on the door, but there wasn't one. I waited. I quietly crept to the window and saw that his car was still here. I saw lights coming too—police lights—and I heard the siren. I opened the closet door and pulled Emmylee tightly to my chest.

"The police are here, honey. It's okay, he's gone."

I figured he must have run away when he heard the sirens. But before the police pulled up, I heard another man's voice.

"Are you guys okay in there?" he asked through the door.

I didn't know how to answer.

"It's okay. This jerk is knocked out, and I hear the police sirens. It's okay. You can come out."

But I didn't want Emmylee to see him.

I yelled back through the door. "We're going to wait until they take him away. What happened?"

"I'm Steve, Sarah's neighbor. I heard the window break and I watched this guy climb in, so I snuck in with a baseball bat and nailed him," he explained. "Are you okay? Did he hurt you?"

"No, we're fine. Just scared," I said.

I heard the police running up the stairs, so I put Emmylee down and started to move the furniture away from her door. The officer opened the door just as they carted Sarah's ex-husband down the stairs in handcuffs.

After close to an hour of questioning, the police left. Steve and his wife, Liz, let us come in and stay in their house. Emmylee had finally calmed down, and we put her to bed with their three-year-old daughter, McKenzie.

They said I could use their phone to call my mom and dad, but instead I called Quentin. I took the cordless into the bathroom and bawled as I recounted the ordeal. He calmed me down and told me if I wanted, he would catch a flight out to Denver right that second.

"Don't be stupid," I said. "You don't need to waste your mission money."

Quentin must have called Dad because ten minutes later the phone rang. He made the same offer Quentin had, but I assured him we would be all right until Monday morning. The guy was in jail, and there was nothing he could do to us now. Steve said he'd call someone to fix the window in the morning.

"Do you think we should call Nathan?" Dad asked. "He did leave you a phone number right?"

"Yes, he did, but I don't want to call him."

"I think maybe we should," he said.

"Dad, listen, they're in the middle of the ocean on their honeymoon. Even if they did find out, there's nothing they could do about it, so why make them worry and have a horrible time. We're fine now. Let's just let them have their weekend and then worry about it when they get home."

"Okay, I suppose you're right," he said. He told me good night and said they would be praying for me. "Get some sleep."

I didn't, though. I lay on the couch the whole night without closing my eyes. I leafed through some books they had on the coffee table, and I even got down on the carpet and stretched around 4:00 AM, but nothing could put me to sleep. The last time I remember looking at the clock was 6:15 AM.

Emmylee climbed up on my stomach in the middle of that afternoon. I opened my eyes and saw the whole family was awake and watching a kids' video on TV.

I sat up, embarrassed. "Why didn't you wake me up? I'm sorry."

Liz laughed. "Are you kidding? I bet you got the least sleep of anyone last night. Anyway the girls were just watching TV this morning, so I'm glad you got a little rest."

Steve walked out of the kitchen with a plate of eggs, toast, and sausage. "The police stopped by this morning and said Sarah already had a restraining order against that guy, so he's going to jail for a long time."

I nodded as I dug into my breakfast. "No one's told you-know-who about who the guy was, have you?" I asked.

"Of course not," Steve said. "In fact you-know-who seems fine today. She said she had a scary dream last night, though. I don't think she even knows it's real yet."

"Oh yeah, and Mitcham's Glass is coming around three to fix that window, but we think you guys should stay here until Nate gets home," Steve said.

"That's okay," I replied. "You've been generous enough."

"We insist," Liz said. "Either that or our whole family is staying with you over there, so you might as well just stay put."

I laughed and nodded.

⊱═━ ❦ ━═⊰

I don't think I really breathed—I mean a deep, relaxing, full breath—until I boarded the plane to Cody on Monday night.

Sarah and Nathan hadn't taken the news well. They wondered how her ex-husband had found them. Nathan said on their honeymoon they'd decided to find another apartment anyway, but now they would speed up those plans.

Surprisingly Emmylee acted as if nothing happened. Still, Sarah planned to take her to a counselor to make sure she wasn't traumatized.

When I hugged Dad at the airport, my tears spilled down his shirt. He held me for a long time.

Liza and Chelsea waited for me in the car as I dashed into the grocery store for more Hawaiian Tan lotion. This was our third bottle this summer.

We spent almost every afternoon in July down at the lake. I was the tannest I had ever been, and the only light part of Chelsea was her blonde hair.

Liza planned to leave in mid-August for BYU, and Chelsea had opted on San Diego State University. I still had no plans to go to school this fall, and this left me the odd man out for many of their conversations.

"Mom has finally stopped crying every time I buy a necessity for my dorm room." Liza laughed.

"My parents aren't too sad," Chelsea said. "They're just worried I'm going to go crazy down there."

"Should they be?" I asked.

She ignored my question. "I mean Mom has already talked to the institute teacher and the singles ward Relief Society president on the phone. I guess everyone will know me before I get there."

Somehow I doubted Chelsea minded this.

"So Chels," I pushed further. "Are you going to join a sorority and everything?"

"I don't know," she said. "What do you guys think? It sounds fun."

"Chelsea, no." Liza looked serious. "All they do is party and drink."

"That's not true," she shot back. "Anyway, you can go to parties and not drink."

"For only so long, Chels," I said. "You learned that once, remember?"

She ignored me and went back to stuffing cotton balls between her toes in preparation for a pedicure on her beach towel. I opened my copy of *Harry Potter and the Sorcerer's Stone* and tried once again to get into the plot. All my sisters raved about these books, but so far I hadn't been able to get hooked.

"All this college stuff is depressing me," I said. "Let's talk about something else."

Chelsea snapped her head to us. "Remember when Gracie got Mr. Nibard for fourth grade, and she cried?"

All three of us laughed. "Well, you would've too," I said.

"No, I just would have put on more green and blue eye shadow," she said, and we all started cracking up. I flipped the book into the sand and pulled my black shades off my head and onto my nose. I walked to the Jeep, held open the broken cargo door, and slid the three black tubes onto the sand.

We spent the rest of the afternoon floating aimlessly, reminiscing. Our lives had been interwoven in so many ways. In the summer sun, with the smell of coconut tanning oil permeating from our black inner tubes, I forgot we were growing up. I forgot these two girls would be leaving in less than a month, and I forgot I had to figure out a plan for my own life.

❦

Quentin was working long hours the whole summer, so we didn't see each other as much as during the school year. We caught up on the phone every night though. Still, I missed our long drives and our comfortable silences. I missed the feeling of adoration I felt with him. I was proud of him, though, because he was saving a ton of money for his mission. The bishop had promised Quentin the ward would cover what he couldn't make, but he was determined to earn as much as possible.

By the end of July, I still didn't have a job, so I begrudgingly went back to Gregory's Farm. I had only been working a week when Mr. Morton, my high school shop teacher, called me. He said there was a volunteer position available, and as soon as he heard it he thought of me.

"Volunteer?" I said. That meant no money.

But as he explained the job to me, my heart started racing.

"There's this organization called Houses of Hope. They build houses for battered women. The women occupy the house for free for a year before they have to start making small monthly payments. Anyway, one of the cabinet builders found a full-time job, so they're down one carpenter." He paused to see if I was interested.

I shook my head to be sure it was real. This sounded perfect to me. Ever since my incident with Sarah's ex-husband, I had been checking out local charities for abused women, but I didn't have the right skills for any of them.

When I didn't reply, he went on. "There are two more houses they want to build here this year before Christmas. I told them how great your work is, and they practically told me they want you if you're willing."

"Wow, that sounds amazing," I said.

"But of course the pay is miniscule really. I mean you get a stipend, but it's not even minimum wage. Do you already have a job this summer?" he asked.

"No," I lied. "Well, yes, but not one I want. I would much rather do this."

"Plus it will be great on your resume if you ever go into the carpentry field," he added.

Mr. Morton gave me the supervisor's phone number, and within a half hour I had a new job and was on my way to pick up my first and last paycheck at the farm. Halfway home it hit me that Mom and Dad might not be elated about my new plan.

I told them at dinner that night.

"Gracie, I just don't think you're too sure what you want out of life right now," Dad said.

"I thought you guys would be glad I'm helping people," I said.

"We are, honey," Mom said. "But you have to think about your future too."

I felt tears coming, but I willed them down. I was going to handle this like an adult.

"I wish I did, but I don't fit the cookie-cutter-college-mold that Nathan and Danielle and Samantha do. There's one thing I've found that I am really good at and that's woodwork," I stammered. "So, I'm going to do what the prophet tells us and develop that talent."

I had them there. I knew they couldn't argue that.

"But the prophet also tells women to have a way to make money, Gracie," Mom said.

"I know I won't make money with this, but I will get experience for jobs in the future," I said.

No one said anything. Had I won?

"I know it's not what you planned for me, but it feels right to me," I said. "Can you trust me with this?"

Dad turned and looked at Mom, and she nodded her head.

"We hope it works, honey," she said.

⁕⧉⋄⧉⁕

I blew the dust off my black and gray toolbox on Dad's work bench. It had been a while since I'd had my hands on these tools, and I was excited to get back to work.

On the first day, I knew I would love this job. We were working on a three bedroom house in a newer subdivision for a family. The mom's boyfriend was currently in jail for a bout of domestic violence that had nearly hospitalized her and one of her sons.

I started on the main-floor bathroom cabinets. They were oak with brass hardware—not my favorite, but we were on a budget. The blueprints were easy to follow, and my work was going smoothly. Most the builders were retired contractors, but everyone was energized by the project. We listened to an old country station turned up loud everyday.

At night I would call Quentin about my day, and he would update me on his money earned. Liza, Chelsea, and I spent as much time together as possible because I knew they'd be leaving soon. And on August 26, the day came.

The three of us met for an early breakfast at Margaret's Café at six that morning, so I wouldn't be late for work. Liza and Amy were all packed, anxious to get an early start for Provo. Margaret's was loud with the sounds of clanking coffee cups and the chatter of middle-aged men—the regulars—discussing the upcoming city council vote. Intermittent shouts of "order up" burst from the kitchen. We sat at a booth toward the back and ordered cinnamon rolls and cocoa all around.

There was an air of uncertainty between us. No one wanted or knew exactly how to say the inevitable good-bye we all faced. I unfolded and refolded my napkin, and Liza kept glancing out the windows toward the parking lot. Amy attempted small talk but was met with short, clipped answers.

Eventually Chelsea pulled a college pamphlet from her purse.

"Check this out, guys," she said, unfolding the paper. "My apartment is only going to be a ten-minute walk from the beach." She pointed to the image of coeds playing volleyball on a sun-drenched beach and waited for our response.

"Wow, Chels," I humored her. "That will be a blast."

Chelsea could sense we weren't up for the conversation, so she put the pamphlet away. But then she dove into the looming topic, anyway.

"Liza, give us some of your advice before you go," she said. "You always have the best advice."

"But you never take it." Liza laughed.

"I will. I will," Chelsea said.

"Okay, let me think. Chelsea: Don't join a sorority," Liza said. Chelsea frowned. "Don't date nonmembers, and don't party."

"Is there anything I *can* do?" she asked.

"Yes, go to institute and meet every person in your singles ward. You'll have tons of friends if you do that."

"Okay, okay, Mom," Chelsea joked.

"And for you, Gracie: Follow your heart. You always make good decisions if you just trust yourself. And, hey, maybe you'll become the most famous woman carpenter someday," she said.

My cinnamon roll covered the entire plate, but I barely made a dent in it. I knew Margaret's was famous for these, but it felt dry and heavy and too hard to swallow. I think the four of us nibbled our breakfasts more out of lack of something to say than hunger.

Eventually Liza pushed her plate back and tossed her napkin onto it. She stood up.

"Well, I guess this is it," she said. "No, wait, I forgot." She quickly sat back down and pulled a huge scrapbook from under her chair. I hadn't even noticed it there.

"I thought you might want to look at this,"

I smiled, relaxing for the first time all morning. Of course it would be Liza who best knew how to handle this moment. What would we do without her?

We flipped through the pages of memories one more time. There were the three of us with huge ice cream cones at Chelsea's birthday party when she turned 11. There was the picture of us all dressed up in Liza's mom's high school formal dresses—

I pointed out Chelsea's makeup. There was the first day of high school when we all rode to school together. We looked at Liza and me, riding our bikes down the dirt road, and Chelsea as homecoming queen.

I knew I was going to be late.

Liza closed the book and stood up. She hugged Chelsea, and all three of us started to cry.

"Be true, Chels. Please be true," I could hear her whisper.

And then she hugged me, and the tears were rolling.

"Gracie, I love you. You are the best friend I could have ever asked for," she said into my hair. I couldn't say anything back.

We walked out to the parking lot and went our separate ways. A page of our lives was over. As I drove to work with tears falling down my face, I wanted to go back to first grade where life was ordinary, things didn't change, and friends didn't leave.

Liza was gone, now Chelsea too, and Quentin would be leaving in just a few months. I didn't like the feeling of being left behind.

***

I left the doors and windows wide open in the Houses of Hope house to combat the smell of the linoleum adhesive I was troweling. I'd finished the bathroom, kitchen, and laundry room cabinets and was starting to lay linoleum—one of my least favorite jobs. The white flooring had gray lines to make it look like tile, and I wished it really was. I'd never done tile before, but I wanted to learn.

I was on all fours when Quentin came running into the house. He was out of breath and sweating. I stood up and placed my trowel across the bucket. He took a giant leap over the exposed adhesive and hugged me.

"Quentin, what are you doing here?" I asked. From the

corner of my eye I saw two of my coworkers peering around the corner.

"I got it," he yelped.

"Got what?" I said.

"My mission call. It's here!" he said.

The floor would need to be laid right away, but Dave stepped into the kitchen, ready to take over.

"Go ahead, take a break," he said.

We ran out to the muddy lot where Quentin had parked just feet from the front door. I climbed up in the cab of the truck and saw the white envelope sitting on the seat.

"Oh my gosh, are you nervous?" I asked.

"No, just excited," he said as he turned the envelope over on his lap. He stuck his thumb under the edge of the paper.

"Quentin, wait. Don't you want to open it with your mom?" I asked.

"Why?" he said.

"She might be disappointed to know you didn't," I said.

"Gracie. I want to open this with you. You brought me the gospel. You're my best friend. I love Mom, but she doesn't get the excitement about this, ya know? Please let's just do it now."

"Okay." I smiled. "But you better go straight home and tell her where you're going."

He made the promise as he clumsily ripped the letter open.

Dear Elder Libbert,

We the First Presidency and the Quorum of the Twelve Apostles . . .

"Stop it." I giggled. "Get to the good part."

He paused as he skimmed down the page. My hands were squeezed tightly together on my lap. Finally he looked up at me with a sly smile.

"Okay, okay, ma amour," he said, grinning.

"French?" I screamed. "You're going to France?

"Nope, Canada." He laughed. "French-speaking Canada Montreal Mission."

I tore the pages from his hands and read them myself.

"Canada, huh? Wow," I said.

I hugged Quentin hard but swallowed a big lump when I read he was to report to the MTC on October 9. That was barely a month away.

We talked a few more minutes about what we knew about Canada—hockey and geese—and Quentin said he was going to the library to see what else he could find on the Internet. Then we hugged again before I climbed out of the truck. I stood in the inside of his open door and said, "Quentin, I'm so proud of you. You're the greatest guy I know, and you're going to make a great missionary."

He smiled and kissed the top of my head. "Love ya, Grace," he said as I walked away.

I went inside and found Dave in desperate need of a partner. The linoleum had gotten hung up on a cabinet corner, but whenever he let go of the other end, it came loose from the adhesive. I jumped in and helped him smooth the floor. While I held it, he ran for the roller.

For the rest of the day I reflected on those few minutes in Quentin's truck, but even more so on that kiss on my head. I mean, it wasn't really romantic. It didn't mean we were a couple. No. Dad and Nathan had both kissed me on the top of my head. But it was so endearing. I couldn't get Quentin off my mind for the entire day. And for the second time in our friendship, I found myself wondering what might be.

twenty-one

It was strange to be up on the stand and see only Mom and Alex and Sheila Libbert down in our family's designated pew. Growing up it had been such a struggle to fit all eight Fremonts on that bench.

I was so glad to see Quentin's mom had come to church for his farewell. Sheila had been completely supportive about Quentin's new life in the gospel. I wondered what his dad thought about the Church from the other side. I tried to remember to ask Quentin if he was planning on getting baptized for his dad after his mission.

The bishop called a week earlier and asked me and Dad to speak that Sunday, along with Quentin. Over the past year I had stopped explaining to everyone in the ward that Quentin and I were just friends. I knew from the outside it looked like we were a couple. We were constantly together, after all. But Quentin wanted everyone to know he was serious about being a missionary, so he was adamant about dispelling any couple-dom rumors.

I spoke about member missionary work and recounted the story of helping Quentin find the gospel. I said he had been a real example of faith to me and that he would make a fantastic missionary. It wasn't until I sat down that I realized I hadn't cried at all.

Dad's talk was a little dry, but a huge smile spread on my face when he bear-hugged Quentin on his way down from the pulpit. Throughout Quentin's talk I watched Sheila dab her eyes with a tissue.

This was Quentin's first sacrament talk, and I was nervous for him.

"Just don't pass out," I'd warned him in the foyer. But he stayed completely calm. It wasn't long, but his message was sweet. When Quentin bore his testimony, I felt the Spirit so strongly. It was like hearing a child share his first testimony. It was so pure and true, and I knew he was choosing every word carefully.

Quentin was absolutely flabbergasted when we drove up our driveway and saw how many people had shown up for his open house. We had to park a ways down the road by Liza's place. We walked inside, and he was met with a near movie-star reception. It seemed that most of our ward had come.

Quentin introduced me to his grandparents for the first time. By now his mom had learned most of the Mormon culture, so she fit right in. She had told Quentin's grandma and grandpa there wouldn't be any coffee, and she'd even brought a Jell-O salad. It looked right at home among all the member-created Jell-O salads, molds, and concoctions.

Quentin made his way confidently through the crowd. I went to find Mom and watched my best friend from the kitchen. He was sitting on the arm of the couch, and I saw him loosen his new tie while he visited with the bishop's wife. A thought came to me. *Maybe I should kiss him tonight before it becomes "illegal."* Quentin was being set apart as a missionary Monday night and flying out Tuesday morning.

Just as quickly, my logic returned. This was Quentin. This was a skinny, red-headed, goofy kid who I had made my project two years ago.

So why couldn't I stop thinking about it?

Quentin looked up and saw me watching him. He excused himself and came over.

"Whatcha doin'?" he asked.

Had I been too obvious? "Just sitting here, watching your missionary skills in action. You know two years ago, you wouldn't have talked to an adult like that for more than ten seconds," I said.

"You're right." He laughed. "Thank you."

"Thank you? For what?" I asked.

"For everything. For changing me. For showing me life could be better," he said. "It's all because of you."

I hugged him.

After the party we helped clean up and went for a walk down the road. We talked about what our new lives were going to be like: He with a new home, new food, and a new language. And me—here in the same place I'd been for eighteen years but without the people I loved.

The sky was a bluish purple, and we climbed to the top fence rail to watch the sun go down. The thought came to me again about kissing him, but I pushed it back with logic. Anyway, I reasoned, Quentin would never think of me as more than a friend. I knew he put me leagues above him in his mind.

We said good-bye that night. I tried not to cry, but the tears came anyway. I reassured Quentin that I was glad he was going, but that I would miss him. We promised to write, and then he left. My pillow was still wet when I woke up for work the next morning.

"I love your Mom for putting you on an unlimited minutes plan," I said to Liza.

"I know. Isn't she the best?" Liza said. "Hey, give her a hug for me, okay?"

"Sure. I'll talk to ya next Sunday."

"Love ya, bye."

I willed myself not to be jealous of Liza. She was having so much fun with her new friends, roommates, and student ward at BYU. I really missed her.

Work life was busy with installing the last of the trim in the current house. But at home, life was dull. Dad and Mom spent every free moment following Alex's grueling sports schedule.

The highlights of my week were the Sunday-night calls with Liza and my weekly letters from Quentin. I expected his first few letters to be lonesome ones, but he remained totally upbeat and optimistic. He made two good friends at the MTC, and I thanked Heavenly Father for answering my prayers.

I didn't think anyone had noticed my mood until Mom came into my room one night. I put down my worn copy of *Pride and Prejudice* and gave her my attention, fully expecting another "go to college" talk.

"Is Mr. Darcy any different this time around?" She laughed, pointing to my book.

"Nope, still a great guy, misunderstood as an arrogant you-know-what."

Mom walked toward the bed, and I rolled over to make room.

"Gracie, the bishop suggested you go to the singles ward," she said.

"I thought you weren't supposed to if you weren't in college," I said.

"Well, that's what I thought too, but he said since you're eighteen and working full-time instead of going to school, you should go and meet some people."

"What do you mean meet some people?" I asked. "I've lived here my whole life. Who could there possibly be that I don't already know?"

"They combined the singles ward with the community college ward this summer, and they all meet in our building," she said. "I'm sure there are lots of kids you don't know."

Oh boy. Did I really want to deal with this?

"I don't know, Mom. All those wards are about anyway is getting married," I said.

"Well, what's so wrong with getting married?" Mom laughed. "It worked out pretty good for me."

"Well, I'm just not going to rush off when I'm eighteen like Hope did and have a house full of kids and no money," I said.

"Gracie, Hope did things her way, and you do things your way." She looked serious. "I wasn't trying to get you married. I just thought you might want to meet some new people."

She got off the bed and briskly walked out of the room. I knew I should have bit my tongue before I put down my sister, but it was too late now. In reality, I did want to check out the singles ward—I just didn't want anyone to know it.

On Sunday Mom, Dad, and Alex sat around the table with a huge pile of waffles in between them. I came down, still in my pajamas, pulled up a chair and piled three waffles onto my plate.

"Why aren't you ready yet?" Dad asked.

"I decided I might go over to the singles ward today. It's not until later," I said as if I had thought of it first. I reached for the butter and syrup.

I tried not to look, but out of the corner of my eye I saw Mom smile at Dad.

"Fine. But you better not come home with a diamond ring," he joked.

"Very funny."

After they left, I borrowed a pink calf-length skirt from Alex's closet. I pulled on a white short-sleeve shirt with a ribbon around the neckline. I did my makeup as if I was going to a formal dance, and I even wore earrings and perfume. No, I didn't want a husband, but I was in desperate need of a social life.

One of the counselors in the bishopric greeted me with a program and handshake as I walked in the chapel. I sat on the back row. Why was I always so early? There were only a couple people I recognized. As they filed in, everyone seemed to congregate toward the center pews. I started to think this might have been a bad idea. Two girls turned to look at me, and I watched as the news of a new girl rippled down the row.

While I was focused on the gossip I had created, an incredibly short guy sat down next to me. He had huge glasses and a huger bald spot, and he smelled of foot powder. No one had to warn me that this was the token weird guy of the ward. I quickly scanned the room for the nearest exit.

"Hi, I'm Jim," he said. He must have been at least a decade older than me.

"Gracie," I said shaking his sweaty hand.

"Do you go to the college?" he asked.

"Nope." I hoped short answers would help him get the hint.

"Do you have a boyfriend?"

"Hi, Jim," I turned to the other side of me. A girl with shoulder-length brown hair and a pretty floral dress slid in the pew next to me. I hoped she had come to rescue me.

We quickly exchanged introductions, and the girl, who I had just learned was named Wendy, asked if I'd come sit with her. I politely excused myself and breathed a sigh of relief as I moved up to sit with her group. It was strange, I thought, how I'd been in this chapel since birth, but in a new ward it felt completely foreign. All forty or so kids were huddled like sheep in the very center of the room. But even more notice-able was the lack of noise. I was afraid to sneeze or even shuffle because of the silence. Everyone sat with rapt attention turned toward the bishop. I guess I had never before noticed the noise that rambunctious children and their accompanying stressed-out parents brought to our family ward, but this was a pleasant contrast.

⚜

One of the guys to introduce himself that first Sunday was Mason Helm. He was only slightly taller than me, but he was stocky and muscular. He had dark brown hair and deep blue eyes. He was an easy flirt, and I could tell he enjoyed being the life of the party. Mason gave me directions to the bishop's house for a dinner that Tuesday.

My hands gripped the steering wheel tightly as I pulled up to the yellow two-story house on Bay Street. Maybe this was a bad idea. I sat in the car, pretending to fiddle with the stereo controls, and contemplated turning around. I jumped when I heard a tap at the window. It was Wendy and two other girls I didn't recognize.

I stepped out of the car, and Wendy introduced me. I stuffed my hands in my pockets and tried to push down my nerves. We walked through the side gate and into a monstrous backyard complete with volleyball net and horseshoe pits. On the oppo-site side of the house, I saw a large group of guys and a few girls playing football with fallen leaves scattered all around them. It was only a few days from Thanksgiving, but the weather was fantastic. Most of the guys had shed their jackets and were playing in T-shirts.

The party was supposed to be an inside dinner, but when the forecast called for upper-60s, it was changed to a barbecue.

We found a few lawn chairs and settled in to watch the game. Mason seemed to be taking the game more seriously than the others, and Wendy told me he played running back for the college team here. With some casual prodding, I found out a bit more. He was from West Virginia and had served a mission here a few years back.

The bishop bolted through the middle of the game, snagged the ball, and ran toward the steaming grill. The crowd followed. After a blessing we filled our plates with burgers, baked beans, potato salad, and the singles ward version of desserts—mostly store-bought cookies and pies.

Mason found me with a plateful of food and sat down next to me in the browning grass.

"So you build stuff, huh?" he asked.

I had a mouthful of hamburger that suddenly seemed impossible to swallow. *Perfect*, I thought. Finally I got it down.

"Um, yeah, I guess," I replied, confused. "How'd you know that?"

"Oh, I know the Rawlings. They filled me in."

Hmm, had Mason Helm actually asked someone about me? *Interesting.*

After the superficial getting-to-know-you chatter, I was surprised Mason kept talking. I knew I looked good for me that day, but not good enough for this guy. I rationalized he must be the elder's quorum president.

The hamburgers were great, and Mason was easy to talk to. But when the volleyball came out, I strained my brain for an excuse to leave. I had never been very athletically inclined.

"Come on," Mason pulled me up by the hand. "It'll be fun."

I tossed my plate in the trash and took the longest possible route to the net. Mason was waving me over the whole time. At least there were twelve people on our side of the court, so unless the ball came directly at me, I was pretty well covered. I didn't move my feet the entire match, but two balls did come at me, and I was able to bump them each without too much disaster.

I breathed a sigh of relief when Sister Marchant threw open the screen door and yelled, "Root beer floats!"

We lined up and each took a tall drink from the trays. A circle formed around the empty fire pit, and someone started talking about new home teaching assignments. I realized Mason wasn't the elder's quorum president when another guy started handing out the little white slips.

"Mason, you're still with Trent, but you have two new people now," he said. He handed each of them a paper, and Mason caught me watching him. He gave me a nod that told me my guess was right—the cutest guy in the ward was my new home teacher. I was almost giddy driving home.

I must have sounded like Chelsea on the phone with Liza Sunday night. I sat on a kitchen chair with my feet soaking in a huge bowl of steaming water. It had been a long time since I'd had a pedicure.

"He is way too cute for me," I said. "So I don't know what the deal is, but he is such a flirt!"

"He sounds great. Tell me more about him," she said.

I tried but realized that except for football and the fact that he was from back East, I didn't know much. Nonetheless, I had never had a boyfriend before—or even been on a real date before—so I couldn't get Mason off my mind.

Liza was doing well in school and getting along with her roommates, she said, but her love department was mostly stagnant. I sympathized, but only for a minute before turning the talk to my new home teacher again.

"So what do you think I should do?" I asked, cradling the phone with my shoulder and chin so I could wrap my feet in a towel.

"What do you mean?"

"About Mason," I said.

"Well, I guess just be flirty and stuff so he knows you like him back and then see where things go from there,"

"I don't know how to be flirty, Liza," I said.

"Um, yes, you do. You've had a glaring example right in front of you for over ten years. Just think of Chelsea."

We both laughed.

After we hung up, I scrubbed my feet with a pumice stone and then painted and repainted my toenails purple. It was getting late, but I was too keyed up to lay down so I pulled out a notebook and started a letter to Quentin. I wrote that I'd met a guy in singles ward and hoped we might go on a date. Then I quickly scratched it out, deciding it might hurt his feelings. I rewrote the sentence at the end of the letter. Quentin and I were just friends anyway.

❧✦❧

On Wednesday night Mason called me. I didn't expect him to do his priesthood duty for a few more weeks, but home teaching wasn't why he called.

"Hey, I just wanted to tell you there's institute on Thursday nights at the college if you want to come," he said.

"Don't you have to be a student?" I asked.

"No, no. There are even old married people in the class," he said, laughing. "And our teacher is really awesome. You should come."

I pretended to think it over. "Yeah, that sounds good, I guess," I said.

"Afterwards we all go to Schneider's for dinner, if you want to join us," he said.

"Sounds good. I'll see you then."

"All right, see ya later," Mason said.

"Okay. Bye. Wait, Mason?"

"Yeah?"

"What time?" I asked.

"Oh, seven," he answered.

"Okay, bye."

"Later," he said coolly.

The conversation wasn't romantic, I'll admit it, but I was on cloud nine the rest of the evening. I set the table for Mom, humming a tune the whole time. Even Alex asked, "What's up with you, Gracie? You've had perma-grin all night."

I let her suffer in wonder as I just shook my head and widened my grin.

I conscientiously chose an end seat at institute the next night because the worst possible scenario I could imagine was sitting between Mason and "old guy" Jim. Mason walked in with Trent and another guy and led them in my direction. He pushed the chair a bit closer to me and sat down. My heart was thumping. I flashed a smile and was about to say something—probably totally stupid—when Brother Long cleared his throat to get started. I had a hard time following the scripture references and quotes. I simply couldn't concentrate with Mason only inches from my elbow. *Oh, I am being so Chelsea,* I chastised myself.

Mason invited me to pile into his car with his buddies and ride to Schneider's. Trent, Spencer, and Sterling looked like sardines squished in the backseat, but they didn't complain. I could hardly believe my luck. The hottest guy in the ward was into me! He'd asked the Rawlings about me, he sat by me at the barbecue, he invited me to institute, and now I was riding in his car. There was no writing this off as home teaching duty.

We walked into the restaurant and saw that literally the entire institute class had converged here. I thought I saw one of Wendy's friends, Maris, glare at me. I could sense my face turning red, but just then Mason grabbed my hand to introduce me to a few more friends. We seated ourselves at the far end of the banquet-sized table.

We only ordered drinks and French fries, but I was out until almost midnight.

On Sunday, Mason surprised me again. This time when he walked toward me, I was certain he was going to ask me on a real date. Instead he said, "So can Trent and I come over to home teach tonight?" The way he said it though, with a smile that couldn't possibly be mistaken for anything else but flirting, quickened my pulse. I knew I'd never in my life been so pumped up for home teaching. I flashed him back my best grin and gave him directions to my house. Mason said he'd be there about an hour after church.

I skipped the usual female chit-chat and raced to the parking lot as soon as Relief Society was dismissed. I had to warn my family to be cool before he got there.

All the way home, I contemplated what to say. I desperately wanted the Fremonts not to embarrass me. At the same time, I didn't want them to know I liked Mason. All my planning was ruined when I walked in the door, donning that same smile I'd worn for the past week.

"Can we straighten the house and you guys please leave because my home teachers are coming," I blurted out.

"So that's who it is!" Alex teased. "You're going for your home teachers, Gracie? Lame."

"What are you talking about?" I said.

"It's obvious you've had some guy on your mind, and I'm definitely not leaving the house now. I want to see what he looks like." She laughed.

Mom walked in from the kitchen. "Of course we'll help you straighten up, but I'm with Alex. We can't leave until we get a glimpse of him."

"Give me a break." I sighed.

Even Dad pitched in, straightening up the living room. I wolfed down a peanut butter and banana sandwich and ran upstairs to change when I heard the doorbell. I guess I'd have to stay in my dress. *At least I had a chance to brush my teeth*, I thought.

Dad was shaking hands with Mason and Trent when I came down. Then Mom walked in and motioned for me to introduce everyone. Thankfully, Mom and Dad went out back once the introductions were done.

First, the guys checked out the pictures on our walls and half-teased, half-flirted with me about mine. I cringed when I remembered my hairdo in a family picture taken about six years ago. It was still long and straight, but I'd attempted bangs for a short while. Mom curled them for me, and they were incredibly out-of-date, even then. The back section was fanned to the side, and the front half curled under. It was so embarrassing. I laughed off the ribbing, and in no time we were joking about how Trent had been served a burger with a bite out of it the night before.

Next, we discussed the most recent corny Mormon movies we'd seen. If this was singles ward–style home teaching, they could come ten times a month!

When Trent started the lesson, I heard a creak on the stairs and cocked my head to the side a bit. I saw Alex's head peek out, and I did my best to shoot her a nasty glare without my guests noticing. It must not have worked because next she walked coolly through the room to the front closet, reached inside, and grabbed her backpack. I noticed she'd changed into new clothes and fixed her hair different than it had been after church. *Little brat*, I thought.

Trent announced that the title of the lesson was "Buoying Each Other Up." I caught that much. But then my mind drifted from the lesson to my sister. It was the first time I had realized she had grown out of her awkward goofiness. Of course, she was still incredibly athletic and funny too. But Alex was really pretty. I was sure she had plenty of guys after her in her own school, and now she was going to flirt with these two?

Alex didn't even acknowledge the guys, but Trent set down his *Ensign* and stood up to meet her when she walked by for a second time. Now I would have to introduce them.

"Alex, this is Trent and Mason," I said shortly.

"Nice to meet you," she said. I thought she lingered too long before going back to the kitchen, but Mason and Trent didn't seem to notice.

I swore Alex came up with as many excuses to strut by the living room as she could think of. I couldn't help but notice how both guys glanced up each time. *Hello, she's sixteen!* I thought.

But a half hour later my fears were put to rest. Mason asked Trent to go out to the car and get a ward list for me. As soon as his partner was out of earshot, Mason smiled at me and said, "So I've gotten you to a barbecue and institute and I've home taught you once. Can I take you on a date now?"

I laughed nervously. *Ah, let me think. Yes. Of course. I thought you'd never ask!* But I knew I better play this cool.

"Is it part of your priesthood duty?" I joked.

"Oh, yeah," he smiled. "It would be strictly for service purposes."

We both laughed. But before I could answer, Trent walked back in. A few minutes later when they left, Trent went out the door first, and Mason turned back to me, "So?"

"Yes. Give me a call," I said as if I had done this a thousand times.

I shut the door, ran to my room, and screamed into my pillow.

⋆⟶❧❦☙⟵⋆

All week I talked to Alex on a need-to-only basis, but I made a truce with her on Friday night because I wanted to borrow another shirt. I swore this girl had more clothes than the rest of us sisters combined. Her best friend had a job at Youth—a hip retail store—and always gave Alex her discount.

After I did my hair, she helped me with my make-up.

"You really ought to think about getting highlights," she said.

"Really?" I asked. With all her recent changes, I wasn't

above listening to her fashion advice. With mascara and lipstick in place, she looked at me seriously.

"Why don't you get me a date with the other one?" she asked.

"What other one?" I said even though I knew she meant Trent.

"I mean Mason is cutest," she thought out loud. "But the other one is pretty good looking himself."

"Alex!" I smacked her arm. "You're sixteen. They're in college!"

"Who cares?" she snapped back.

"I do. And I guarantee Mom and Dad do too," I said. Alex just shrugged.

A few minutes later, the doorbell rang and Alex shot out of my room and down the stairs. Mason looked great. He had on a faded pair of baggy jeans and a white T-shirt under a short-sleeved button-down plaid shirt. The blue in his shirt made his eyes stand out even more. His short hair was gelled and spiky.

When he told me we were going bowling, I was glad I'd changed the skirt for a pair of jeans. I wore a purple baby doll shirt with little white buttons and a tie in the back. We made our way down Sheridan Avenue to Nite Lanes—a black-light bowling alley. Bowling was the one sport—if you could call it a sport—that I felt comfortable with. Still, I was no pro. By the fifth frame of the first game, we were both doing horrible. I didn't mind, though, because every time I guttered a ball, Mason gave me the cutest little smirk. My score was 22 and Mason had 28.

"I have an idea," he smiled. "Let's just do tricks instead."

"Tricks?" I wasn't sure what he meant.

"Yeah. Okay, I'll go first and you have to do what I do."

"All right," I agreed.

For his first "trick" Mason turned his back to the pins and rolled the ball between his legs. He actually knocked five pins down. When it was my turn, the ball rolled so slow I swore it was going to stop. But instead, just before it reached the pins, it guttered. And there was that smirk.

For the next frame, Mason left-handed the ball. It looked awkward, and I burst out laughing. But when it was my turn, it couldn't have been much better.

By our third "trick," bowlers in the adjacent lanes were giving us funny looks. I pretended not to notice. I was sweaty and nervous—I wanted him to like me so bad—but as the night wore on, I felt more and more comfortable.

We finished the game and climbed on two stools at the snack bar. I leaned my arms against the smooth cherry wood bar and sipped a slushy. With almost every word he said, Mason would smile. He made me feel like I was the only one in the room, and when he looked into my eyes, the room started spinning.

I didn't want to get out of his car that night for two reasons: I wasn't sure what the end-of-date-protocol was, and I was having too much fun to go home. Mason ran around, opened my door, and walked me up the steps. He seemed completely at ease, like he'd done this thousands of times.

"Hey, call you tomorrow?" he asked.

"Sure," I said. "Thanks." And I stepped inside.

⁕⇢•❧⊱❀⊰❧•⇠⁕

The next night I went out with Mason and his friends. There was only one other girl, Trent's girlfriend, Lissa, but I didn't mind. We played video games at Trent's apartment. Even I got in on the action when they broke out the old games Hope and Nathan used to play, like Super Mario Brothers and Duck Hunt.

That night Mason put his arm around me when he walked me to my car. It could have been construed as a "friendly" gesture, but my heart was beating so hard, I wondered if he could hear it. When we got to the car, he opened my door. I got in and rolled the window down.

"Thanks for inviting me," I said. "I had fun."

"Of course. I really like hanging out with you," he said. "Don't forget tomorrow is break the fast after church. I'll expect you to bring something delicious."

I laughed.

My mind began racing as I drove away. *Okay, Mason has one year left of college. That means we could get married in about a year and a half. Yeah, I think I would like a spring wedding. Wait, no, I'd have to wait for Quentin to get home so he could meet him.* Speaking of which, Liza would be home in a few days for Christmas Break. I couldn't wait to update her on my new guy.

I got up super early and enlisted Mom's help on a chocolate pecan cheesecake. We had to make two, I insisted, so we could taste one and leave the other one looking nice. I told her I wouldn't dare take something to church that I hadn't tried.

"This doesn't have anything to do with this Mr. Mason, does it?" she asked.

"No." I smiled teasingly.

I slid the cheesecake into the fridge to cool and turned the dial to colder. I only had a few hours until church. I went upstairs, took a shower, dried my hair, and found a long black dress I hadn't worn in a long time. It had cap sleeves and silvery-blue butterflies and flowers from the knees down. I curled the ends of my hair under and pulled the sides up in little diamond covered clips.

My dessert got rave reviews that afternoon. I knew next month I'd have to find a treat equally as impressive.

❧⟡❧

It was hard to stop smiling at work the next week. I was enjoying the trim work I was assigned to, but I was mostly thinking about Mason. I was completely smitten with him! I even informed a couple of coworkers that he was my boyfriend, or at least I thought he was.

Mason and I went out again on Tuesday. On Wednesday, he came over to my house for dinner. I invited Liza too so they could meet.

Liza rushed in the door without knocking and almost bowled me over with her hug. It was the first time we had seen each other since August, but we picked up right where we left off. After Mason left, Liza listened wide-eyed as I recounted all the details of the past few weeks, even though she'd already heard it all over the phone.

As much as I missed Chelsea too, we hadn't stayed in touch too well. We saw a movie together when she had flown home for Thanksgiving, but we didn't have much to talk about. Chelsea wouldn't be home for a few more weeks because the Copelands were taking a cruise during the holidays.

On Saturday, Mason took me out one last time before he went home for Christmas. We were going snowshoeing. He picked me up early and helped me load my mountain of gear—black snow pants, pink and white coat, gloves, hat, and scarf—into the back of his car. The Carter Mountain road was packed with snow and ice, so the drive took over an hour. On each side of the road, the snow was piled higher than Mason's car. And only occasionally could we see the tops of signs poking out of the heap. Finally we rounded a corner and saw the huge lodge. It was made from massive logs—probably eighteen inches in diameter. There were tall windows and a beautiful snow-covered deck on the side. We parked and went inside to rent our snowshoes. The air was cold and crisp, but the sun was shining. I was glad I'd brought sunglasses.

Apparently Mason had been snowshoeing before because he navigated the prairie expertly. It was a bit more awkward for me. It took me about an hour to get used to my huge feet and stop tripping over myself. We made our way through the first prairie and then into a cluster of lodge pole pines. I brushed the snow off a fallen log and sat down.

Mason pulled a canteen from his pack and passed it to me. "Thanks," I said. "I had no idea this was so much work."

I took a long drink from the canteen, and the water tasted wonderful. He reached for it, but I quickly snatched it back and drank again. Mason laughed.

"You're going to make me fight you for it, huh?" he asked.

I screwed the lid back on and smiled as I attempted to hand it back to Mason. But instead of taking it, he tackled me, and I fell off the back of the log and into a pile of powder. I started laughing and couldn't stop. Mason lay down next to me and I shoveled two handfuls of snow into his face. I felt the damp snow on the back of my head, but I didn't care. I jumped up and attempted to run away, but only fell again.

When we emerged from the trees, a few minutes later, the scene was breathtaking. A huge valley was flanked to either side by steep ridges covered in pine trees. The wide meadow was completely white, and the sunlight sparkled off the snow. A frozen stream ran the length of the prairie. Mason pointed to brown specks that seemed a mile away. I looked at him, confused. He set down his pack, extracted binoculars, and focused them for me. When I pulled them to my eyes I saw the large herd of elk. There were over fifty head, I estimated.

We spent the day exploring the terrain of the natural corral, and by late afternoon, I was feeling much more confident on my snow shoes. Then we started the long trek back. Although before it had seemed rather flat, it felt like we were hiking more uphill now, and after just a few minutes, I had to shed my coat. I tied it to the top of my pack and kept moving. By the time I saw the red metal roof of the lodge rising over a hill, I was about spent. I had also shed my sweatshirt and only had on a red Houses of Hope T-shirt. Still, I felt soaked in sweat. Our date had proved to be quite the workout.

I grabbed my jeans and long-sleeve white shirt from Mason's car and changed in the lodge bathroom. My hair had been mashed in every direction from my wool hat, so I brushed through it and pulled it into a ponytail. I met Mason at a small table near the huge stone fireplace. A fire crackled quietly. He had already ordered hot chocolate and two heavy moose mugs sat in front of us. My legs ached, but I smiled. I didn't want to be anywhere else. It was so romantic. I sipped my cocoa and set the mug back down. Mason reached across the table and grabbed my hand.

"Gracie, I really like you," he said, staring into my eyes. "I hope we can keep dating when I get back next month."

"You better call me before then. I can't wait that long," I said. He pushed his chair back and leaned forward over the table. I closed my eyes and felt his lips on mine. When he sat back down, I was embarrassed at my huge grin. I couldn't stop it, though. I couldn't have imagined a better first kiss.

When Mason dropped me off that night, he kissed me one more time.

"Wow," was all I said before I ducked in the front door. I waved from the window as Mason drove away.

twenty-three

I sat on a stool with my arms folded on the kitchen counter and stared at the phone. *Ring. Ring.* I silently begged it.

Mom's yell from the garage brought me back to earth.

"Gracie, can you help me carry in these groceries?"

"Sure, Mom. Be right there," I shouted back. I jumped off the stool but turned around and grabbed the cordless phone. I clipped it to my jeans' pocket—just in case he called.

"Wow, Mom, who are you planning on feeding?" I joked when I eyed the loaded-down minivan.

"Our family's growing, honey," she said. "Oh, I can't wait to all be together again."

Everyone was coming home for Christmas this year, except Danielle. She wouldn't be home from her mission until March, but at least we'd get to talk to her on the phone. Even more than seeing my family, I was looking forward to Mason calling me. He'd only called once since he left.

"Sorry I can't call much, but my dad freaks out if I go over my minutes," he had said. I was pacified, but only for a few days.

Waiting for Mason's calls had been exacerbated by more boredom. At work we finished building our last house three days before Christmas, so now I was sitting at home all day.

The house turned out beautiful. My favorite part of the job was the Move-In Ceremony when we met the women who were taking over the house. Their tears of joy overflowed with mine. Even though I hadn't earned much more than tithing and a bit of spending money at this job, the feelings I got from helping the women were invaluable. Now our crew would be laid off until the spring, when the next year's grant money kicked in.

On Christmas Eve, after the dinner dishes had been cleared, the ladies made their way into the living room where Dad, Nathan, Anthony, and Damon sat watching TV. We squeezed our way onto the couches and chairs beside them. The thunder of the kids upstairs muted the football commentator. Hope cleared her throat and announced that baby number five was on the way in July.

"And this is the last one!" Anthony swore.

"Sure," we all laughed.

"This time we're not going to find out the sex," Hope said. "Maybe that way we can finally get our girl."

I glanced across the room and saw Nathan and Sarah looking into each others' eyes. They both wore huge smiles, and Nathan leaned down to kiss her.

"Well, since we're doing announcements," he said. "I guess we'll tell you that Emmylee is going to have a little brother or sister in July too."

Mom covered her mouth and started to cry.

"Please, Mom," Alex said.

Immediately Sarah and Hope launched into a pregnancy discussion that was over my head, but I caught that their due dates were less than a week apart.

Dad turned to my sister, "Sam, Damon, do you have any news to add?"

We all laughed but waited. Her face was turning the color of the red-wrapped Christmas gifts.

"No, we don't," she stammered. "Well, at least not until August 2."

"Are we turning into The Fremont Family Baby Factory?"

I asked. If Danielle, Alex, or I were in need of any familial attention over the next year, I knew we were out of luck. Three new grandkids in one month!

The rest of the weekend was spent talking about babies, of course. Whenever I'd had my fill, I walked over to Liza's house. And once Chelsea came home, she usually joined us there. California had made Chelsea even more appearance-crazed than she was before. She tanned three times a week and wasted all her book money on new clothes. Against Liza's advice, Chelsea had joined a sorority. The worst news was that Chelsea was seriously dating another nonmember.

The three of us stayed the night at Liza's and sat around her table the next morning. We were still in our pajamas. I poured myself a bowl of cereal and a glass of orange juice.

When the conversation turned to Chelsea's boyfriend, she ran into the hallway and grabbed her polka-dot purse from the hook. She came back to the table, pulled out his picture, and gently set it in the center of the table.

"Isn't he the most gorgeous thing you've ever seen?" she asked.

He was cute. Very cute, in fact. But what was she doing, I asked her point blank. "What's with the sorority and the non-member and everything else, Chels?"

"What do you mean?" She looked surprised. "I don't party with everyone, I just do the other social stuff, and besides Matt is a really great guy. I only get to go to college once. I might as well experience it, right?"

"I guess," I shrugged. I knew we hadn't stayed close enough for me to start lecturing Chelsea now. I'd just have to pray for her instead.

Liza was loving BYU, and by New Year's, she was ready to go back. I asked her probably twenty times over the break if there were any special guys in her ward, but she just shook off the question.

MASON COMES HOME was scrawled across my calendar in red marker for January 6. I'd been counting down the days. I waited by the phone, but the day came and went without his call. I predicted he would for sure call on Friday.

That night I tried watching TV, doing a crossword puzzle, and even cleaning out my closet. Nothing worked. I could not get my mind off of Mason. By 6:00 PM, I hadn't heard anything and I was going completely crazy. The ground was covered in a thin layer of ice, but I pulled on my coat and went for a walk anyway. I walked down to Liza's house and reflected on how many times my feet had crossed this dirt. I went further toward the Bronsons' house, but halfway there I turned back. I had to see if he'd called.

I walked in the door and yelled to Mom, "Did anyone call for me?"

"No, sweetheart."

In the den that night, I tried to read a book Nathan had bought me for Christmas, but I couldn't concentrate on the words. Between pages, I found myself staring at the phone across the room. Nothing.

On Saturday morning Alex walked in my room. "I thought Mason was getting back this week," she said.

"I think maybe he stayed home longer," I said, but she saw right through me.

"Why don't you just call him?" Alex asked.

I ignored her. But that night, I finally gave in. I took the phone into my room and shut the door. I sat down in the middle of my floor and crossed my legs. I took a deep breath and dialed the number.

His roommate answered.

"Hi, is Mason there?" I stammered.

"Um, who is this?"

"Oh, this is Gracie." My hand was shaking.

"Oh. Uh, hi, Gracie. Well, let me check." I heard the phone rustling around.

A few minutes later he got back on. "He left for a little bit, but I'll tell him you called."

"Okay. Yeah, thank you," I said.

I set down the phone and lay back on the carpet. My heart sank. Mason must have been there but just didn't want to talk to me. Their apartment definitely wasn't big enough to have to "check" to know if someone was home or not. Tears came to my eyes and dampened my hair just above my ears.

The next morning at church I sat in my car and watched Mason walking into the building. I waited until I knew I was a few minutes late. Then I walked in hurriedly and sat next to Wendy in the back row. I didn't hear a word the speakers said. I stared at the back of Mason's head and pleaded for him to turn around and look at me. If he would just wink or smile or something, I'd know we were all right. But he never did.

I contemplated escaping and never coming to this ward again, but I couldn't. Even if I didn't have Mason, I knew the people in this ward were my only friends.

I sat down in Gospel Doctrine class and let out a huge sigh when Mason walked in and sat next to me. Okay, this was going to be fine. I knew it. The lesson was starting, though, so we didn't get any chance to talk. When class ended, Mason grabbed my hand. My heart jumped into my throat like it hadn't since he'd left.

"Let's go talk," he said.

Oh, no. I followed him out of the classroom, down the long drab hall, and into the parking lot like a student headed to the principal's office. I knew he was about to dump me. We sat down on the curb in front of the building, and I stared at my shoes.

"Gracie, you are such a great person," he said. "You're fun and you are so nice and everything."

I was already crying.

"While I was gone, though, I realized we'd make better

friends than a couple," he said.

What? In my mind Mason was my first boyfriend, and if life went the way I planned, he was going to be my last.

"Okay," was all I could say. I wiped my face on my sleeve. He hugged me, but I wished he wouldn't. As we walked back in the foyer, he made some small talk about institute on Thursday and then slipped into priesthood meeting. I turned back around and walked out the glass doors.

~≈☼≈~

Even after driving around for an hour, my eyes wouldn't return to white, so I went home anyway. I was glad Mom was the only one home.

"What happened, honey? Are you okay?" she asked.

"Do I look okay?"

"No. Come here." She hugged me, and my body shook with sobs.

"Mason just wants to be friends," I cried.

"Oh, honey," she said. "I'm so sorry."

I was glad Mom didn't ask any more questions. She just held me for a long time. When I heard the garage door open, I went upstairs to my room to cry more.

How could this be? Mason had kissed me! I was sure I was falling in love with him. In fact, I told Liza I was.

"I hate my life," I said aloud and pulled a pillow over my face.

Somewhere in between sobs, I fell asleep and didn't wake up until nine that night. Of course, then I couldn't go back to sleep. So in typical damaged girl–style, I spent an hour reading through my journal from the moment I met Mason until now. Then I took out a red pen and poured today's feelings onto the page.

I dialed Liza's number, and she offered what solace she could from hundreds of miles away. She told me Chelsea was having a hard time too, and I ought to call her. Sure, that's just what I needed: someone else's problems heaped on top of mine.

I called her anyway and a half hour later I was still listening to Chelsea rave about her boyfriend's family's beach home outside San Diego. Having a hard time? What was Liza talking about? Yeah, Chelsea's life sounded pretty tough. She kept going on until I was sick of the details. Mid-sentence I interrupted her.

"Chelsea, my boyfriend just broke up with me," I said.

"Oh, Gracie, I'm so sorry. What happened?" she asked.

"He said he wants to be just friends, and I think—"

"Matt told me that a week after we started dating, but now look how things turned out. We are totally serious," she said.

Same old Chelsea—completely focused on herself.

"Yeah." I didn't feel like making an effort. "Well, I guess I'm going to go."

"Okay. Hey, wait. I have advice for you," she said.

This ought to be good.

"Go on a date."

"What? With who?" I asked.

"It doesn't matter. With anyone. That way if you see him dating other girls, you'll be okay. You might still be thinking about him—what's his name again? But anyway, seriously, it would be good for you."

We hung up and for the first time in our twelve-year friendship, I found myself considering Chelsea Copeland's advice valuable.

Yeah, maybe I'll go on another date. Even with my resolve, I was cranky the rest of the week. I skipped institute on Thursday, but I promised myself that I'd scope out the ward on Sunday for a date selection. But when Sunday morning came, Mom and Dad looked surprised when I came downstairs, ready to go to church with them.

"Aren't you going to your ward today, honey?" Dad asked cautiously. *Mom must have told him,* I thought.

"I don't feel like it. Can I just go with you?"

Mom nodded her head, "Of course you can." She gave me a hug.

I cried that afternoon when I wrote Quentin his letter. I wrote that I missed him. I wrote that I got dumped. I wrote that life was really sucking right now. I quickly folded the letter and stuffed it in the envelope without re-reading it. After I stuck it in the mailbox the next morning, I regretted it. I remembered a Young Women's lesson from a few years back: "You should only write uplifting and encouraging letters to missionaries." *Oops.*

By mid-week even *I* was getting sick of my pity party, but I couldn't get through a day without crying. I shouldn't miss Mason this bad. All I wanted was for Quentin to come home. I wanted him to drive me up a steep hill and shut off his truck so I could tell him all that hurt in my life.

Or I'd take Liza or even an unmarried younger version of my brother. I just needed someone.

I was facedown on my bed when the phone rang. Alex yelled upstairs, "Gracie, it's someone named Jim."

Oh my gosh, could this get any worse? What a sick joke, Heavenly Father. Yeah, I need someone, but not this *someone!*

"Gracie, hi. This is Jim. You know from the ward?" he said. "I was wondering if you wanted to go to a movie tonight."

"Sure," I almost gasped at my own acceptance.

"Really? You mean it?" he asked. I could tell he was much more accustomed to rejection.

"Yeah, sure." I hoped I wouldn't regret this.

Two hours later, sitting in a dark movie theater, I prayed Jim wouldn't try any moves. He didn't. Rather he was a perfect gentleman. I let my mind wander and I didn't follow much of the flick. Instead I thought of Mason and Quentin and everything except the place I was in. When Jim dropped me off, I knew I'd better clear the air.

"Jim, I really appreciate you taking me out tonight," I said. "It was great for me to get out."

"Sure. I think you're really nice and, well, really pretty too."

Oh, great.

"Um, but Jim I don't think we'd better go on any more dates by ourselves," I said in the kindest voice I could muster.

His smile fell, and he put his hands on the steering wheel. "I understand," he said.

"You're a really good guy—" I stopped myself. Was this what Mason had done to me? It was rejection in its purest form. I didn't want to hurt someone the way I had just been hurt. I wanted Jim to be happy—not spend the rest of the month wallowing because of my dismissal.

I quickly reasoned with myself. Maybe I could go on one more date. He wasn't too bad of a guy. But then my conscience got the better of me.

"Jim, the truth is, I don't think this would work out between us, so I think you should spend your time dating a girl who is as interested as you are."

I pushed back the urge to hug him, remembering how Mason's hug had just stung deeper. I waved as he drove away. Then I sat down on the step and considered calling Chelsea. She was right. Her advice hadn't gotten me a boyfriend, but it was a good idea. Even I could admit, I felt better.

***

I went back to the singles ward the next Sunday and gasped when I saw Mason walking in holding a girl's hand. I had never seen her.

My eyes started to sting. How could I get out of here without anyone noticing? I thought I saw Maris glaring at Mason's new girl. She was the same one who had given me a dirty look at the restaurant that night. What was her problem?

Wendy saw my face going crimson and grabbed my arm. "Gracie, can you help me get something out of my car."

I calmly stood up and quickly walked out of the chapel. The tears started falling when we reached the parking lot. I thanked Wendy for once again rescuing me.

"Let me guess," I said. "There's nothing in your car?"

"Nope. You just looked like you needed to get out of there."

"Yeah," I said. I didn't feel like explaining, but to my surprise, I didn't have to.

"Don't worry about him," Wendy said. "Mason is like that."

"Like what?" I asked.

"You know—a flirt. He dates almost every new girl who comes into the ward."

"What?" I was shocked. "Why didn't anyone tell me?"

"Would you have listened?" she asked.

I considered it. "Probably not, I guess."

"I didn't listen a couple years ago when someone warned me about him," she said. "I mean who doesn't want to be liked by the best looking guy in the ward. Right?"

"You dated him too?" I asked.

"Gracie, I don't think anyone here hasn't."

I shook my head and wiped my eyes. "What a jerk."

She rubbed my shoulder. "He's not a jerk. It's just his way. Besides the standards say we should date a lot of people, right?"

"I guess," I agreed. "Still, he shouldn't go around breaking hearts."

"True, but that's just it with Mason. He seriously doesn't know he's hurting girls. He thinks its fine to hop from one to another," she explained.

"So is that why Maris glares at his girlfriends?" I smiled.

"Yeah, she was a Mason dumpee once too. The difference with her is, she hasn't gotten over it yet," she said.

"Oh."

"Now let's go to church," she said, and we walked back in.

On Monday I didn't get out of bed until after noon. I didn't feel like showering, so I dragged myself to the couch and started flipping through stations. I was glad no one was home to see my pitiful state. I ate half a big bag of Peanut M&Ms. When I heard the garage door open, I ran upstairs and shut my door.

I pulled my scriptures off the shelf. Something had to help. Before I read, I decided to pray first. I opened to 2 Nephi 22:2 which had become my favorite verse since Mom pointed it out to me that one night years ago.

It lifted my spirits, but it wasn't exactly what I needed to get out of this funk. Instead I turned to where I was currently reading in Alma. I read the chapter but didn't feel much better. It was about war and one leader killing another leader.

I looked in my mirror to assess how horrendous I looked, but I noticed a little note card I had put there a few years back. I pulled it from the mirror and held it in my hand.

"The best advice for a bad day is to serve someone else."

Yeah, I thought. Wouldn't I be a lot of help to someone now?

I looked awful. My hair was in a ratty ponytail, and my mascara was smudged from yesterday. It was a blessing I hadn't talked to anyone today because I hadn't even brushed my teeth yet. My gray sweatpants had a growing hole over one knee.

I threw the paper on the floor and fell asleep facedown on my bed. Alex woke me up awhile later.

"Are you sick?" she asked.

"No."

"Oh, then you're just pathetic."

"Please get out," I said.

I didn't get up again.

That night I dreamed that I was sitting on a curb, watching beautiful people walk by. They were well-dressed and happy looking. I kept saying "hi" and waving, but none of them heard me. No one even looked my direction.

I woke up at 10:00 AM the next day and decided I had better take a shower. When I started to take off my sock in the bathroom, it stuck to my hand. What in the world? I must have stepped on that quote from my mirror, because it was stuck facedown on my foot. Without taking it off I tilted my head and read it again.

"The best advice for a bad day is to serve someone else."

I read it three or four times before getting in the coldest shower I could handle.

❦

"So what do you think?" the beautician swiveled my chair around, and I stared at a new me.

"I love it," I said, running my fingers through my shoulder-length, highlighted hair.

I paid and walked across the street to the drug store for some new make-up. *Nothing like a makeover to jump-start your mood,* I thought. I picked up a complete lineup of Almay products: powder and blush, eye liner, eye shadow, mascara, and lipstick.

On my way home, I stopped at Gibbs Books and picked out a mystery—totally unusual for me. I took the Beacon Hill way home instead of my normal route on the Greybull Highway. When I got home, I read Mom's note. She was at the family history center. I ran upstairs, tested out my new makeup, and decided to make dinner for everyone. What would have taken Mom a half hour took me two, but by 6:00 PM we had a tasty chicken casserole on the table. I threw together a spinach salad and of course baked my signature cookies. I had even washed the cooking dishes before anyone was home.

After dinner I forced Mom out of the kitchen so I could clean. This drove her nuts. Instead of relaxing in the living room, she hovered around the kitchen entrance. When I finished, I hopped in the car and drove to Hope's house. When I pulled up, I was immediately glad I'd come. She had two boys fighting with plastic swords in the front yard and one urinating out the back door while she wrestled to bathe her youngest over her expanding belly. Anthony was roofing in Montana,

Hope explained. She looked close to tears.

I made up a cleaning game and tricked the three oldest into helping me straighten the house. Then we played their version of Monopoly—not even close to the real version—and I helped Hope tuck them in.

She flopped onto the tan corduroy couch.

"Sometimes life is so hard," she sighed.

"You're right," I said, thinking of my own past few days. "Hey, do you have the stuff to do pedicures?" I asked to chase away the cynicism creeping in.

"Yeah, I guess."

We scrubbed and polished our feet and then painted each other's toenails while watching reruns of the "Wonder Years." By the second show, Hope's mood was almost giddy. I ended up staying until after midnight.

She walked me out to the car and bear-hugged me. "How did you know I needed you?" she asked.

"I don't know. I think I needed you too," I said.

She gave me a strange look and then hugged me again.

When I got home, I saw a note from Alex that said my work had called. It surprised me because we still had almost two months until we started the next house. I stuck it on my dresser and knelt down for prayers. I thanked Heavenly Father for helping me to help myself, and I thanked Him for getting me through a day without crying. I fell asleep seconds after hitting the pillow.

The next morning I called Carry, the director at Houses of Hope.

"Thanks for calling, Gracie," she said. "I have something to ask you."

"Okay?"

"Well, David and his wife are retiring and moving down to Florida, so we're out a building supervisor for next year," she said quickly.

"Oh, no," I said. "Everybody loves Dave. And he does such a good job."

"Yeah, it's going to be a hard loss," she agreed. "But talking to everyone about what to do has brought out some interesting ideas," she said.

"Okay, what are you thinking?" I asked, honestly hoping the program wouldn't suffer.

"Well, I know you're young, but—"

What? Were they actually considering me?

"The board of directors voted unanimously for you to be our new building supervisor if you're up to it," she said.

"Me?" I asked. "I don't have any degree or experience, and I've only worked on a few houses."

"Yeah, we know. But Dave said he'd love to train you for the next few months before he leaves. I'm sure you'll pick it up quickly. You're such a natural. And the fact is, well, you're the glue in our building team," she said.

Me? Glue?

"I'm not sure, Carry," I said.

"Well, of course it's up to you, but let me tell you the specifics of the job. I would come to you with the families, and you would meet with them to determine their needs for the house. Then you would direct the framers, electricians, plumbers, roofers, and any other subs on what we're looking for. And of course, you would oversee the regular crew every day."

"You mean I would actually work with the families?" I asked. That sounded awesome to me. I loved building, but I had gotten into this to help the women.

"Yep," she said.

"That sounds amazing. I just don't know if I can handle it." It was freezing outside, but I was starting to sweat.

"Everyone has confidence in you. You've done every job there is in those houses, and you're so talented—you pick things right up. We know you'd do great."

I was quiet for a minute.

"Why not? I'll do it," I shrieked.

"Great. Well. I'll let everyone know. We're going to get you out of the Stone Age and finally get you a cell. And you, Dave, and I can meet tomorrow if that will work for you," she said.

"Sure."

"Oh, and Gracie," she said.

"Yes?"

"You do know about the salary, right?"

"Salary? I thought everyone was on a stipend," I responded.

"Everyone except for me and you. You'll make $34,000 a year with benefits."

My mouth dropped, and I couldn't speak.

"Um. Okay," I finally said.

Sensing my shock, Carry started laughing. "You're going to be great, hon. In fact, you'll be the youngest building supervisor the organization has ever had."

"Will I be the first girl?" I asked.

"Second," she said. "I was first."

"That explains you wanting me so bad." I laughed.

"Yeah, I guess it does. But it also means you'll have someone here to help you whenever things get tough. I was in those shoes for fifteen years before Dave came around."

After I hung up, I jumped the stairs three at a time to tell Mom the news.

For a full week, I felt like I was floating. Mom had called everyone to tell them. Was Heavenly Father finally showing me why He wanted me to stay here when all my friends had left town last fall?

My confidence was still riding high by Sunday, and I asked Liam, a guy I had talked to in institute a few times, if he wanted to go out on Valentine's Day.

"Can you believe it?" I asked Liza on the phone. "Me, asking someone out!"

She was laughing. "And he said 'yes!' Not just 'yes,' but an excited 'yes.'"

I filled Liza in on all my meetings at work, and she seemed genuinely happy for me. Toward the end of our conversation, I asked Liza, "So there are still no guys you're interested in?"

She got quiet.

"Liza?" I prodded.

"Well, there is this one guy," she said shyly.

"What? And you haven't told me about him?" I joked.

"Well, it's probably nothing," she said. "We just have this class together, and he's pretty nice."

It seemed like she was downplaying the situation, but I decided not to push. We promised to talk next Sunday.

I never did get to talk to her on Sunday, though. I was in too much shock. After church that day, our bishop called me into his office and asked me to be the new Relief Society president. I didn't take this new job with quite the same enthusiasm I had mustered when I was on the phone with Carry. Mom, Dad, and I talked late into the night.

"Heavenly Father gives these callings, Gracie, not your bishop," Dad said.

"I know. I know. But it's still hard."

"It's going to take lots of prayer on your part, honey," Mom said, "but you're going to be wonderful."

I wasn't so sure.

I fell asleep feeling overwhelmed. In the morning, though, my happy excitement was back. Energized, I wrote out a daily schedule for the next month to help me accomplish everything I needed to do.

Wednesday was Valentine's Day, and Liam and I planned a totally creative non–Valentine's Day date. He brought me weeds instead of roses. I gave him a box of jelly beans instead of chocolates. Instead of going to a fancy restaurant, we ate in the playland at McDonald's and watched the kids run around. After they left, we even jumped in the ball room ourselves. Then we opted for a cheesy horror flick instead of a romantic one.

Overall I had a great time. There wasn't a huge spark, but Liam made me laugh. I burst into my date recap when Liza called the next night. She listened, but I could tell something else was on her mind.

"Wow, I'm glad you had fun," was all she said.

"What's up for you?" I asked.

"Well, I have two questions for you," she said. This sounded rehearsed.

"Okay . . . ?"

"First of all, do you remember the road trip we planned?" she asked.

"Of course," I said.

"Well, I was wondering if you could take that trip with me at the end of April?"

"What? What made you remember that?" I asked.

"Just answer," she demanded.

"That would be awesome, but I'll have to check with our building schedule to see where we're at then," I said. "So, 'Yes, hopefully.' Is that good enough?"

"Sure. Okay, the second question is, will you be my maid of honor?"

"What?" I shot off the couch and was literally screaming into the phone. It took me a full minute to calm down.

"You're getting married?" I screamed.

"Just answer. Then I'll give you the details." She was being so matter-of-fact.

"Yes. Yes. Yes. Of course I will."

I sat back down, captivated, as Liza unfolded her story. She was introduced to a new guy in a bowling class when the teacher assigned them to the same lane. They hit it off immediately and had started talking about marriage in less than two weeks. Within the month, they were completely serious, and last night, on Valentine's Day, he'd given her a ring.

I was amazed. It wasn't that Liza getting married young was too strange. I could easily picture her as a wife and even a mother. However, I couldn't believe I hadn't heard a word about this guy until now.

She said they were being sealed in May at the Idaho Falls

Temple and having their reception the next weekend, here at the stake center.

"Liza, why didn't you tell me about this?" I asked, a bit hurt. "For weeks you've been letting me blab on about my new job and my dumb date, and the whole time you were about to be engaged?"

"Well, there's one thing I was worried about," she said.

"What?" I asked.

"I didn't want to hurt your feelings—"

"Just because my life wasn't going great didn't mean you couldn't share yours," I said, offended.

"No, no, it's not that."

I waited.

"Gracie, I'm marrying Justin Fram."

"You mean *the* Justin Fram?" I asked.

"Uh-huh," she gulped.

I was shocked. My mouth opened, but no sound came out.

"Oh no, you're upset?" she asked, her voice almost trembling.

"Upset? What are you talking about?" I asked. "That's wonderful. He was such a great guy. And cute too."

"But you were in love with him," she said. "I was so scared you'd be mad at me."

I burst out laughing.

"You can't be serious," I said.

She was quiet for a second and then she started laughing too. I was almost rolling on the ground.

"I was twelve." Tears of laughter formed in my eyes. "How dare you, Liza Roberts," I said sarcastically. "Or should I say Liza Fram?"

We talked for another hour while she gave me more dating details and the basic wedding plans. When we hung up, I wished it wasn't so late. I couldn't wait to tell Nathan.

twenty-four

Everyone but Samantha made the trip to Cody for Danielle's homecoming in March. Sam couldn't come because her blood pressure kept spiking, and her obstetrician wanted to keep a close eye on her. I swore Hope and Sarah compared belly sizes at least twenty times—Hope's beat Sarah's by a landslide.

"Well maybe by your fifth one, you'll look like this too." She laughed.

Danielle seemed so different when she got home. She wouldn't be starting back at school until the fall, so we saw a lot of each other. At times it felt like too many adults living under one roof, but for the most part, Danielle, Alex, and I became closer than we had ever been.

Just when I was getting used to the workload with my new calling, we started my first house at work.

I loved the family. Laura, the mom, was so humble and grateful for what we were doing. She had only one daughter, so the house was only about 1,500 square feet. When I met with her to talk about what they wanted in their new home, she wouldn't suggest a thing.

"Just four walls where no one can hurt us," she said. "That's more than we've seen in a long time."

This brought tears to my eyes, but I maintained my professionalism and worked out a basic floor plan for two bedrooms, two baths, and an office. The blueprints were approved a week later, and then it was time to get to work.

It didn't take long to realize there were several steps in this process I had never done before—like working with the excavators and setting up the house for city water and sewer. I called Carry and Dave almost every day. I wondered if Dave wished he hadn't left his phone number behind.

The hardest part was working with our outside contractors. I can't count the number of guys who looked at me like "You're in charge?" Our crew was my cheering squad, though. They had total confidence in me.

We put the finishing touches on the house in mid-April. It went pretty fast because of its size and because I really wanted to be free for the road trip. For our reveal, I bought fifty pink balloons at the grocery store and placed them throughout the house. Laura and her daughter were so excited, they ran from room to room to see what we had done for them.

When Laura hugged me, it felt like she'd never let go.

"You're my angel," she whispered into my ear.

That night I ardently thanked Heavenly Father for making my life happy and full. Sometimes it felt almost too full—but I wasn't about to complain about that.

⤞⊶◈⊷⤝

My plane touched down in Salt Lake, and I marveled at the beautiful day. Spring could always bring a smile to my face. I planned to stay one night in Liza's dorm before we left for our trip. While she was finishing her last final, I pulled open a new photo album she had on her shelf. It was loaded with pictures of her and Justin. I could see glimpses of the old cute Justin Fram I'd known years ago, but he looked much older and mature now. They seemed so happy.

For the first time, Liza had dipped into the money she'd been left when her Dad died and bought herself a new Honda. We threw our suitcase and atlas inside, topped off the tank, and took off. There wasn't a lull in conversation from Salt Lake down to Bryce National Park. We had so much to catch up on.

We camped the first night and then hiked among the red hills and canyons until late afternoon the next day. I realized my work must have gotten me in shape already because I wasn't huffing and puffing like I expected to be.

Liza brought along a CD of the old songs we loved in high school, and we blared it most the way to Phoenix over the next couple of days. It was already in the upper-80s there. We went to a great restaurant out in the boonies where there were dollar bills stapled all over the walls. We had our picture taken with a seven-foot man there—all three of us were pointing Old West rifles at the camera.

In no time we were on the road again, heading south to San Diego. We stayed with Liza's uncle who had Disneyland connections. He got us cheap tickets and we drove up to the park the next day.

Liza and I stood just inside the gates, contemplating which version of Mickey Mouse ears we wanted to buy when Chelsea grabbed us both from behind.

"I'd definitely go with the pink," she said.

Liza glanced at her watch. "It's about time!"

"Sorry. Sorry. I got a late start," Chelsea said. "Now why don't you let a local show you around the place."

We ran to Star Tours where the line was remarkably small. As I catapulted from side to side in my seat, I couldn't help but bonk into Liza again and again. She giggled through the whole ride. Next we hit the Jungle Cruise, the Haunted Mansion, and of course, It's a Small World.

"It's a world of laughter; a world of tears . . ." blared from the speaker system for the umpteenth time as our boat slowly rounded a bend. Chelsea sat between us and pulled us in close for a squeeze. It was great to all be together once more. I couldn't help but wonder if the three of us would ever do something like this again with Liza getting married so soon. A wave of depression crept in, but I quickly pushed it away. After all, who could be sad in the happiest place on earth?

We stopped for lunch and then headed toward the huge mountain—the Matterhorn. The afternoon crowd was in full force, and the line took well over an hour. Chelsea spent three quarters of it on her cell phone, apparently with her boyfriend, Matt. Finally we boarded our bobsled and crept to the summit of the mountain—narrowly escaping the hungry abominable snowman. When our sled tipped out over the peak, I could see the entire park. We seemed to pause for a moment before the plunge, and I thought of one thing: Quentin and I in his pickup truck. I wished more than anything that he was here with me.

⁕⁂⁕

The next morning we packed swimsuits, towels, and Liza's uncle's directions and made our way through morning traffic to Del Mar Beach. I was surprised when the beach was barely occupied. A few families were scattered here and there, but for the most part we had a long stretch of clean, fine sand all to ourselves. Liza and I selected a spot, spread out our towels, and relaxed. I pulled my latest book—Crane's *The Red Badge of Courage*—from my bag and stretched out on my stomach. I scooted down on the towel so my toes hung off the edge and dug them down into the warm sand.

"I'm so glad we did this," I said to Liza.

She stared out at the ocean and nodded her head.

A few hours later we saw Chelsea coming down the beach toward us with Matt and three of his friends. Her swimsuit was shocking. To say it was skimpy was an understatement. The top was strapless and barely covered the required areas while the bottoms had to have been less than a total of six square inches of material. Honestly, I hadn't been looking forward to a day with Chelsea's boyfriend. When I saw the way she was plastered to Matt's side, I knew it would be just as frustrating as I'd imagined.

"Hey, guys, this is Matt, Jeff, Jamison, and Trig," Chelsea said. Liza and I were met with a round of "hey's" and "whassups." The guys were all I imagined California surfers would be. They were all shirtless, buff, and tan. Matt, Jeff, and Jamison sported similar blond hairdos of shaggy messy locks, while Trig's head was shaved clean. The tattoos were countless. I quickly scanned Chelsea's body but didn't see one, and there wasn't much space where a tattoo could be hidden.

Trig lugged a cooler forward and tossed it into the sand. He flipped open the lid and fished out three beers. He tossed one to each of his friends and then looked at Chelsea. She quickly shook her head no. Jeff and Jamison started scoping out the waves while Matt and Chelsea sat down next to us.

"So how was your night?" Chelsea asked.

"Fine," we both said too quickly.

"We went out to eat with my aunt and uncle," Liza added.

"Sounds fun," Chelsea said, distracted. Matt was kissing her neck on the opposite side. Liza and I pretended to get back into our books. Chelsea attempted small talk a few more times, but it was obvious to all that her two clusters of friends didn't mesh well. Eventually, Matt joined the other guys, and we were able to talk a bit more candidly. But even then, we didn't have much to say. The air was thick with our disapproval and Chelsea's acknowledgment of it.

After a few minutes I stood up and walked down toward the water. I tread slowly through the sand, letting the waves lap at my ankles. Regardless of my disappointment in Chelsea, I couldn't deny this was a magnificent place. I laughed aloud when I wondered what the oceanfront property owners of California would think of our sage-brushed prairies. Still, out of everything we'd seen on our trip so far, nothing felt as incredible as home. I loved Wyoming's mountains. Even more specifically, I loved how in Cody I could get in a car, drive in any direction, and be in the mountains in half an hour. I loved knowing almost everyone I graduated with, and their parents, and their siblings. And I loved the clean, fresh air; the nonexistent traffic; and the safe feeling I always got when I reached the top of Skull Creek and saw the lights of Cody glowing from below.

I walked away from the water and climbed up a sharp black rock. I pulled my journal out of my bag and tore out a few pieces of paper.

Dear Quentin,

I wish you could see what I see right now. I am on the most gorgeous beach near San Diego. It's fantastic. The sand feels so good on my feet, and the water isn't even too cold. This trip with Liza has been awesome. We even got to see Chelsea down here, although I can tell she's not making great choices.

I put down the pen and listened to the ocean. It was so beautiful.

⊱⭒⊰

We said good-bye to Chelsea the next day and made plans to see her at Liza's reception.

We drove all day and into the night and found a deserted spot to camp on a northern California beach. The bottle of mace Dad had taught me how to use was under my pillow, but I wasn't scared. Instead I didn't sleep because I couldn't stop listening to the waves crashing.

We went to Portland and onto Seattle the next day, where we stayed on the pier. The weather was sunny and bright—not raining like everyone had warned us it would be. We rode the ferry to Bainbridge Island and back and then spent the day walking around the pier. The market was unbelievable. Bushel baskets overflowed with orange, yellow, pink, and red tulips and roses. Jewelry, tapestries, scarves, and quilts bulged from booths.

I slowly perused the book vendors and then found a whole hall devoted to wood crafts. I was in heaven. I found gorgeous wooden spoons made from cherry, maple, and walnut. Another booth was dedicated to wooden toys: cars, trucks, and even ferry boats. The next artist created a variety of wooden puzzles. When I came across the Fine Grinds stand, I fell in love with the man's work. He sold a variety of salt and pepper mills made from exotic woods. Some were only six inches tall, but he also made some mammoth twenty-four-inch mills. When I told the artist I enjoyed woodworking, he told me to pull up a chair and we got to talking. He showed me several mills that were still in the early lathe processes and gave me a few tips for building my own. I bought one for Mom and moved on to the next wood-worker, who crafted hardwood cribbage boards.

By the time I caught up with Liza, she was lugging a box of handmade gifts for her wedding party. She'd found beautiful fresh produce baskets, bath soaps and salts, huckleberry jams and jellies, and even a pretty pair of turquoise earrings for her mom.

We found a cart and made our way back toward the foods. We loaded up on treats for the rest of our ride: apples, pears, candies, éclairs, and macaroons. We had to stop to take pictures at the fish market. I couldn't help but smile at the fishermen singing and tossing their fish high in the air to each other. More than once I found myself thinking, *Quentin would love this.*

We'd barely made a dent in our goodies by the time we pulled into the Spokane KOA campground the next night. The five-hour drive had been the first quiet one of our trip. We were both exhausted.

"How far do you want to go tomorrow?" Liza asked, once we were settled into our sleeping bags.

"Home," I said. "I'm ready to go home."

"Good," she agreed. "Me too."

We made the long drive home the next day and didn't get

there until about eleven. I could barely bend my knees to get out of the car that night. I stretched my arms up high above my head and unenthusiastically unloaded my stuff from the trunk.

"Can you believe we actually did something we've been planning since we were thirteen?" Liza asked.

"Yeah. That was such a blast," I said. I hugged Liza and turned up the walk.

"That was the best bachelorette party I could imagine," Liza said. "Thanks, Grace."

I walked in the front door and mock-collapsed onto the carpet when Mom and Dad asked me how the trip was.

"I need another vacation to recover from that one," I said.

twenty-five

Liza and I stood in front of the hotel mirror practicing her hair and makeup. She decided she liked the silver eye shadow best, but wasn't sure on a lipstick color. We were having a hard time getting her hair exactly right too.

"Where's Chels when we need her?" Liza laughed.

It was the night before the wedding, and there was actually less for me to do than I had planned. As always, Liza was quite prepared.

"I brought this in case we got bored," she said as she pulled a box from the closet. It was full of her old mementos. We laughed at the clay figurines we'd made as little girls. We looked at the pictures of our classmates in elementary school and reminisced. A pink journal with a pair of ballet slippers on the cover lay in the bottom of the box. Liza pulled it out and flipped it open.

I didn't even remember making these lists, but there they were.

Liza:

> • *I think I will be married by the time I am 20.*
> • *I want to have eight kids, so they never get stuck being the only child like me.*

• *I want to go to college but I don't really know for what.*
• *I want Gracie to always be my best friend.*

Gracie:

   • *I will get married in the temple someday.*
   • *I think I'll have three or four kids.*
   • *I don't know what else to write.*
   • *Liza is the bestest friend ever!*

"Well, you beat your prediction," I told Liza. "You're not even twenty."

"We'll see what Justin thinks about those eight kids, though." She laughed.

"But you're still my best friend. That was right," she said, hugging me. "Well, no. Gracie, I think you're more like my sister."

"Wait a minute. I forgot something," I said, running to my suitcase. I pulled out a package and tossed it to Liza. "My wedding gift."

"You want me to open it now?" she asked. I nodded yes.

She tore open the white wedding paper and pulled out a yellowed pillow with "The Frams" crookedly embroidered across the front. Liza gave me a puzzled look.

⊱━━❈━━⊰

We got up early the next morning. Amazingly Liza's hair and makeup seemed to fall into place perfectly. She looked gorgeous. I quickly pulled on my lavender top and matching full skirt that Amy had sewn. I dabbed on my makeup and pulled my hair into an easy updo.

I couldn't go inside for Liza's temple sealing, but she asked me to stay in the waiting room. I was glad I did. It was so peaceful and relaxing in the temple, and this time I didn't have kids to babysit. I had been through this so many times with my siblings, but I had never really thought about what was going on inside.

185

This time I tried to imagine it, but I really wasn't sure.

When Liza and Justin came out glowing, I knew it must have been special. She looked positively radiant.

On the ride home, Mom and Dad talked about what an awesome sealing it had been. I asked a few questions, but their answers were vague.

"You'll see soon when you get married, honey," Dad said.

"Soon? Right," I shot back. "More like *never.*"

They both laughed.

⚜

Friday night, back at home, the church gym was set up for a traditional Mormon reception. I loved Liza, but her idea of a party was pretty boring. White cake, 7-Up punch, and silver-wrapped wedding gifts were the main components. I spent most the night bouncing between Amy's table and Mom and Dad's.

I wished Nathan and Sarah were there, but with the baby coming in a couple of months, money was too tight. Besides, Nate said that he and Justin hadn't really kept in touch after their missions.

Of course the party seemed to liven up when Chelsea walked in. Her strapless, green-striped dress definitely wasn't up to par with church standards, but it did manage to get the attention of most the guys in the building. She wore her platinum hair straight—only held back by a pair of huge black sunglasses, expertly balanced on her head. She exchanged congrats with Liza and spent the rest of the evening gushing about her California life. Thankfully Liza was too in love and preoccupied to notice.

I heard her talking with some younger girls from our family ward about how great college was. I found myself gritting my teeth as I listened to the way Chelsea made partying sound so fabulous. I excused myself from the receiving line and pulled her out into the hall.

"This place is so boring, Gracie," she said. "How can you stand it here? I've only been here one weekend, and I can't wait to get back to Cali for the summer."

I ignored the question.

"I mean, in San Diego we have stuff going on every night. Matt and I have such a blast down there."

Talking to her, let alone trying to influence her, seemed like such a chore. I just didn't have the energy. I let Chelsea dominate our quick conversation and then politely excused myself. She ended up leaving the reception early to call Matt. I was outside grabbing more crackers from Amy's car when Chelsea got into her Dad's Camaro and cranked up the music.

"You know it makes me sad," I later told Mom. "Chelsea can get everyone's attention without even trying, so why does she think she needs to act like this to do it?"

"I don't know why she's doing what she's doing, Gracie," she said. "But I do know it's breaking her parents' hearts."

"She's so stupid." The more I thought about it, the madder I got.

"All you can do is love her, honey. Sometimes it's hard to watch our friends walk away from the gospel, but we just have to pray that they'll make their way back."

It didn't seem like much of a solution to me.

***

I carted a watermelon under one arm and a case of soda in the other.

"Did you get the red, white, and blue tablecloth?" Mom yelled, her head stuck into piles of groceries in the back of the minivan.

"Yes, Mom," I said. "I think we're completely loaded."

A few minutes later we were headed to Hope's house for our annual Fourth of July picnic when Anthony called. Hope had gone into labor the night before, and they were at the hospital.

He had gotten a babysitter for the night but asked us to go pick up the boys and bring them to our house. We hastily turned around, unloaded the food, and then drove to Hope's house.

On the way to the house, Danielle and I worried something might be wrong. Hope was still almost a month from her due date.

We dropped Mom off at the hospital and brought the boys home to hang out with us. The older boys played in the yard, but the rest of us paced around the house nervously. Finally Alex put in a movie, and Dad, Danielle, Alex, Matthew, and I crammed in together on the big couch. Still my mind was on Hope.

"I think it's a girl this time," I said to no one in particular. "That's probably why it's different from the others."

Around two that afternoon, Mom called. Dad answered.

"Yes. . . . Yes. . . . Uh-huh. . . . What?" There was a long pause. "You've got to be kidding me."

The three of us girls stood around Dad like a pack of wolves panting for the privileged information.

"Well, isn't that something." Dad was laughing now. "We'll come down this evening then," he said. "If she doesn't want visitors, just call us back. Otherwise we'll be down around five or so."

He hung up the phone, wiggled his way out from our circle, and sat right back down on the couch. His smile stretched from ear to ear.

"Dad!" Alex screamed. "What? Is it a girl?"

He laughed, knowing his silence was killing us.

"Well. No, it's not a girl," he said slowly.

"Oh man," I said. "Another boy."

Dad looked confused. Finally, he said, "Actually two more boys."

"Twins!" Danielle said. "What? No, she never told us she was having twins."

"Hope didn't know she was having twins." He laughed.

"How could you not know?" I asked.

"I guess Hope and Anthony asked their doctor not to do an ultrasound on this baby because they didn't want to be tempted to find out if it was another boy." Dad was cracking up. "The doctor agreed since they'd always had healthy pregnancies."

"Still, wouldn't they hear two heartbeats?" I asked.

"I guess not. The doctor said about three percent of twins are undetected before birth. Hope was in that three."

I was in awe. Twins. My sister had twins and now she was up to six boys and not a single girl.

"Well, this ought to teach her a lesson," Alex said. "I hope she's done having kids now."

We all laughed.

"Oh yeah, and they couldn't think of anymore good 'M' names, so they went with Evan and Ethan," Dad added.

"Finally they picked something good," Alex said.

Instead of our barbecue, we ate lasagna in the hospital cafeteria that night. The boys couldn't wait to meet their new brothers.

Even though it was unplanned, the twins were completely healthy. They were even big for twins at six pounds, one ounce and six pounds, four ounces. Hope was exhausted and out of it, but I noted the real dread in Anthony's eyes. I saw his dad take him out into the hallway later. I assumed he was passing along some words of wisdom.

The other boys stayed with us for the rest of the week, and by the time we dropped them off Friday, Hope seemed to be recuperating. Amazingly to me, she had figured out how to nurse both babies at the same time, holding them like little footballs at her sides.

The next night Nathan called and announced the birth of Colter. Sarah's labor had progressed so quickly they didn't even have time to call until the baby made his entrance. He was a little early too, but he was healthy and ready to go home in a few days. Sarah's mom was flying down to help out with Emmylee, so Mom and Dad planned to wait to meet the newborn.

The rest of July was a whirlwind. I was busy at work and

church, but I was also busy helping Hope. Getting used to six little boys was sinking her quickly. Danielle and I took turns taking the older boys out so Hope could get chores done around the house.

Every now and then, I caught myself thinking about marriage and children. I had been dating guys from my ward off and on, but whenever I dreamed of forever, none of them seemed to fit.

One Sunday afternoon, I stopped in the middle of writing Quentin a letter and got out my journal. Instead of writing, I started reading the old entries. It was hard to believe that just six months ago, my life was so empty. I smiled, realizing who I'd become.

Still, that afternoon I caught myself counting the days until Quentin would get home.

⊱⊷⧖⊶⊰

In the first week of August, Mom flew down to be with Sam. She claimed her belly was already the size of a baby cow, and if she didn't deliver soon, she was going to go insane. The heat was getting to her too. She said she sat in front of an oscillating fan spraying herself with a squirt bottle most of the time. They had a healthy baby, though—another grandson, Brayden, born on August 6.

I couldn't wait to meet my two newest nephews, but I knew we wouldn't all get together until Thanksgiving. Both Samantha and Nathan sent pictures, though.

My next letter to Quentin began,

> *Can you believe it? Eight boys and no girls. It's mind-boggling.*

Then I remembered.

> *Well, I guess there is one girl—Emmylee. She's just like a niece, but you know, technically, she's not a Fremont. I wonder*

190

if it's in our blood or something not to have girls. I sure hope not.

My next letter back from Quentin was filled with congratulations on the new babies.

Gracie Fremont, are you getting old on me? You're starting to sound like you're thinking about kids yourself. Just because Liza went and got married doesn't mean you have to join the oldies too! You better knock that off. We have plenty of four-wheeling years ahead of us!

The thought brought a smile to my face.

Hope and Anthony caught me reading another letter when they came home from dinner one night. It'd been their first time to venture out without the twins. I had babysat for them and amazingly still had my sanity. All six boys were asleep.

When they walked in the door, I put the letter down and had to do a double-take of Hope's face. She looked rejuvenated for the first time in ages. I hadn't noticed before they left, but she looked really pretty. Her black hair was curled, and she was wearing makeup and a pretty silver bracelet. Anthony was smiling and held her hand like I hadn't seen them do since Michael was born. He even kissed her as she slipped her heels off. Their stern parental image was gone, and they looked happy—in love, even. Maybe married folk could keep the romance alive.

"So how is that Quentin doing anyway?" Hope asked, setting down her purse.

"Good, I guess," I said. "He's had a few baptisms so far."

"Are you waiting for him, Gracie?" She smiled.

"Yeah right." I laughed nervously. "Quentin? I don't think so."

I ignored the sly look Hope shot Anthony and gathered

my stuff to go home. Nathan and Sam's families were arriving in the morning, so I had to get my room cleaned. Besides, it looked like Hope and Anthony could use the privacy.

I should have brought home a pair of earplugs from work, I thought. Everyone showed up in a matter of minutes of each other, and I think it was the loudest our house had ever been. We had eleven adults and nine kids—four of them between three years and four months old. They were adorable. The twins were smaller than Colter or Brayden, but they made up for it in lung power. Whenever one was hungry, wet, or otherwise upset, he would scream, and his brother always took the cue to join in. I knew this year my older siblings would be spending Christmas with their in-laws though, so I tried to be a good sport.

The girls, now women, of the family—Hope, Danielle, Sarah, Sam, Alex, and I—made a pact to give Mom a break this Thanksgiving. On Thursday morning, we chased Mom out of the kitchen and sentenced her to a day of Grandma Duty, something she absolutely adored. Our first chore was one of damage control. The Fremonts had been staying up past midnight every night playing charades, Yahtzee, Pig Mania, and cards. Popcorn kernels filled the bottoms of countless bowls across the counter. The recycling bin was overflowing with pop cans. Half-eaten boxes of candy littered the table top. The disaster was monstrous, but nothing six women on a mission couldn't deal with in a matter of minutes.

Sarah volunteered to take on the turkey, and Hope got busy chopping celery, carrots, and onions for the sage stuffing. I pulled out three pie plates and began stretching the pastry into the dishes.

"Thank goodness Mom bought the pre-made crusts this year," Alex laughed.

"What are you talking about?" I asked. "When it comes to baking, I'm the bomb!"

My sisters laughed.

I was planning three pies: apple, sweet potato, and pecan. I also wanted to try out a recipe Wendy had given me at the last break the fast. It was a pumpkin ice cream cake that was fantastic.

Danielle started on Waldorf salad, and Samantha searched for Grandma Fremont's famous roll recipe. Alex sat on the counter, dangling her legs in my way.

"What's your job, missy?" I asked, mock-pulling her off the counter.

"I think I'm head supervisor."

"I don't think so," Hope said. She pulled three cans of green beans from the cupboard and shoved them in Alex's direction.

"The recipe is on the back," she said.

"Oh no, you don't. Green bean casserole? How boring," Alex whined.

"You could come pull these gizzards out if you'd rather," Sarah said, dangling the giblets away from her body. She slowly walked toward Alex and was met with a scream.

"Get away from me!" Alex said. She jumped down and started opening the cans of beans.

Within a few hours, we had most of the dishes in the oven or refrigerator and sat around the kitchen, gossiping. The buttery aroma of the rolls filled the room. Two of my pies sat cooling on the window sill, and the ice cream cake was setting up in the freezer.

Hope sat behind Danielle, French-braiding her hair. Sarah leaned back in her chair, nursing Colter while Sam and Alex finished up some cooking dishes.

"Don't Mom and Dad seem so old to you guys now?" Danielle asked.

"Yeah, it's cute though," Hope said. "They make such good grandparents."

"Mom can't even read without her glasses," Alex said,

sounding annoyed. "And Dad's salt-and-pepper hair is getting more and more salty."

We all laughed.

"One thing will never change," Nathan said, walking into the room and stealing a black olive from the tray. "I'm still your big brother and I can still whip you all."

With that challenge, we dove on him. Hope easily pinned Nate's shoulders down while Sam, Danielle, Alex, and I took turns tickling and pinching his mid-section. His wife just sat back and laughed.

"Maybe you're not so tough any more, babe," she said. "Marriage has softened you up."

"Oh, don't let him fool you, Sarah," I said. "Nate was always a wimp."

Once he spun himself out of the mess of his sisters, he took a low wrestler's stance. One by one, he threw us to the ground until he was suddenly accosted by the nephews. I moved out of the way and sat back against the wall. I had to catch my breath. I smiled as I looked up at my family and suddenly knew being a Fremont was my greatest blessing.

twenty-six

"So, guess what," Liza said, "You're not going to believe this."

"What? What?"

"No, I take that back. You're totally going to believe this," she said.

I could tell the surprise wasn't a good one by Liza's tone.

"I guess Chelsea's 'fun times' have finally expired," she said. "She's pregnant."

I pulled my hand up to cover my mouth.

"No," I said.

Liza said Matt dumped Chelsea as soon as she gave him the news. She didn't want to stay in California, pregnant and alone, so she decided not to go back to school after Christmas break. I hung up with Liza with a sick feeling deep in my stomach. What was Chelsea going to do?

That night I picked up the phone to call her, but I wasn't sure what to say, so I hung up before anyone answered. I prayed for Chelsea long into the night. When I told Mom the next morning, it was obvious she already knew.

"Gracie, Chelsea needs you to be her friend now more than ever. Don't abandon her," she said.

I called her again the next day. As soon as she picked up, I could tell she'd been crying. We exchanged awkward pleasant-ries, and then she broke down.

"How could this happen to me?" she wailed.

It took every ounce of energy I had not to scream at her, "I told you so!" If she had just taken Liza's or my advice once, this might not have happened. I wanted to tell her this didn't just "happen" to her, but that she chose this life, when she had to walk on that edge.

Chelsea talked for over an hour about her life and Matt and how she felt lost without him. She said she'd come home at Christmas and then decide what to do.

At work we were pushing hard to get our last family moved in for the holidays, but I couldn't stay focused. I was going through the motions, but all I could think about was Chelsea. It repeated in my head so many times. I envisioned Liza in her wedding dress and her happiness as a newlywed. She and Justin had done this the right way. And Chelsea knew what was right too!

She got home a couple days before Christmas, and I went to the Copeland's house to see her. When Chelsea came to the door, I was surprised she was already showing. Even with a baby bump, she looked cute as ever in her black pants and pink fitted maternity shirt. I didn't know the baby was due in March.

"I didn't tell anyone for as long as I could," she explained. "Sorry. I just didn't know what to say."

She pulled me in the door, and I hugged her. We made our way to their living room where we sat on the same floral couches we had years ago, waiting for James Fromberg on Chelsea's six-teenth birthday. I thought it strange that their stiffness hadn't lessened at all over the years. Chelsea said her parents were over their initial shock, but her siblings were outraged. Two of her older brothers wouldn't even talk to her.

"Do you know what you're going to do yet?" I asked.

"You mean keep the baby or not?"

"Yeah." I swallowed hard.

"No. I don't know. I have no idea what to do," she said.

Chelsea sat a few feet from me, and we both looked at the floor, ceiling, and coffee table—anything but each other. I tried to change the subject, talking for a minute about work, but it was awkward and obvious. Finally Chelsea stood, walked to me, and grabbed my hands, "Gracie, I know you think I'm stupid."

I just shook my head.

"You're right. I was stupid. You and Liza always did what was right, but I had to test the water. I wish I was you, but I'm not," she said.

"You didn't have to be me or Liza, but Chels you knew what you were doing was wrong," I said.

"I know I knew. But please don't hate me right now. I can't handle one more person looking down at me. I need a friend, Gracie. I want to get my life back the way it's supposed to be, but when everyone is pushing you down, it's too hard."

I looked into her eyes and knew she was right.

"I'm here," was all I said.

⁕⁂⁕

Chelsea asked me to go to LDS Social Services with her that week for her first counseling appointment. I was a little nervous, but I decided to be supportive anyway. I worried the counselor would be too judgmental and Chelsea would give up right away. I couldn't have been more wrong.

Her counselor, Janice, looked only a few years older than us and was so friendly. She introduced herself, and we followed her into her office. We sat on a comfy futon-style maroon couch, loaded with black pillows, while Janice sat across from us in a squatty leather chair. Janice's mild manner set me at ease immediately. She thanked me for coming to support Chelsea. The counselor first got to know Chelsea and then began discussing LDS adoption with her. She suggested Chelsea pray to know what to do. When the counselor asked her last question, I couldn't wait to hear my friend's answer.

"How do you feel about the Church, Chelsea?"

Chelsea considered the question for a full minute, and I noticed my nerves creeping back in. Then she answered. "I know it's true. I know I made a wrong decision that's always going to affect me," she said. "But I don't want this one mistake to rule my life forever."

Janice nodded. "It doesn't have to," she said gently. "You know if we do all that we can do, we can be fully forgiven. But all we can do is a quite a bit, Chelsea. It's going to be a long, painful road, but it's worth it. Are you ready to begin the repentance process?"

I held my breath.

"Yes. I am ready. I've just been waiting for someone to tell me I can repent." Chelsea started crying.

I held her hand, and inside my heart did a flip.

"I'm here to help with whatever you need, Chels," I said.

"I know I'll need your support, Gracie," she said. "But it's something I need to do on my own."

twenty-seven

My jaw almost hit the floor when Mom yelled up the stairs at me one evening, "Gracie, Quentin's mom is on the phone."

I hadn't talked to Sheila in a year and a half.

I timidly picked up, but Sheila acted like she'd just seen me yesterday. She gave me all the details of her phone call with Quentin on Christmas Day. She told me about the holidays with her parents, how her job was going, and what show she was currently addicted to on Lifetime. It was great to chat, but when we hung up, I realized I didn't have a clue why she'd called. *Maybe she's just lonely*, I decided.

The next Sunday after church, I whipped up a quick batch of cookies and covered them with saran wrap. I set them on the passenger seat and drove to Quentin's house. I decided it was time to visit Sheila. I felt sweaty, nervous, and nostalgic all at the same time when I saw their house. It brought the memories of Quentin flooding back.

Sheila acted like my plate of cookies was a million-dollar donation, almost to the point I was embarrassed I'd come. She thanked me profusely and then invited me in. Sheila flipped off the TV and turned toward me. She asked about my family, any correspondence I'd had with her son, and how my job was going. The conversation was pleasant, but when I left, I still sensed there was something she'd been trying to tell me.

***

A week later, after church, Mom informed me Sheila had left a message on our machine and I was supposed to call her back. What was going on with that woman? I changed from my church dress into a pair of jeans and a wool sweater. Then I dialed her number.

When Quentin's mom attempted another round of chit-chat, I found myself getting impatient, so I took the plunge.

"Sheila, are you doing all right?" I asked. "I keep feeling like there's something you want to talk about."

She was quiet for a minute. "I was wondering if you have an extra Book of Mormon I could borrow."

A smile spread across my face. *Aahh, so that's it.*

"I mean, I don't want to join or anything like that," she said quickly. "I just, you know . . . Well, I just thought, 'Hey, my son is out there teaching about it, maybe I better find out what it says.' "

"Of course I do," I said a bit too enthusiastically. "I can bring it over right now."

"Oh. Just whenever you're out and about," she said nonchalantly.

"I'll be there in a couple hours," I said before we hung up.

I went screaming down the stairs to tell Mom the news. She helped me get a hold of the missionaries and an extra copy of the Book of Mormon.

A few hours later, I knocked on the door. Sheila hugged me before I came in. She told me about Quentin's latest letter. I acted surprised at all the news, even though my last letter included everything she said. At the first lull in conversation, I pulled the Book of Mormon out of my purse and handed it to her. She grabbed it quickly and set it on the coffee table.

"Oh, thanks," she said flippantly.

Sheila stood up, and I took my cue that it was time to go. She walked me out to the car but stopped and turned toward me.

"Gracie?"

"Yeah?"

"Would you mind not telling Quentin about this?" she asked.

Darn it! I'd been planning on writing the letter as soon as I walked in my house. "Sure," I agreed.

"I just don't want him to go getting excited, you know?"

I made the promise I didn't want to keep and drove away.

❦

Sheila called the house a week later. She was already in 2 Nephi and was lost in chapter 3.

"I'm just not sure who all those Josephs are," she explained. "At first I was just going to skip over it, but it's been bugging me."

I put down the phone and ran to retrieve my own scriptures. I was thankful I had marked this passage well in institute. I explained the Josephs were Lehi's son Joseph, Joseph of Egypt, Joseph Smith, and Joseph Smith, Sr.

A few nights later she called with another question. Then she called again the night after that. Sometimes our talks went on for over an hour. I was impressed at how she was really striving to understand what she read. More than anything I wanted to tell Quentin what was happening, but at the end of every conversation Sheila reminded me of my promise to keep quiet.

❦

We were only a few weeks from our next grant installment at work. Then we'd be able to start a house. Carry called me into her office to discuss the upcoming schedule.

She asked me how I felt about the job after the first year.

"Are you kidding? I loved it," I said enthusiastically. "It was even more challenging than I expected, but it was so rewarding at the same time."

I didn't tell her this part, but I had been able to save close to $15,000 my first year. The salary was great for someone living at home with virtually no bills.

"Gracie, everyone was really impressed with your work," she said. I blushed a bit. "People in high places are noticing you."

"What do you mean?"

"Let's just say, keep your mind open for advancement in the agency, okay?"

"Okay," I said confused. What advancement? I had my dream job. I couldn't think of anything better than what I was doing.

I left her office excited but confused. What could Carry be talking about? *Oh, well,* I decided. There was no sense in worrying about the unknown.

⁂

In February I met Chelsea at a sandwich shop for lunch. I couldn't help but grin as I watched her grab both sides of her car to hoist herself up out of the seat. A blue top stretched across her torpedo belly, but aside from a noticeable waddle, she didn't look pregnant from behind.

We ordered our sandwiches, and I had to laugh at Chelsea. Never in her life had I seen her consume a foot-long meatball sandwich. She seemed to savor every bite. I ordered a six-inch turkey and a cookie. Chelsea barely talked while she ate, but as soon as she finished, she reached her hands high above her head.

"Um, what are you doing?" I asked.

"I can barely breathe if I eat something big like that," she grimaced. "I just have to stretch a bit."

Once Chelsea got comfortable—well, as comfortable as possible with a belly pressing against the edge of a table—we started talking.

I told Chelsea how proud I was of her going to church, even when she knew people might be talking about her. She dabbed her napkin at her mouth and then smiled.

"Gracie, things are going good for me," she said. "I mean, I'm starting to get back on track."

Chelsea had lost many of her church privileges, but she still attended all her meetings and was meeting with the bishop every week. She had been working with her counselor and was now getting ready for adoption. Chelsea selected an LDS couple in Portland who had been trying unsuccessfully to conceive for eight years.

"I know this is right," she told me. "I've never known something was as right as I do this."

"I'm so glad, Chels," I said.

"I'm coming back, Grace. I'm coming all the way back to where I should be. It's going to take me about a year, but I'll get there."

I squeezed her hand. When I looked in her eyes, I knew she was right. This time I believed Chelsea.

"Grace?"

"Yeah?"

"Do you think you could come to the hospital with me and Mom when I deliver?" she asked humbly.

"Of course, of course," I said. I tried to mask the nerves I felt with a fake confidence. "I'll be there."

On March 14, Sister Copeland called. "Can you meet us at the hospital, Gracie? It's time to have this baby."

When I walked into the labor and delivery room, I was shocked. For the first time in almost fifteen years, I could say that Chelsea did not look in the least bit attractive. Her sweaty hair was completely matted to her head and pulled back in some kind of a messy bun. Her face was red, and the blood vessels at her temples seemed to have grown exponentially. She lay back at a forty-five degree angle, and her enormous belly pointed oddly toward the television. She suddenly let out an angry growl from gritted teeth, and I scurried to her side. I felt entirely inadequate to assist her. Thankfully Sister Copeland seemed to have a much better command of the situation.

At every scream I would softly rub Chelsea's back or squeeze her hand while her mom and the nurse held her legs. The adoptive parents were there as well. Their anticipation seemed almost exhausting. The mother would wince at Chelsea's pain as if it were her own. Finally at 12:19 that night, after a particularly lengthy scream, the baby was born. Chelsea chose not to see the baby, so the nurse quickly whisked the newborn and the new parents into a recovery room.

The new mother wept as she carried the baby out of the room. She cried, "Thank you, thank you," over and over, and I wasn't sure if she was thanking Chelsea or thanking God.

Later, while Chelsea napped, I softly knocked on their door, and they let me in.

"Would you mind if I saw the baby?" I asked.

"Of course not. You were a big help in getting her here," the new father said.

"So it's a girl?" I asked. "Chelsea didn't want to know."

"Yes, it's a girl. Her name's Ella Marie," he said.

She was beautiful. She had a soft fuzz of white-blonde hair and beautiful fair skin. Even only a few hours old, I knew she'd look like Chelsea. But no matter who she looked like, these were her parents. It felt so natural. I knew Ella was going to have a wonderful life.

* * *

Getting started on our first house of the year brought on those first-day-of-school jitters, and I found myself barely sleeping. Most of our seasoned crew was returning from last year, but this year we had to work faster than ever. Headquarters had given us the go-ahead to squeeze one more home into this year's schedule. Carry suggested we line up extra volunteers to help over the summer.

We had an afternoon of orientation, which I thought was unnecessary, but headquarters required it. I was so ready to get to work.

The concrete subs finished the foundation, and we were finally ready to frame. Holding a hammer in my hand again felt wonderful. I was like the little sister or daughter of these guys, but I was their boss too. It was a strange situation. They all looked out for me and tried to keep me from any strenuous jobs. I did my best to thwart their efforts.

The day the roof trusses were delivered, I stood with my boots caked in mud and directed the semi to where he'd be unloading. My cell phone rang, and I recognized the number. It was Sheila. I plugged one ear and tried desperately to hear what she was saying. The truck's reverse beep was piercing.

Eventually, I caught the gist of her call. Sheila wanted me to line up the missionary discussions for her.

"Just to find out more," she explained.

I quickly agreed. I could see one of our laborers nearing an argument with the truck driver, so I decided I'd have to get a hold of the missionaries later.

Keeping Sheila's investigation from Quentin was nearing impossible. Sometimes when I'd write his letters, I wanted to scream. In fact I had written the whole story in one letter, but I tore it up. I knew breaking her promise might jeopardize our friendship.

⊱⊰

Mom and Dad were thrilled when Sheila opted to take the discussions at our house. She settled in right away. She had many more questions than Quentin had, but I loved researching answers to her questions. I was studying the scriptures more than ever before.

She moved through the discussions quickly, taking a couple each week. She was going to church with us too. Our family prayed she was feeling the Spirit, but I couldn't be sure.

It was the last discussion, and we all sat quietly around the table. Sheila's Book of Mormon lay on the table next to her reading glasses. Mom and Dad sat on either side of her with the missionaries, and I on the other side.

Elder Bauer bore his testimony, followed by Elder Love.

"Sheila, would you like to be baptized?" Elder Bauer asked. I envisioned her accepting, but still I held my breath.

"Oh, no, no, no," she said, quickly, pushing back from the table. I was shocked. "Thank you very much, but no."

I shifted nervously and glanced at my parents. We all seemed unsure of where to go from here. Sheila abruptly excused herself and went to her car, leaving the missionaries, Mom, Dad, and I dumbfounded.

"I hope I didn't jump the gun there," Elder Bauer said. "But I thought she was totally ready."

"I think we all did, Elder," Dad reassured him, shaking his head.

I didn't hear from Sheila for over a week, so finally I gave into the urge to call. Sheila seemed just as pleased as always to hear from me. But I was incredibly anxious.

"I was just wondering how you felt about what you've learned about the church?" I asked, my voice wavering.

"I think it's a great church that has done a whole lot for my son," she answered.

I waited for her to say more, but when she didn't I went ahead.

"What about what it could do for you?"

"Gracie, I told you in the beginning, I just wanted to learn about it. I hope you didn't plan on me joining your church."

Why hadn't the Spirit touched her? I knew personally that

the promise in Moroni was real. I hung up feeling completely dejected.

❋⋙🌿⋘❋

The next day on my lunch break, I grabbed a soda from the work cooler and drove out to her house. Sheila let me in and offered me a seat, but I declined. I didn't want to waste any time.

"Sheila, I know you just wanted to learn about the church, but I couldn't live with myself if I didn't tell you this," I said.

"Okay." Sheila took a half step back and folded her arms across her chest.

"I didn't always have a strong testimony, either. But I prayed and prayed and prayed and finally learned for myself that the church is absolutely true. I know it is, and I couldn't live without that knowledge," I said. "And Sheila, Quentin knows it too. He's so sure it's true, he would do back flips if he knew you were learning about it."

She just nodded with a little laugh.

"Don't you owe it to him—no, to yourself—to find out if it's true?"

I grabbed her Book of Mormon off the TV and opened again to the promise in Moroni. I read it aloud. Sheila hugged me and agreed to pray about an answer.

I left her house feeling confident Heavenly Father would come through for her. But when I didn't hear from her for close to a month, I had about given up.

❋⋙🌿⋘❋

The day before Mother's Day, Sheila called. She asked if I wanted to come over and talk to Quentin on the phone the next day. I told her I'd think about it. I wanted to more than anything, but I wasn't sure if it was appropriate. Dad said as long as we weren't "together," it would be fine. I assured him Quentin and I had never been "together," and then I called Sheila back.

That night my bed seemed smaller—more claustrophobic—than it ever had before. I counted sheep, wrote in my journal, and even tried reading, but I couldn't fall asleep. I must have eventually dozed off, but when I woke up to the alarm the next morning, it felt like I hadn't had much rest.

Throughout church I couldn't keep the phone call off my mind. The minutes of sacrament meeting and Gospel Doctrine seemed to crawl by. I had to teach in Relief Society, though, and the sisters offered tons of comments, so the third hour went much faster. I went home for a quick bowl of soup and then grabbed the keys to take off again. Dad stopped me at the door.

"Remember, keep it professional," he said, referring to the phone call. I just laughed.

The phone rang only minutes after I came in the house, and I felt my voice box constricting. I prayed Sheila wouldn't make me talk to him first. I cleared my throat over and over, but I couldn't seem to find my voice. I was so annoyed at myself for feeling this way. Quentin was my friend, and I knew that was all. Why was a phone call from him making me behave like a love-struck school girl?

After talking to Quentin for just a minute, Sheila smiled at me.

"I have a surprise for you," she told her son. "Hold on a minute."

She handed me the phone. My hand was trembling as I reached for it. I cleared my throat once more and mustered up a squeaky, "Hello?"

"Hello . . . Gracie?" he said.

"Yeah, it's me."

"Woo hoo," he shouted. He must have set down the phone for a minute because I heard more screaming followed by a muffled, "No flippin' way!"

"I can't believe this. How are you?" he asked, gaining composure.

It felt like I had to swallow ten cotton balls at once. "Um, good, I guess," I said. I was so glad Sheila was standing right in front of me because I knew I'd be bawling if she weren't. That voice was the best sound I'd heard in nearly two years.

We talked for about thirty-five minutes. Quentin updated me on the families he'd been working with and his latest transfer. I had never heard Quentin's voice so full of energy. He sounded like he was going to burst with excitement, and it was all from the gospel.

Before I gave the phone back to Sheila, Quentin said, "So, are you still going to hang out with me this October, or are you too big and important now?"

I laughed.

"I mean, the youngest building supervisor and the Relief Society president; you are way too cool to be a geeky kid's friend now."

"I'll never be too cool for you, Quentin," I said honestly. Then I handed the phone back to Sheila.

It felt awkward listening to them, so I picked up my purse and slowly backed toward the door. Sheila waved her arm, signaling me to stay. I sat down on the kitchen chair and listened to her end of the phone call. It seemed like they had talked forever when she finally said, "I have something to tell you too. I read the Book of Mormon."

Long pause.

"No, no, no, just to see what you were up to out there in Canada."

My heart sank.

She was quiet for a long time, listening to Quentin.

"I wasn't finished. What I wanted to say was, I just read it to find out what it was about. Nothing happened to me, though." *How could the promise not have worked*, I wondered. "That was until this week."

What?

"I hadn't really prayed about it until a certain friend of yours told me to get to it," she said. I felt my face blush a bit. "Then I prayed and I prayed and I prayed, and finally I was just about to give up."

I was sitting rigid in my chair, wishing Sheila would get to the point.

"Quentin, last night I saw your father in my dream. He told me this church was true and that he wanted me to be a part of it."

I gasped and tears started streaming down my cheeks.

"That's not all, though," she said. "He wants you to make him a member too. Can you do that?"

I nodded my head yes as Quentin explained baptism for the dead to her.

"So, son, will you baptize me when you get home?"

She had to hold the phone away from her ear because Quentin was screaming again. I leapt up and hugged her, and we spun a circle in the living room.

The promise hadn't failed.

***

"Earth to Grace!" I snapped my attention up to the beam that Lewis, one of my framers, sat on and realized he must have been calling to me, unnoticed.

"What's with you lately?" he asked.

"Nothing, sorry," I said.

It wasn't the first time I found myself staring off into space. After that phone call with Quentin, everything I did was entwined with images of him. *What would my life be like shared with him?* I'd wonder. Usually I'd shake my head to clear the thought. My life was busy enough when my brain wasn't wandering all over the place. This was too much.

Seeing Sheila after church every Sunday only reminded me of Quentin more. She attended the family ward with Mom and

Dad and then usually came over for dinner afterward. By mid-summer, she was having a hard time waiting to be baptized. The missionaries assured her they would be happy to dunk her whenever she was ready, but she was intent on waiting. Sheila was going through the motions of being a full-fledged member, but her hunger for the gospel was obvious.

Now that she had spilled the beans, I was free to write about her conversion to Quentin. What a relief! The first letter I wrote after Mother's Day was over five pages long. I was so proud of Sheila and the decision she'd made. And that dream she'd had—how amazing!

Then, in early August, I received a letter from Quentin that surprised me. He mentioned a sister missionary who he'd become good friends with. He told me all about Sister Kendra Elliot and what a strong spirit she had. He said she was from California, and they planned to visit each other sometime after she went home—just one week after he did. I knew Quentin didn't mean to, but his words stung. I found myself reading it over and over, looking for a clue that he might have romantic feelings for her. Quentin wasn't a casanova; in fact, I was the only girl friend—let alone girlfriend—he'd ever had. I reflected on the days when I was dating Mason, wishing I had never written to Quentin about the situation. I wondered if he'd felt this same way then.

twenty-eight

It felt odd to be on the Roberts' front porch without Liza, but then everything about this situation was odd. Liza had informed me over the phone that her mom was getting married. Amy called a few days later to enlist my help with wedding invitations in lieu of Liza. We sat at a card table she'd moved outside, surrounded by white and silver invitations, envelopes, stamps, and a list of friends and family.

"I feel ridiculous doing all this at my age," she said. "But for some strange reason, Tom really wants the whole hoopla."

"I don't think it's ridiculous at all, Amy," I said. "If anyone deserves happiness it's you."

The Fremonts hadn't had a clue Amy was even dating. But she and Tom—a widower who lived on his own farm in the Burlington stake—had found each other at a singles' activity and were ready to make the commitment. He had three kids who were all grown and married. Liza was thrilled to be gaining her own brothers and a sister for the first time.

I had only seen Liza and Justin twice since their wedding a year and a half ago, so when Liza came home, we had tons of catching up to do. I helped decorate the house for an open house after the ceremony at the church. As we made hors d'oeuvres, we talked about our families.

Chelsea arrived about an hour before the party and asked if we could use her help. There wasn't much left to do, though, so Liza sent Justin on an errand, and the three of us went up to Liza's old room. It was mostly how she'd left it two years ago when she left for school. We talked about married life and college and work for me. When we heard the first cars pulling up, we went downstairs.

Amy looked beautiful in her elegant white silk skirt and top. She seemed younger and more vibrant somehow than I had seen her in a long time. I liked her new husband too. Tom was gentle and kind, and from what Liza said, a hard worker. I was disappointed though when I heard they'd be selling the house.

I couldn't imagine anyone else but the Roberts living three doors down from the Fremonts on our dirt road. I wished I could buy that house and live there forever. It definitely wasn't my dream home, but there were so many memories I didn't want to lose.

"Isn't this hard on you to lose your home?" I asked.

"It's just a house," Liza said. "Home is wherever you make it. Besides," she added, "they still haven't paved this darn road."

We both laughed at the old joke. She was right, but still I hoped my parents would never move off Appaloosa Lane.

The three of us kept the punch bowl full and helped serve cake. We showed guests to the bathroom and visited with old family friends.

It wasn't until later that evening I noticed Chelsea hadn't been the center of the conversation upstairs. In fact the whole night she was being friendly but laid back. She seemed content just hanging out with her family. It was strange seeing Chelsea in this new, grown-up way, but she had told me she was going to change, and if this was part of her changing, then I was going to embrace it.

When I got home that night, I had a message to call Carry

from work. It had seemed like she was up to something lately, so I was hoping this would explain it. I apprehensively dialed her home number.

"Headquarters called today," Carry said. It scared me.

"They've been watching you and they think you're great," she said.

"That's good news," I said, smiling. "But what else?"

"Well, in the big cities right now, Houses of Hope is working triple-time. Next year the Governor of Illinois is expected to give the agency double the budget they've had in the past. They have so many projects in the works, they can barely keep up as it is." She was talking fast.

"Uh-huh. So what does that have to do with a girl in Cody, Wyoming?"

"They're hiring three new project managers there, and they want you to be one of them."

I didn't say anything for a minute. "Chicago?"

"Yeah, Chicago. There's so much going on there right now."

I was quiet again, and Carry sensed my hesitation. I kept picturing that huge 23 on Michael Jordan's front gate that Alex was always talking about.

"Gracie, you could be getting three or four times as many families into houses as you do in Cody. And the salary would jump to $50,000," she added.

"Wow, it sounds great," I said, unconvinced. "How soon would I go?"

"Not until the new grant kicks in around February. But they need you to decide by November."

"Oh, good. I have awhile," I said.

I hung up feeling crestfallen. This was a great opportunity—a promotion. Why wasn't I jumping for joy? I dragged myself upstairs and went to bed. It had been a long day.

twenty-nine

I usually looked forward to "move-in day," as we called it, for weeks, but not this time. I had been so disappointed to hear this event was on the same day as Quentin's homecoming. For two years I'd envisioned meeting Quentin at the airport, but this ceremony had been scheduled for months, and there was no way I could miss it.

I downed a cup of orange juice and a powdered doughnut, trying to relieve my nerves; instead it made me nauseous. I glanced at my watch at least a hundred times.

Mr. Allison, a senior board member, noticed my jitters.

"What's going on with you today?" he asked.

"I'm just really excited to see a friend I haven't seen in a long time."

"A boyfriend, you mean?"

Before I could stop myself, I nodded my head yes.

"Oh, no. I mean. . . ." I must have looked like an idiot. "Well just a friend that's a boy, that's all."

"Uh-huh." He smiled indulgently.

I wanted to race to Quentin's house that night, but instead I decided to run by my house and change clothes. Why was I acting like this? *It's just Quentin*, I told myself. *It's not like I'm attracted to him*. Still, I pulled on a heavy gray sweater and folded the neck over. I tried on a new pair of jeans and stood in the mirror. "Nope," I said, tugging them off again. Instead I opted for an older, faded pair—I didn't want to be too obvious. I pulled my hair up into a fresh ponytail and curled the ends. Then I dabbed on a quick coat of mascara before I ran down the stairs. Thankfully no one was home to ask where I was headed.

When I came over the hill and saw his house, the butterflies in my stomach nearly made me lose its contents. *Should I turn around?* I squeezed the steering wheel tightly.

"Gracie Fremont, get a hold of yourself."

I laughed nervously, realizing I'd said it aloud.

I pulled through the front gate and shut off the car as Quentin came bounding down the stairs to meet me. I just stared. My mouth was wide open, and I couldn't move.

No letter I'd received over the past two years had prepped me for this. This wasn't my old Quentin. There were the warm eyes that smiled along with his mouth, but now they weren't hidden behind thick glasses. Quentin must have gotten contacts.

This guy was at least two inches taller and forty pounds more buff than my old best friend. His red hair had faded to strawberry blond, and it was cut in a short but spiky do. His freckled teenage skin had transformed into a smooth tan.

Quentin was hot.

He flung my door open. "Aren't you going to get out?"

"Uh. Yeah," I gulped. He yanked me from the car and swung me around in a hug. My shock gave way to laughter.

"So I look different, huh?" He laughed.

"Yeah, a bit." I smiled.

"Well, I'm the same old country boy, Gracie. Do you want to go four-wheeling?" He laughed.

I stood statue-still.

"Just kidding. Let's go inside."

I was glad he had already met with the Stake Presidency that afternoon to be released. It would have been misery to see him and not hug him.

We visited with Sheila, and for the first hour I felt so awkward. He talked about the families he'd served and how strong his testimony was now. He seemed so mature.

I couldn't stop noticing how great he looked. It was like everything I had always loved about Quentin on the inside was now on the outside too. I stared at him while he spoke animatedly to his mother and me. His smile captivated me.

I was done convincing myself he was just my friend. There was no way I could ignore it now. Quentin Libbert owned my heart, 100 percent. But now that I was able to acknowledge my feelings, I didn't know how to act.

Finally he suggested we go for a walk. I jumped at the chance to get out of the house.

Once we were outside, Quentin slung his arm around my shoulder the way he had a thousand times, but this was the first time it sent tingles down my spine.

"So why are you being weird, Grace? It's the same old me." He smiled. "Hey, you're different too. I like your hair."

"I know. It's just weird having you home," I stammered.

"Do you want to race?" he asked. And before I could answer, he took off. I chased him until we got to the tire swing by the creek, and then he swung me around until I was dizzy.

Okay, maybe this *was* my old Quentin.

He stopped the swing and laughed goofily.

"I like you better this way," I said, comfortable for the first time that night.

"What way?" he asked.

"Immature and dorky."

Over the next three days, we spent every spare moment together. We cruised our old mudding roads, finding not much had changed, and watched movies at my house, finding much had. Quentin wanted to see the Houses of Hope houses I had supervised, so I introduced him to each of my families, and we toured the houses. I hung out with Quentin while he repaired a sink and a cupboard for Sheila. And he joined me for my lunch break every day.

One night after work, I drove to Quentin's house. He led me down to the creek where he had a dinner set up on a folding table. There were two chairs, a red checkered table cloth, and two covered plates. I could smell the sliced garlic bread in a basket.

"Wow," I said. "This looks amazing."

"Well, you know. I didn't have much to do today while you were slaving away, so . . ."

I sat down at the table and pulled the cover off my dinner. I could hear the water gurgling over the rocks. It was already dark out, and Quentin lit two tall candles. I picked up my fork and was immediately chastised.

"Hey, I didn't pray yet," he said.

"Oh, sorry, Elder Libbert," I joked. There were moments when Quentin was still a little missionary-esque. Quentin blessed the food, and I dug in. He was about to eat too but instead jumped up and tuned a tiny radio to a country station. The music played softly behind us.

"What are you doing here, buddy?" I asked. "Are you practicing up for your real dates?" Neither of us had mentioned anything more than friendship yet, but by the looks of things, I was beginning to think tonight was the night.

"Yeah, something like that." He smiled.

The scene was dreamy, and the conversation came easy. Quentin's energy was catching. When a moment of silence came, I gently laughed.

"What?" he asked.

"Nothing."

"What? You know I'll get it out of you," he said.

"It's just that I can't believe that you were scared to even say hi to me back in high school."

"You've always been way out of my league, Gracie," he said. "Always."

I wanted to refute him, to let him know that we were a perfect match, but somehow I wasn't sure how to cross that line. The friendship we'd had before he left was back, but now there was an undeniable attraction tied to it. I knew I had never experienced this with Mason. This was so much deeper. It was absolutely amazing. I was falling for Quentin.

I drove away from his house that night feeling extraordinary and miserable at the same time. Realizing I loved him meant the world to me. I think the feeling was the same for him. Still, the moment would have been so much sweeter had one of us known how to admit it.

~•~

The next night was Sheila's baptism, and I thought my heart would explode as I watched Quentin raise her out of the water. The Spirit tingled through me throughout the entire meeting.

After the baptism was over, he drove Sheila home, but I beat them there. I waited on his front porch swing and when that truck came around the corner, I caught his eye. He smiled at me all the way up the lane. Then he jumped out of his truck and laughed as he leapt up the steps.

"Hold on," he said. Sheila stopped to hug me on her way in the house.

There was a cool breeze, but I hadn't noticed. I had my arms wrapped around my knees to keep warm.

Whatever he was doing in the house took longer than I expected. Finally he came out with a huge red and white quilt and wrapped it around my shoulders as he sat down next to me.

He stopped the swing and turned toward me.

"Gracie." He was serious.

"Yeah?" My stomach tightened. Here it was. After all this time—he was going to say he loved me too.

"What are your plans for awhile?" he asked.

"Well," I said slowly. "I'm going to keep working for the agency and living with Mom and Dad, I guess. Is that what you mean?"

"Are you going to Chicago?"

"What? How'd you know about that?"

"Your mom told me," he explained.

"I haven't decided. I'm definitely not set on going." I would stay if he wanted me to, and my eyes begged him to realize this.

"I'm leaving for awhile," he said.

"What?" I gasped.

"Kendra is home—remember, from my mission—and I'm going to meet her family and just hang out down there for awhile."

I jerked a bit, and the swing pushed back awkwardly. *Don't cry, don't cry.* I just stared.

"I didn't know you two were still close," I said flatly.

"Yeah, she's great. We always planned on doing this after our missions, so I guess now we're finally getting to."

I nodded my head.

So that was it. He'd grown into the man of my dreams, I finally realized it, and now he just wanted to be friends.

✦❧✦

I sat in my car at the airport that Friday and watched his plane lift into the sky. I wiped my eyes, reached for my phone, and dialed Carry's number.

"Hi, Grace," she said. "How are you doing?"

"Fine," I lied. "I just wanted to call and let you know I'll accept the job."

"Fantastic," she said. "I'll let headquarters know right away."

thirty

I wished my family would shut up about my job! So what? I had a great job; I was saving tons of money—I didn't care. It wasn't what I wanted.

The past month without Quentin had gone slower than the entire two years he'd been in Canada. What in the world was he doing out there?

To make matters worse, my whole family knew what I was going through. When I'd finally realized my feelings for him, I'd let Hope, Nathan, Danielle, and even Alex in on it. Now I wished I'd kept my mouth shut.

Life was miserable. I didn't want to go to Chicago, but at the same time, I was counting down the days until I could escape.

When Quentin called on the first day of December, I didn't know what to expect. His voice was totally flat, lacking the energy I so loved. And the news he delivered was worse than any scenario I'd concocted.

"Gracie, I just wanted to tell you Kendra and I are getting married," he said.

I covered the receiver and started sobbing. It was a long silence.

"Wow," I finally forced out.

"I thought you'd be more excited for me," he said.

"No, no, I am. Congratulations." I didn't even ask when the wedding was planned.

Quentin talked for about thirty more seconds before I lied that I was late for a meeting. I hung up the phone and let the tears fall.

The next day was the first time I had ever called in sick to work. It was freezing outside, but I pulled on a pair of cotton shorts and drove over 100 miles before I stopped. I was in the middle of the badlands, and I pulled to the side of the road, laid my head against my steering wheel, and bawled.

I sat that way, crying in the middle of nowhere for thirty minutes. How could I have been so stupid? All along I thought Quentin had feelings for me too. I was completely fooled, just like I'd been with Mason, but it had felt so different—so right. I got out of the car to stretch but jumped back in quickly when I realized the snow was over my tennis shoes, soaking my socks. I wanted to go anywhere but back to my life. Finally, when I couldn't think of anywhere else to go, I turned the car around.

<hr />

The distraction of crying babies was exactly what I needed. Seeing my family for the holidays was the first thing to uplift me the whole month. Everyone was here this year, but there were no more baby announcements. One night after dinner, Nathan pulled me out to the front steps.

"You've got to get on with life, Gracie," he said.

I was stunned. Was my jerky older brother back in place of the one I had grown to love?

"Thanks," I said sarcastically.

"I'm not trying to be mean. I'm just telling you the truth. The only person who can make you happy is *you*. Not Quentin or any other guy. You need to quit *looking* for someone and get back to *being* someone. Grace, you were the highlight of this family before this set you back," he said.

"Really?"

"Yeah, really. What you do is amazing! Look how you've put your talent to use. Sarah especially thinks it's awesome how you help women like her," he said.

"Thanks."

"All I can say is, you're going to be an awesome wife some-day, but for now, just focus on being the Gracie we all love."

That night I wanted to crawl in bed and lose the world, but I knew Nate was right. I had to do something.

❧⟡❧

For the first time since Christmas, I looked around my room and noticed how messy it was. The new purple fleece blanket Hope and Anthony had given me was strewn across the bed, and the rest of my gifts were scattered about. I'd gotten a toaster, towels, microwave, and smoothie maker. I guess everyone wanted to help me set up my apartment in Chicago. My desk was overflowing with materials about the city: magazines full of apartment rentals, visitor's guides, maps, and a stake directory Mom had somehow gotten her hands on. I had been surfing the web, looking for apartments, but I still hadn't picked one. Mom reminded me over and over again that time was ticking. But if I thought too long about leaving, my hands would start to shake. I knew it was a fantastic opportunity, but it just didn't feel right. Still, I had no reason not to go. I was dreading two things like the plague: the first was getting Quentin's wedding invitation and the second was boarding a plane to Chicago. I knew I could survive both, but I didn't know if I wanted to.

I flopped down on the bed with the phone, snuggled up in the blanket, and called Chelsea. She was so different now. Since the adoption, she was much more reserved. So humble. I never thought I'd say that: Chelsea Copeland, humble. But it was true. Since she'd been home, we'd spent hours talking about her and the baby, but we'd also spent equal time talking about my life and my fears. She genuinely cared.

"Hi Chels, its Grace," I said.

"I was wondering when you'd call."

"Whatcha doin'?" I asked.

"Just hanging out with Mom and Dad," she said. "What about you?"

"Sitting in my room, staring at all this Chicago stuff, and feeling sick."

"Gracie, you better make some decisions or you're not going to have anywhere to live when you get there," she said.

"I know. I know. It's just so scary, you know?"

"I know you, Gracie Fremont. You're not scared to be in a new place. You've always been brave."

I laughed. "Me? Brave?"

"Yes! I think what's holding you back is Quentin."

I started to protest, but she stopped me.

"And it's okay. We both know I've based my life around guys for . . . well, most of my life. But you're better than that. If he doesn't know what he's missing, then you need to move on too," Chelsea said. "Go make the most of the woman you've become."

I was crying, and Chelsea knew it.

"Hey, do you want me to come over?" she asked.

"No. No, I'm fine," I said.

"Pick out the fanciest apartment you can afford, and you're going to have a blast. Me and Liza will have to come visit our friend in the city all the time," Chelsea said.

I wiped my tears and took a breath. "Maybe you'll see me on *Oprah*."

"And then you can tell the world Chelsea Copeland taught you everything you know," she joked. "You're going to do great, Gracie. Everyone knows it but you."

The air was crisp, and I could see my breath in the garage. I had half the boxes on the shelves down around my feet and was reaching deep into a shelf for an old hammer I wanted to take to Chicago. The plane tickets in my purse said I was leaving in four more days.

I pulled another box down and noticed GRACIE written in big black letters on the top. I dusted off the lid and set it on top of a tall pile. I pulled open the flaps.

There was a layer of tissue paper on top and underneath was the apple, potato, pear, ear of corn, and cornucopia that had caused me so much distress almost a decade ago. As I ran my hands over its fading paint, I realized this "masterpiece" wasn't as great as I'd once believed. In fact I was glad it hadn't seen the outside of the box in a long time. My talent had taken me so far since then.

I'd been furious at my family that night, and yet they'd made a huge fuss about that dumb cornucopia. I stood there shaking my head when I heard the door open behind me.

The light in the garage was dim, and I couldn't tell who opened it.

"Gracie? Are you in here?" I froze. It was Quentin's voice. He stepped inside, and I jumped out from my maze of boxes.

"What are you doing here?" I was completely shocked.

Quentin crossed the garage in two giant steps and grabbed me in a bear hug. He didn't say a word. I wanted to, but I couldn't let myself melt into his embrace. Instead I pushed him away, and when I stood back I saw a tear fall down his cheek.

"Quentin, what's wrong?" I demanded. "Are you okay?"

He just shook his head no. It must have been Kendra.

"We're not together anymore," he said, reading my mind.

"I'm sorry. I can see you really loved her," I said. The words stung as they came out.

"I'm not crying because of that," he said. "I'm crying because I messed up."

I raised my eyebrows in confusion. "What do you mean?"

"Gracie, I called it off. I called off the wedding." What was Quentin saying?

"What do you mean you—"

"It's you!" he nearly yelled it. "It was *always* you I loved."

I didn't move. My eyes widened, and I opened my mouth, but nothing came out.

"Gracie, I love you. I've loved you since wood shop in high school, but I knew I never had a chance," he said. "I love your laugh and how you hate being scared but love it at the same time. I love how you want what's best for everyone and how you're willing to do anything for those who need you. I love your smile and your blue eyes and your eyebrows. Their little arch drives me wild."

"Quentin—"

"Shh. Let me finish," he said. "I thought I could make it work with someone else, but all I've ever wanted was you. I'm sorry if I'm just 'friends' material, but I wanted you to know the truth."

I jumped into his arms. He held me for a minute before I could find any words.

"Quentin, I love you too. I wanted to tell you so bad, but when you told me about Kendra, I just couldn't."

He put his hands on my head and leaned back. Quentin stared into my eyes. "Gracie, are you going to Chicago?"

"I told them yes," I said slyly. "But things could probably be arranged."

Quentin pulled my head to his and kissed me hard. In his kiss, I felt everything I'd known and everything I'd watched grow over the last four years. I loved him.

Finally he loosened his grip and took a step back. "Would getting married be a good enough excuse to cancel?"

I stopped breathing as Quentin went down on one knee on the concrete floor. He reached in his pocket and slid a cold ring onto my finger as he stuttered, "Gracie Fremont, will you marry me?"

I was silent. *Heavenly Father, please help me to know.* It only took an instant.

"Yes. Yes. Yes! I'll marry you," I said as I yanked him up from the floor into our second kiss.

We spent the rest of the evening snuggled together under Joseph's tree in the backyard. It was freezing out, but I wasn't cold. We contemplated going inside to announce our news but decided better of it. This was our moment, and we didn't want to share it with anyone.

thirty-one

Finally it was my turn. Quentin and I were being sealed in the Billings Temple on June 1, 2009, and for the first time I was glad so many of my friends and siblings had gone through before me. My parents, Liza and Jason, Amy and Tom, Hope and Anthony, Nathan and Sarah, Samantha and Damon, and Danielle were all inside waiting for us. Chelsea and Alex were the babysitters this time around. Sheila also hadn't been endowed yet, and we asked her over and over again if she wanted us to wait, but she insisted we shouldn't.

Of course I hadn't slept the night before, and I rolled out of bed a bundle of nerves before we left the house at 5:00 AM. But when I joined Quentin in the temple, every fear was put to rest. Our sealing was more than I had ever imagined or hoped for. Following Hope's advice, I tried my best to truly listen to our sealer's beautiful words.

I had never before felt so whole.

When we made our entrance into the waiting room as husband and wife, Sheila was crying. She told Quentin that her husband's presence had enveloped her the entire time she was there. Quentin promised her she could be sealed to him one day too.

We walked outside, and Quentin hoisted me into his truck,

which I now had to claim as half mine. I slid over close to my new husband and nuzzled my face into his neck. He looked down and kissed me. Then he fired up the engine, and we drove toward home for our reception, with our family and friends waving good-bye.

***

I closed my eyes and held my arms out wide. I had to be sure this was real. When I opened them again, I gasped. Alex had begged to be completely in charge of our wedding reception, and the fairyland she had created was amazing. Quentin and I picked a red barn about twenty-five miles north of Cody, and then we let Alex do the rest.

A long dirt road that was lined on both sides by cottonwood trees led to the huge English-style brick-red barn. The barn was trimmed in a crisp white, with three white stars decorating each outside wall. The huge doors were swung open, leaving an entryway that was close to twenty-five feet wide and tall. A white steeple rose from the center of the roof.

Just to the south of the barn sat Lily Lake, which was actually more like a large pond, named for the owner's daughter. The road forked and led to the barn or the wide dock on the lake. Willows lined the lake to the far side while grass rose out of the other side and created a huge lawn up to the barn wall. A barrier of white tulips—at least twenty rows deep—surrounded the entire lawn.

Alex, with the help of Mom and Dad, had lined the sides of the dock with huge metal bins, full of more white tulips. For Sheila's sake and the rest of Quentin's family, we'd decided to have a short ring ceremony at the beginning of our reception. About seventy-five chairs were set up on the lawn, with a line of elegant satin ribbon connecting the rows. The ceremony would be performed on the dock.

Inside, the barn was gorgeous. The plank floors shone in

the candlelight that seemed to be everywhere we looked. Alex had enlisted the help of the college art students in crafting distinctive twig chandeliers and centerpieces. The lights were hung from the barn's huge wood timbers. Every table was set with white linens and adorned with romantic sparkling twigs and metal troughs of floating white tulips. The smell of the roast beef was already emanating from the kitchen, and the cook hollered out that the potatoes had thirty more minutes. Cheesecakes topped with cherries, strawberries, and chocolate lined one table and another was set up for gifts. A large square was left open for our country dance—something Quentin had informed me was absolutely essential.

Quentin grabbed me from behind and spun me around and around. I felt like a princess.

"What do you think, Mrs. Libbert?" he asked, spinning me so our faces were just inches apart.

"I think it's gorgeous," I said.

"I think *you're* gorgeous."

"Well, thank you, husband." We both laughed. Quentin pulled me to him and kissed me, and the lights overhead seemed to whirl around us.

"Excuse me, lovebirds," Alex said, bringing me back to earth.

"Yes?" I said.

"Does everything look okay?"

"Alex, everything is perfect. I can't believe you did this for us. Thank you so much," I said.

Alex stepped back in a mock curtsy and said, "I made it my personal mission to dispel those rumors that Mormon receptions are lame. This one is going to go down in the history books."

We met with the photographer, and he got right to work on Quentin and I. He posed us on the dock, in the barn, and my personal favorite: a shot of us from behind walking through the tunnel of trees down the dirt road. We were hand-in-hand, and I was staring up at Quentin. I knew all this smiling and saying "cheese" wasn't Quentin's cup of tea, but he didn't complain once. Soon we heard cars coming up the road, and we knew family pictures were next. That took another half an hour. Finally, it was time for our reception. Quentin and I hid in the barn while the guests filed into the seats outside. Alex had timed everything perfectly, and the sun was just beginning to set over the lake.

Pachelbel's "Canon in D" created a hush in the crowd, and Quentin and I walked slowly toward them. He was irresistible in his black tux with a white vest and a single tulip pinned to his lapel. In my left hand, I carried my tulip bouquet, held together by a wide pink satin ribbon. Walking through the crowd, I couldn't help but get teary-eyed. There sat both my high school and junior high shop teachers, my coworkers from Houses of Hope, my eight nephews, and my little Emmylee. Chelsea and Liza were both dabbing their eyes with tissue, and I winked at them as we passed. I saw Sheila sitting with Mom, and I thanked Heavenly Father for joining our families in this way.

We passed our family and friends and stepped out onto the dock. Dad's back was to the crowd, so Quentin and I passed him and then turned back to face him. Every eye was on us, and for once I didn't mind. I glanced down at my dress and smiled at how beautiful I felt. My simple satin gown was fitted on top and made my ribs and waist look tiny. Four thin satin ribbons wrapped around my middle. The flowing skirt of the dress splayed out in front and behind me, completely hiding the white flip-flops I wore underneath. My hair was done in a French twist with only a few strands hanging loose around my face.

Dad said a few words about the importance of our temple sealing and the love that can bind us together forever. Then we exchanged rings and finally got to Quentin's favorite part—the you-may-kiss-the-bride bit. Quentin reached his hand behind my back, dipped me low, and planted a romantic, passionate kiss on my lips. The crowd stood and clapped, and then Quentin did something that will forever be remembered about the Fremont-Libbert wedding reception. He let go of me, turned toward the crowd, and yelped a "Yee haw" as he back-flipped off the edge of the dock and into the lake.

Unexpectedly, the hardest person to say good-bye to was Chelsea. She stood with my family outside Quentin's and my apartment. Quentin put the little cooler of sandwiches on the floorboard of the truck and stood talking with Dad about the upcoming drive to Pullman, Washington, where Quentin had enrolled in school. Chelsea walked toward me and took my hands.

"I'm so proud of you for getting back on track," I told her.

"I'm so proud you stayed on track, Gracie," she said. "Now look at your life." She pulled me into a hug and whispered into my ear, "You deserve every blessing that comes to you."

I felt the tears coming down.

thirty-two

It was Valentine's Day and my turn to come up with a date idea. So far, I didn't have much. I decided I better at least get pretty for the day and hopped in the shower early. I was putting on my deodorant in our tiny apartment bathroom when I heard Quentin outside the door. I looked down just in time to see him shove a pregnancy test stick under the door. I started laughing and pulled the door open.

"Can I help you, Mr. Libbert?" I asked.

"Come on," he said. "Just take one."

We had bought the tests a week earlier, but so far I was afraid to take one. Quentin was growing more and more impatient with me, though. He clasped his hands together as if begging and gave me his best puppy-dog eyes. I bent over and picked it up.

"Fine. I'll do it," I said. "But get out of here!"

I managed the awkward test and set it on the counter. I almost ran out the bathroom door.

"So, what's it say?" he asked.

"I don't know. I think it takes awhile."

"Well, go see," he said.

"No. I'm not doing it," I folded my arms across my chest and shook my head like a stubborn three-year-old. "If you want to know so bad, you do it."

233

Quentin slowly walked in the bathroom, and I went to the couch. I sat down and picked up the latest issue of the *Ensign* and pretended to read.

I expected him to hoot and holler, so when I didn't hear anything, I figured it must be negative. Quentin walked out and sat down beside me on the couch. He put his hand on my knee.

"Honey?"

"Seriously, Quentin, don't get all worked up. So I'm not pregnant, it's no big deal," I said. "It was our first month of trying."

He grabbed the magazine from my hand and tossed it to the coffee table.

"Gracie, you're pregnant!"

"I am?"

He smiled and scooped me up in his arms. He spun me around the tiny apartment—my feet banging on the wall with every revolution.

"We're going to have a baby," he sung.

A few minutes after the announcement, Quentin was shoving his books into his backpack and running out the door—he was going to be late. As soon as the door clicked, I lunged for the phone and did a three-way call to Chelsea and Liza.

"Good morning, girlies," I said. "I have some news for you."

"You're pregnant," Liza guessed.

"You brat!" I said. "You ruined my surprise."

We all laughed.

"How far along?" Chelsea asked.

"Oh, I don't know," I said. "Probably just barely."

"I'm so happy for you!" Chelsea said. "Hey, I guess I have some news too."

"What?" Liza asked.

"Well, do you guys remember Liam Johnson from the singles ward?" she asked.

Liza didn't know him, but I did.

"Yeah, I went on a date with him once," I said.

"Oh, you did?" Chelsea said. "Well, we've gone out a few times, and I think I like him."

Liza and I swooned for a minute. "Chels, good job to pick a good one," I said.

Liza was also expecting, so I immediately launched into questions for my two girlfriends. Chelsea gave me a few tips on abating morning sickness—crackers and citrus—and Liza brought out her due date calendar to give me an estimate of when the Libbert baby would make its debut. After close to an hour of baby talk, Chelsea got serious.

"Girls, I have an idea," she said.

"Uh-oh," Liza and I said simultaneously.

"Let's go on a trip. My dad has that condo in Playa del Carmen—in Mexico—and we could just hang out on the beach for a week," she said.

Liza and I were quiet, and I knew we were both contemplating being away from our husbands for a whole week.

"Oh, come on," Chelsea begged. "You're both going to be mommies soon and won't have time for us. Let's do this."

We finally hung up with a plan to discuss the trip with our husbands and report back tomorrow. In the meantime, Chelsea attempted to convince us with emailed pictures of the condo. They were hard to resist. Situated on a private white-sand beach, the condo was gorgeous. The room had a huge jetted tub, walk-in shower, kitchen, and big screen TV. A pair of French doors led to the wide balcony overlooking the beach.

<hr>

By the time Quentin came home from class, I had a romantic Valentine's Day date completely planned. Without explanation, we hopped in the truck, and I popped our wedding CD into the stereo. We reminisced at how far we'd come and remembered that first non-date in this very truck. We drove an hour and a half to Spokane and parked downtown. I knew people were looking at us like the country bumpkins we were, but I didn't really care.

Quentin ran around to my side of the truck and opened the door for me. We made our way toward the park where we crossed a bridge and found a nice lawn, overlooking the falls. There wasn't snow on the ground, but we could still feel the frozen earth through the quilt I'd spread out. Quentin sat with his legs straight out, crossed at the ankle, and I lay back onto his lap. He ran his fingers through my hair. I stared up at the stars, trying to understand how I could have been so blessed. Finally I sat up and unpacked our picnic dinner: cold chicken, potato salad, baked beans, and chocolate chip cookies.

We strolled through Riverfront Park, taking plenty of breaks for kissing. Quentin raced me to the top of the gigantic Radio Flyer wagon in the park, and we slid down the slide together. Then we made our way to the ice rink. I sat on the bleachers under the warmers for a minute and rubbed my red hands. Quentin sat behind me and softly caressed my neck. Eventually I walked toward the ticket booth and Quentin stopped me.

"Are you sure it's okay?" he asked rubbing my tummy.

I laughed. "We've only known there's somebody in there for like twelve hours. I'm sure its fine."

We were the most uncoordinated skaters on the ice, but it looked like we were having the most fun. Time after time we landed in a tangled heap—several times with a daredevil kid jumbled in with us. Toward the end of the night, Quentin gushed when we made it through an entire song without falling. He spun me into his arms and hugged me tight. I looked up into his eyes and said, "I love you."

After we turned in our skates, we sat down on the bleachers, and I brought my Valentine's Day present out of the backpack and handed it to him. He turned the heart-shaped box around a couple of times in his hands.

"Hmmm," he said. "Fortune cookies?"

"Just open them," I said.

Quentin carefully broke the first cookie and pulled out the tiny sheet of paper I'd spent all afternoon stuffing in the cookie.

"I love the way you put your hand on my back to lead me into a room," he read. He smiled and leaned forward to kiss me.

Then he opened the next one: "I love the way you always ask if I'm okay."

"You make me so happy. I can't wait to spend eternity with you," he read. By now he was almost blushing. Quentin finished breaking the cookies and met my eyes.

"Take me home, Mrs. Libbert," he said.

thirty-three

"Girls, can you please keep it down," the stewardess asked us. This was her second time back to our seats, and this time she looked serious. "The other customers are trying to get some rest."

We stifled our laughter but busted out again as soon as she was gone. It was 5:00 AM, but Liza, Chelsea, and I hadn't slept a wink the whole night. The red-eye was close to $300 cheaper. Within minutes, though, the sun was rising and our laughter changed to awe as we neared the Yucatan Peninsula. Liza sat at the window, and Chelsea and I hovered over Liza to see the view. The deep blue ocean changed to azure, cerulean, and finally, almost turquoise, as it reached the sand of the gorgeous beaches. In some spots, we could see the dark shadows of the reefs in the shallow water. Resorts, hotels, beach huts, and chairs lined the narrow strip of land as far as we could see. And then the ocean began again on the other side. For a minute I felt sadness and a bit of guilt that Quentin wasn't here with me. Chelsea read my expression.

"Hey now, none of that," she said. "You both had awesome honeymoons. Besides, Quentin's going to be a big rich engineer someday, and you'll come back here. I promise."

"I know, I know," I said, shaking it off.

"Let's all do a trip with our husbands here when we're done with school," Liza said, her eyes never leaving the window.

"Promise?" I asked.

"Absolutely," Liza said. "But first we've got to get Chelsea and Liam married."

"Ahem," Chelsea cleared her throat. She reached into the front pocket of her tiny purse and extracted a princess-cut diamond ring. She slid it onto her left ring finger, and Liza and I gasped. Chelsea grinned.

"Yep, he asked me."

Thankfully, most of the "customers" were awake by now because both Liza and I started screaming.

"Why didn't you tell us?" Liza asked.

"I don't know. I just wanted to wait until the right time, I guess," she said.

⚜

Our plane landed in Cancun, and we took the shuttle to the Copeland's condo. The pictures didn't do it justice: it was gorgeous. The complex had four pools and a huge gym. But the best feature was, of course, the ocean out our back door.

The first afternoon, we hit a local market and loaded our kitchenette with junk food. We slept in the luxurious queen-sized beds until ten or eleven each morning and then lazily made our way to the beach. Chelsea looked great as ever in her new swimming suits—much more modest than she'd worn in the past. And Liza's maternity suit was cute. I was over four months pregnant now, and showing a bit, but I was still able to wear my normal clothes. The weather was at a comfortable 85 degrees every day, and even the water was fairly warm. We attempted snorkeling through the colorful reefs but found none of us were huge fans. Other snorkelers carried fish bait in their pockets to draw the creatures, but when a fish got anywhere near me, I'd squirm for the surface. For the most part, we just laid on the beach, read, talked, tanned, and then read, talked, and tanned some more.

In the interest of saving money, we didn't do much touring, but we decided to visit a cenote on the last day of our trip. The bus ride was loud and sweaty, but the wait was well worth it. When we reached the cenote, we stashed our bags in lockers and made our way down a deep cavern on slippery rock stairs. The cavern was probably seventy feet deep before it reached the still pool of crystalline water. I had never seen such clear, pure water. Our guide explained the cenote was part of a complex system of underground rivers that had been ritualistic during the Mayan period. He said the pool was forty feet deep, and as we descended the stairs, we could see the bottom of it. The ridges inside the cavern were covered with mossy vegetation, and thin green vines hung the length of the cave. It was completely enchanting. We stopped several times during the descent for pictures but then realized the scene from the bottom was just as beautiful.

Once we reached the bottom, we climbed into the cool refreshing pool and swam through the vines. Other visitors were jumping from raised platforms into the pool, and Chelsea climbed out to join them. I considered following, but Liza pointed to my baby bump and gave me a stern, motherly "no."

We swam at the cenote until the next shift's guide informed us it was closing time. Reluctantly, we climbed out, toweled off, and began the long trip up the stairs.

Back at the condo we sprawled out in the living room, surrounded by wedding magazines, two versions of "What to Expect When You're Expecting," and baby name books.

"Here you go, Liza," Chelsea laughed. "Edwina."

"Sure, sure Chels," Liza said. She had an open bag of a Mexican version of Cheetos resting on the top of her belly.

"No, I think Liza should name her daughter something that rhymes with Fram," I said. "Like Pam Fram."

Liza nearly choked on a Cheeto.

"What exactly are you referring to, Gracie?" she asked.

"Oh, I don't know, Liza Miza."

Chelsea looked confused for a minute, and we filled her in. That memory brought back scores of others, and we talked late into the night. I realized life had changed in so many ways, but inside each of us were those same little girls who had been linked for the first time when we were six.

Close to midnight, there was a lull in conversation, and I pulled myself from the floor. I looked around the trashed condo in search for my suitcase.

"Well, girls, let's pack," I said. "I miss my husband."

thirty-four

It was a particularly stunning autumn, and I seemed to notice the leaves and enjoy the crisp air more than I ever had before. Quentin's class was released early one afternoon, so we drove to Manito Park in Spokane. We slowly wandered through the rose garden and fed the ducks in the pond. We found a high fence with a sign announcing the Nishinomiya Japanese Garden and went inside. It was like entering a hidden wonderland. We followed a pebble path around traditional bonsai trees and into hidden coves. Quentin splashed the toe of his boot in the waterfall. Then we sat down on a bench near the huge koi pond and watched as the giant orange and white fish huddled near rocks and under the arched bridge. Quentin followed the fish around the pool, and I dug my journal from my bag. My bulging belly served as a perfect shelf for writing.

I sat there with pen poised, but nothing came to me. *That's weird*, I thought, as I closed my journal and set the pen down beside me. I watched as a pile of yellow-orange maple leaves grew taller with each breeze. I closed my eyes and thanked Heavenly Father for my life. The past year had been a long string of magical moments. When I opened my eyes, I saw Quentin kneeling down near the water's edge, swirling his finger in it. I picked up the pen again.

Dear Baby,

You are growing inside me, and I can't wait to meet you. I want you to know I love you more than you can imagine and your daddy does too. We know you will be beautiful and smart and special. The only thing we don't know is if you're a boy or a girl. Of course, all the Fremonts are betting on a boy. We didn't find out because I love surprises.

You are going to be making your grand entrance in about a month, we think. I am sure life on Earth is going to be hard for you to get used to, and it will be difficult for us too, but I promise I will try my best to be a good mother to you. I want so badly to do what's right.

There is a lot I don't know about life yet, little one. But there are a few lessons I've learned that I want to share with you.

Heavenly Father loves us. He loves you so much. He loves every single person on Earth—whether other people do or not—He does.

Each of His children is special. There was a time I didn't know what made me special, but I have learned there are many things. What defines our lives is if we are willing to find these special gifts and share them with others. I know there will be many talents and characteristics that make you special.

Family is our best gift. Daddy and I are so excited to begin our family with you. Family is Heavenly Father's gift to us, and we should always cherish it. Every day my family has showed me how much they loved me, and I hope we can do the same for you.

A good friend is forever. I hope you have many good friends—or at least a few special ones. I have had two good friends my whole life, and they have meant the world to me.

When life gets us down, our best medicine is to help others. I hope you learn to serve others and that you can remember to get busy when all you feel like doing is crying.

Only you can make you happy (with the help of Heavenly Father, of course).

Prayer is vital. There are so many times prayer has made a difference in my life. I promise to teach you to pray always.

And finally, follow your heart. Sometimes other people will tell us how to act, what to do, and who to love. But only you and Heavenly Father know what's right for you. By following my heart, I found the love of my life—your daddy—and I hope you find someone special to share eternity with too.

We love you, baby. We'll meet you soon.

Love,

Mommy

❦

Five weeks later, Quentin held my hand while he read the letter aloud to Eliza Grace Libbert. I held her in my arms and tears came to my eyes.

the end

book club questions

1. What did the Fremonts do right in raising Gracie and the other Fremont children?
2. At what point should Chelsea have altered her course to avoid major negative life consequences? How could she have changed at that point?
3. What aspects of Liza's and Gracie's friendship make it one that could last a lifetime?
4. What did Gracie learn from her relationship with Mason?
5. How did developing her talent change Gracie's confidence?
6. What factors were most important in Gracie developing a personal testimony?
7. How did Gracie's integrity shine through in her friendship with Quentin?
8. How did sharing the gospel with Quentin and Sheila affect Gracie's testimony?
9. What did Gracie discover is most important in life?

about the author

Maggie Fechner was born and raised in Wyoming. She wrote her first book in first grade for the Young Author's program. Maggie received a bachelor's degree in journalism and has worked as a reporter for several newspapers. Maggie, her husband, and their four children make their home in Idaho. She enjoys writing and portrait photography.